THE INN

THE INN

JULIAN STRYJKOWSKI

TRANSLATED FROM THE POLISH BY
CELINA WIENIEWSKA

A Helen and Kurt Wolff Book
Harcourt Brace Jovanovich, Inc.
New York

ISBN 0-15-144415-3
Library of Congress Catalog Card Number: 78–184121
Printed in the United States of America
B C D E F

In memory of my sister
Maria Stark,
who died in Vienna
in 1922

Can a man hide fire in his bosom, and his garments not burn?

Proverbs 6: 27

Yes, it was sheer luck. Not to have escaped with the others had been the greatest luck. The bullet which killed beautiful Asya, the only daughter of Wilf, the photographer (curly-haired Boom was madly in love with her), might have hit, God forbid, Old Tag's daughter-in-law, Minna, or his thirteen-year-old granddaughter Lolka. He had not tried to stop them from leaving. Old Tag did not mind being left by himself. He was born here, as was his father before him; his parents died here, so did his wife, and here he too wanted to die. If a man cannot feel safe in his own bed, where can he feel safe, I ask you? Among strangers? The fools! Ah, let them go ahead, since they have already left. They needn't worry about him. He will manage. The cows won't starve. Yevdocha will help out with the farm and with the guests at the inn. Besides, it will soon be autumn. When July is over, summer is over. And, either way, the inn won't be of much use to anyone. As if anything could be of much use to people who are doomed anyway. Old Tag never said this out loud. Minna and Lolka would not have understood him. Would anyone else?

From Passover on, when engaged couples began their walks into the country, people used to drop in at Old Tag's inn. Before him, his grandfather and his father had run it. He was the last of the line. Elo, his only son—his wife's second pregnancy had ended in a miscarriage and she had never recovered her health—worked as a book-keeper in Axelrad's steam mill, nearby. The inn stood by the main road to Duliby, which also led to Skole and the Carpathian Mountains, in almost complete isolation on the edge of the town, far from the school and the synagogue, and the young ones would certainly have moved into town if Elo's job had not been so conveniently near.

When July is over, summer is over; and, in the autumn, when the Days of Awe come—with us Jews even Holy Days have to be called Days of Awe—the rains begin and no one thinks of country walks any more. So it has been in peacetime, so it is now. When school starts (it's doubtful whether there will be any school at all this year) the children are busy; Lolka's cheeks glow under the lamp while she leans over her books, which smell of fresh paper. The skating and tobogganing have not begun yet. And the grownups: how they have sinned, how they have sinned all year long, O Lord! Thou who knowest all! But before the Day of Atonement people suddenly remember that the Almighty exists: the synagogues resound with contrition and the houses of prayer are thick with lamentations. Even those who are tied to Judaism by a mere thread, like doctors and lawyers, those who scarcely remember during the rest of the year who they are or who their parents were, feel uneasy in their hearts. The Great Accountant tots up how many cigarettes have been smoked on the Sabbath, how many pounds of ham have been bought from Pyc, the pork butcher. But, in point of fact, these sins are not the worst: they are the noisy ones—the silent ones are much worse. The All-Knowing One remembers every sin, and if He Himself should forget there is always somebody to remind Him and make Him enter the sin in the Book of Life together with the sentence—whether the sin is to be forgiven once more or whether the sinner, God forbid, is to be struck from the Book of Life. The most pious fathers and sons get up in the deep silence of an autumn night when there is no creaking of wheels to be heard, when even the dogs are curled up in their kennels asleep and only the cocks can be heard crowing in every Jewish house. One knows that the Day of Atonement is approaching; the poultry has been fattened in the sheds and coops—roosters for the men,

10

hens for the women; they flap their wings, screech, and writhe when you crush their beaks underfoot so that their death may redeem the death of a man, and even on occasion keep from him sickness, want (God save every Jew from it), and worries in the home and in business. Afterwards one must wait all through the heavy, somnolent winter for the earth to dry out in the sun and the hens to lay their Easter eggs with their springtime cackle; and only then did people resume their daily walks into the country and to the inn. What people liked most was the sour milk, the best in town. Along with the milk came warm rolls of whole-wheat flour, covered with melting May butter, yellow from the dandelions which grew in profusion in a meadow beyond a dried-up stream bed where Yevdocha used to drive the cows out to graze. People cared more about food than the good air of the nearby wood where black alders grew. Who else provided milk as good as Old Tag's! Doctors recommended it to consumptives; the General Hospital ordered it for its patients, during peacetime of course, before it was converted into a military hospital. It did not last longer than a few days in that capacity, however, because yesterday the wounded were evacuated in a hurry. Now only the white cloth on the roof, with its red cross, remained, fluttering in the wind like a scarecrow. The red cross, it has been said, is the best protection in the whole world. It has been agreed that the wounded should not be fired upon. There may be some people who abide by this, but not the Russians. An aeroplane came flying in, in bright daylight, as bold as brass! And this one could not even aim right! And while people stood there looking up at the sky, it dropped a bomb! An enormous ball of fire erupted from a small house not far from the hospital. The whole town came to stare at its torn-off roof and partly collapsed wall. A real display of Goyim might! The Baroness came in a carriage driven by two grey horses, with Amalia Diesenhoff, the first Esperantist in the town, who used to gather together all the children playing in the streets and teach them free of charge. The school chaplain, who liked Jews, came along with Mrs Henrietta Maltz, the wife of the attorney, and her younger sister Erna, both daughters of Mr

11

Lorbeer, the Jewish landowner, who owned Stynawa. A collection of money and clothing for the refugees was organized on the spot. A soup kitchen was opened in Toynbee Hall. It was holiday time and homeless people could be accommodated in the school founded by the Czacki family. The sight of the sudden destitution of people reduced to sleeping on rotten straw might have warned the others against leaving their homes. Various rumours about the Cossacks began to circulate. Most frightened of all were the women and children. Half the inhabitants of the town, which means the Jews, were alternately packing and unpacking, depending on the news spread by the rumour-mongers, who had never been busier. In the morning the Russian forces were getting closer, in the evening they were in retreat. Last night gunfire could be heard.

Today, the guest hall at the inn was full.

People came to rest and fortify themselves before their flight. How far did they plan to escape? As far as Vienna? How far could they get on foot? A few kilometres. Why wait until the last moment? They might have gone in comfort by train. A week ago the frontier station of Podwoloczyska was taken. It was "retaken". What do they mean by "retaken"? You can only retake something you once owned, something that once belonged to you. And Russia never owned Podwoloczyska and had never given it to us. Who would have thought that the Emperor had made such enemies of those Russkis! But Podwoloczyska had fallen to the Russians and there had been enough time to consult one's wife about what to do next. Town after town had fallen like so many skittles; the enemy seemed to be in a hurry. He obviously had no time to spare. Why? That is another story. But people who did not leave by train, and now had no money to hire a cart, or had enough money but did not want to spend it, ought to be staying at home.

"*Sydy i ne rypaj sja,*" says Yevdocha in Ruthenian to a cow, and the cow understands that it has to stay put and not move, but a man does not understand.

12

But to get back to our subject, the enemy seems to be in a hurry. But why? Is it possible that our forces are unable to contain him? Or is it perhaps part of the plan of our General Staff?

In the morning, the town was quiet. The professional gossip spread the news that our side had repelled the Russian forces. And at dinnertime—it always has to be "at dinnertime"—the lodger rushed in, quite a young man but more sensible than some of the older people, who had been self-employed for a few years, working in his own shoemaker's workroom across the hall in Tag's house; well then, he rushed in with the depressing news that people had begun to pack again. Everybody called him Gershon the cobbler, by his given name, for poor people have no family names. The Cossacks are already at Mikolajow, only thirty kilometres away. Mounted Cossacks. The infantry was a menace to men, because it rounded them up for digging trenches, but the Cossacks were an even greater menace to women. Why were people packing? They would have to leave everything behind anyway. Even if they were now willing to pay the price of a cart in gold, they would not find anybody foolish enough to sell. One might leave with a horse and cart, but to return with it would be more difficult. After all, people had not hidden their wagons or their carts when our side was evacuating the wounded, only to have them requisitioned by the enemy. In war a horse is four times more valuable than a man.

Minna, the daughter-in-law, and Lolka, the granddaughter, were standing by the window, crying softly.

"You can escape if you want to! I'm staying here. I'm not in any danger. What could the Cossacks do to me? Nothing."

"Why?" asked Lolka.

"Silly child. You always pretend to be sillier than you are."

"I can stay," said Minna, "but what'll happen to Lolka? She's thirteen now," she whispered, rolling her eyes, "you mustn't forget that. If only Elo were here . . ."

Minna and her daughter had seen Elo off when the black and yellow posters announcing general mobilization were stuck on all the walls and fences. The men were in uniform and were walking with their suitcases to the station. They were soldiers now and belonged to the Emperor. Oh, beloved Emperor! If only you could see what was happening at the station! . . . a band marched in front, blowing their trumpets, behind it a column in blue. On either side, as usual in peacetime, children were running. From the windows people were waving their handkerchiefs, just as in the song:

> When the soldiers march through the streets
> The girls open windows and doors.
> Why? Because . . .

This may have been appropriate once upon a time . . . Now the handkerchiefs were used for wiping eyes. More than one woman's face was wet with tears.

Ladies in wide-brimmed hats were passing out sweets and flowers to the soldiers, as they did during end-of-term celebrations at school. Mrs Henrietta Maltz, chairman of the welfare committee, the "Women's Hearth", arrived, out of breath, carrying a bunch of cornflowers, almost too late, because together with her husband and her sister Erna (who had suddenly disappeared), she had been packing for her departure. Already on the first day of the war . . . The men, the ones dressed in civilian clothes, were slipping cigarettes to those who were mobilized. On the platform, the same band played the anthem: "God support, and God preserve our Emperor and our land." The men doffed their bowler hats, and stood at attention. The soldiers peered out from the cattle trucks, their eyes fixed on their families, smiled, waved, as if beckoning them to come and at the same time taking their leave. Jokes were cracked. People were winking, wiping the perspiration from their brows; the civilians were unbuttoning their frock coats, and the younger ones their summer jackets. Hands and handkerchiefs were waved. Playfully, some took refuge under the ladies' white parasols. Now it was the soldiers' turn to throw sweets and single flowers at the young girls crowded round the open doors of the cars. Amid the laughter, children caught them, as it would not be proper for young women to do so. From time to time the eyes of the ladies and gentlemen

14

turned toward the Baroness. Perhaps she wanted to remain unrecognized, but the thick black veil covering her face did not help her. The Baroness wore black, as she had done for many years now. She was recognized at once both by her dress and by her carriage, drawn by two grey horses, which was waiting outside the station. Besides, over whom would the first Esperantist in town, Amalia Diesenhoff, hold her parasol (being an Esperantist is even worse than being a Socialist, Mr Maltz the attorney used to say in order to tease his wife, Henrietta), clad as she was in a man's black straw hat, a blouse with a tie, her pince-nez on a ribbon? The Baroness was seeing off a young lieutenant who might have been her son, but wasn't. Miss Amalia handed him as a farewell present not flowers or sweets, but a thick pamphlet with Esperanto vocabulary and grammar. It might come in handy during the war. The Russians were also learning that international language, the language of brotherhood and of the future. The lieutenant was standing at the window of his reserved compartment with a cornflower pinned to the ribbon of his shako. He was a cavalry lieutenant; he was smiling, and surrounded by an aura of glistening brilliantine and the smell of perfume. Suddenly a commotion broke out. People called: "Quiet! Quiet please!" Over the heads of the crowd appeared a high fur hat with an egret plume. It was Mayor Tralka arriving in his Polish national costume. He owed his position to the Baroness, but that was an old story. Next to the mayor appeared the director of the classical high school in full-dress uniform—a braided suit, cocked hat, and sword. The subprefect, on the other hand, was wearing an ordinary frock coat with striped trousers and a bowler hat. The Catholic school chaplain, the one who liked the Jews, took a step back and ranged himself next to the town rabbi in a sable hat and fur-lined overcoat; the two men, tall and slim, were quietly carrying on a conversation. The mayor was lifted up onto a chair, which creaked under his weight. He wiped his neck with a red kerchief and shouted: "Soldiers!" Silence fell. "We, Poles, loyal subjects of our gracious ruler, will stand as one man behind our Emperor, Franz Josef the First, to defend freedom under the sceptre of His Sovereign

Majesty . . ." Cheers and applause broke out, cries of "Long live!" were heard, and tears appeared in the eyes of some ladies. The military band played again "God support, God preserve . . ." Everybody, even the small children, stood at attention. When the last sounds of the anthem died away, the "Women's Hearth" welfare committee moved toward the train. The ladies carried flowers in their hands. But first their chairman, Mrs Maltz, made a speech. In a tremulous voice she read from a sheet of paper her piece about brave officers and loyal soldiers ready to defend the Fatherland and the Emperor, their mothers and children, their wives and sisters, who would all loyally wait for the return of the victors. In God's name and with His help! See you all again in four or six weeks, at the latest. Long live the Emperor Franz Josef! She ended just in time, for the train began to let off steam. The sliding doors of the cattle cars were shut. Women and children rushed toward them crying, their arms outstretched. The train started, at first slowly, so that one could still keep pace with it. Through the slits between the sliding doors people were grabbing hands, anybody's hands. A great cry full of names went up. The locomotive had its nose turned to the east. The train took Elo to the front. Minna and Lolka stood sobbing in one another's arms. Straight to the front! They went on and on, all day long, stopping at every station. This was unheard of! They stopped for several hours at a time. Supply trains with arms, ammunition, hay and fodder for the horses, and meat for the soldiers were let through first. Thank God, this meant that Elo's train had not been sent to the front yet. They were safe for the time being. Thank goodness for that, we'll pray for the rest. They stopped at Horodenka, not far from the Austro-Russian frontier. Even in peacetime it was frightening to look beyond that frontier, let alone now! We are in a certain town, Elo wrote. This letter had no sender's address, only a field post number as a precaution against spies, of whom there were many everywhere, but the name Sarah—his aunt's name—was enough for them to guess where the 29th Infantry Regiment was stationed. On Saturday, Elo wrote, he had got a pass to go to the synagogue together with Nathan Wohl, the son of the baker from Lvovska Street, the one who delivers bread in his own cart. And who has another, younger son, a well-fed young fellow . . . What a story! Old Tag stopped reading. To need a pass in order to go to the synagogue on the Sabbath! Soon they'll be issuing passes for God knows what! . . . But Elo did not go to the synagogue at all but to Aunt Sarah's for a good Sabbath dinner. Dear Auntie burst into tears when she saw two Jews in uniform in the doorway. They had many laughs together on that sad day, the first Sabbath away from home, because, for Nathan Wohl's benefit, Elo told a story of a poor man who took another poor man to a free meal at a rich man's house, passing him off as his son-in-law whom he had to support. Aunt Sarah laughed at the story through her tears; she was not cross at all, on the contrary, she was very pleased that Elo had brought a visitor, for in times such as these Jews have got to help one another. For who will have to bear the blame? Who will be the scape-goat, if not we? But dearest Minna is not to worry, Elo said in his letter, everything will be all right. If for a packet of tobacco (here followed a few words in Yiddish so that the censor should not understand) you can get a pass from the sergeant himself, things cannot be too bad. With God's help our offensive will begin soon and our gallant armies will give the foe such a beating that he'll never forget it, he'll get sick of fighting and he'll never get back on his feet again. They will be together for the New Year, in a few weeks' time. The war cannot last much longer. For the Feast of Tabernacles, Elo will build a sukke or hut in front of the house, in the garden, and not in the yard next to the cow-shed, as he used to do before the war. But dearest Minna must take care of herself and of dear Lolka and look after herself and Lolka. One hears so many stories about the Cossacks. In a certain village, the name of which he cannot give for military reasons, a Jew was hanged in the market square because some tele-phone equipment had been found in the house. Everybody was assembled and forced to witness the terrible death of an innocent man. The town rabbi went to the commandant to ask that his soldiers not be allowed to harm Jewish wives and daughters, and he never returned. This was not a rumour.

People from that place told him the story. And as to dearest Father, he should be careful not to overwork and on no account must he intervene on behalf of other people, as he likes to do. As to the farm, Yevdocha must work more and must not be allowed to spend so much time lying in bed. Besides, there will probably be less work in the inn now anyway. It might be more profitable now to make cheese and butter rather than sell the milk. And to bake rolls once a week, on Thursdays, for the household only. There will be fewer customers now, fewer all the time. Has anyone rented the little attic room? Does Gershon still meddle in other people's affairs, instead of working in his workshop? Because he too likes to mind other people's business. He's safe, though, he's still young, he won't be called up for a while yet. Let's hope that when his age-group comes up the war will be over. Father should not worry so much about various things. He himself has forgotten when the anniversary of Mother's death is, he only remembers that she died during the summer, when it rained so hard that the stream carried away the top of the old dam by Axelrad's mill. . . .

The talk was already getting loud at the long table in the guest hall, when Wilf the photographer entered the room with his second wife and his only daughter, Asya, with whom the curly-haired Boom was madly in love. The stepmother's name was Blanca, and she was only a few years older than her stepdaughter. Asya was tall, and Blanca short and plump; she wore an old-fashioned dress with a train in back and very tight in the waist. At once she sat down and took off her boots, sighing with relief. Wilf knelt down and, shaking his head, looked at Blanca's swollen toes.

"I told you they would be too tight," he said.

"I'm half dead," said Blanca frowning. "Asya, my dear," she added, turning to her stepdaughter, "let me see your boots. Perhaps yours will fit me and then you can try mine."

When Lolka saw Asya, whom she knew from school—Asya was three years ahead of her—she burst into tears.

"Mummy, I'm still young, I want to live. Let's escape too. Everybody's leaving."

18

Gershon, the cobbler, heard this and scowled.

"Lolka! What's the matter with you? What are you talking about? There's no need for you to talk that way. Your grandfather and I won't let you come to any harm."

"Why take it out on the child?" asked Minna. "Come, Lolka, let me change your dress while your grandfather makes up his mind what to say."

She took her daughter's hand and they went up to their bedroom. She took some old clothes out of the cupboard not only for Lolka but for herself. She threw them onto the bed, shut the door, and began to change.

All the wives and daughters of the town had changed clothes. Blanca had changed too, but not poor Asya, for whom she cared little. Blanca was wearing an old-fashioned dress but tried to look young in it. So the masquerade was quite useless. Mrs Soloveytchik, for instance, and Mrs Kramer and her daughter Rose wore their oldest clothes and kerchiefs on their heads like ordinary peasant women. To protect their new clothes from the dust, supposedly. They were trying to conceal the real reason from the youngest members of their families, and the daughters pretended not to understand.

Gershon was grinning. "What's this? A carnival? A masquerade ball? It won't do any harm, but it won't help you either. Whoever invented this method of protecting oneself against the Cossacks?"

As a matter of fact, there was a lot of dust that year.

A rainy spring was followed by a hot, dry summer. The weather, thank goodness, did not affect the harvest. Throughout the district, especially at Duliby, where the soil was best, the corn had grown like a forest. If war had to break out, this was the summer for it. The enemy was only waiting for the peasants to bring in the corn and thresh it. The army would then take the grain, and the straw would be used for the horses and for mattresses in the barracks.

There had been another sign. A practically infallible one: locusts.

At that time Gershon showed what he was capable of. He went to see people in the town and collected together all those living near the General Hospital, urging them to fight this plague. First of all he organized the members of "Future", the shoemakers' union, and of "Star", the needleworkers' union, which shared premises on the square.

"Locusts? What locusts?" Old Tag had asked doubtingly.

"What are they, then?" countered Gershon irritably.

"Some other kind of insect, more than likely."

"Why's that? What do you mean by 'some other kind of insect'?"

Admittedly, Gershon did not go to the synagogue even on the Sabbath, preferring his union, which had elected him to the post of librarian at their last general meeting, preferring to read his *World History*, in German in six volumes bound in leather with gold lettering, at first not being able to understand, but reading on and on without understanding, until suddenly he began to understand all the words, for which he was indebted to Comrade Simon of the needleworkers' union—Comrade Simon, who had finished four classes of high school and was better educated than many a student. And so Gershon preferred books to the synagogue; he also liked going to the cinema on Saturday afternoons to see films with Max Linder, Asta Nielsen, or Waldemar Psylander, and his heart beat faster when the man who collected the tickets closed the shutters, and the lamps under the ceiling of the Ruthenian "People's House" went out, and Henry Mund began to play his violin and living pictures moved across the screen, yes, but all the same he remembered enough from the Pentateuch which he had learned at the Jewish school to know that locusts were an Egyptian plague and he more or less could imagine what the plague looked like, for although many centuries had passed since those days plagues had not changed much.

Old Tag raised his hand to his mouth.

"Yes, yes," he agreed, "now I see that you are right! And anyway, if you've got your mind set on seeing locusts, it's all right by me. If that's all you need ..."

The locusts descended suddenly.

At noon it grew very dark, and a thick cloud moved in from the direction of the General Hospital. It was high in the sky and it looked as if it were about to rain or even hail, until it blocked the sun. The noise did not resemble the roaring of the wind, because not a single leaf moved on the trees, not a speck of dust rose on the road. Darkness fell on the earth slantwise, in clouds, one after the other. The noise was so great that it drowned the voices of the cattle lowing in fright, the howling of the dogs, and the shouts of the people. Shut the windows! Close the stable doors! Children were hurriedly brought indoors from the streets. Nobody could tell who was calling or screaming. The swarms of insects hit people in the face. The metallic whirring of wings reminded one of May bugs; it died away after a short while. The insects whirled, collided, broke their flight, fell down like wounded birds, brown, rustling, their red-lined wings looking like a million open, greedy mouths; they flew low over the ground as if made heavy with its proximity, drunk with it, buzzing malevolently, once airborne but now crawling winged bugs, they turned around, fell, and again crawled on the grass, on the flower beds, on the mignonette in the front garden of the inn, on the apple trees and pear trees in the orchard behind the cow-shed, on the black alders by the bend of the stream, on the meadow, the road, the wattle fence, the roof. They made their way into the hall, the kitchen, the living rooms, the cowshed, the milk pails. Their joints cracked, their feet drummed on the tin roof, on the floorboards. They piled up in layers, one on top of the other, a general mating occurring casually while food was being sought, at random, blindly, densely, on the move. The field, the rooftop, the road—everything seemed to crawl like one enormous leathery beast. The chickens ran around the yard madly, heavy with food, their necks swollen with insects. The white cat hid under a wall of threshed sheaves of rye in the shed. In both the Catholic and the Orthodox churches the bells were ringing in harmony. The fire engine roared by, its bell clanging metallically like a broken pot. From its hose a stream of water shot out to the left, to the right, straight ahead, then straight back as if trying to keep the insects away. But it was a drop in the ocean. Not until the locusts disappeared were people able to do anything. Gershon ran back and forth, rounding up boys from the streets and grownups from their homes and from the union building. The boys were easier to persuade, but the grownups preferred on the whole to watch the few who had begun to dig holes. It looked as if trenches were being dug. After the locusts had gone, people kept looking for a long time to the east, west, north, and south. Women kept white sheets, as Gershon told them to do, to chase away the plague, should it appear again. They told one another what they had dreamed of the other night or the night before. They told each other what they had seen. One had seen a crazed herd of cattle, another had dreamed that the madwoman Pessa, Simon the tailor's sister, ran about shouting, clutching boys by their sleeves and repeating: "I love you, I love you, I love you!" Yet another had seen fire over the railroad station, and a fourth had even dreamed of a star with a tail. People did not believe them, but everything is possible: hadn't one seen the town idiot, Shulim, telephoning the Emperor from every waterspout just before his body was found on the railroad track, flattened by a train? Everything is possible. Illness is foretold by many omens: shivering, fever, itching, a rash, excess perspiration, or an abscess. War is the same. And after the locusts, an epidemic might follow. Gershon was already setting fire to the dead locusts piled high in the holes which the boys had dug, when a policeman suddenly appeared with a drum hung on his shoulder and drumsticks in his hands. From a sheet of paper he read an order that all manure heaps, gutters, sewers, and privies should be sprayed with lime and carbolic acid. Those who refused to obey the order would be fined a sum of up to five crowns. There was danger of a cholera or typhus epidemic. Next, posters signed by the "Women's Hearth" welfare committee and other committees appeared appealing for gifts of soap to be distributed among the very poor. It was then that Erna, Mrs Henrietta Maltz's sister, fell in love with Simon the tailor who lived in a wooden hut in the worst street in town— Crook Street—infested with thieves and drunkards. Mayor Tralka himself drove around the town in his official carriage, inspecting backyards, looking into rooms. He praised the

22

courage of the inhabitants who had heroically withstood a natural disaster. He praised Gershon for his idea of burning the dead locusts. The mayor dropped in at Old Tag's inn, but he was in such a hurry that he had no time to have any sour milk and asked only for a glass of water, so sick did he feel from the smoke and the smell of the burning insects. Meanwhile Gershon had another idea. Having harnessed himself to a rusty roller used for spreading gravel and levelling stones on the road, he trudged blindly ahead, crushing the sluggishly crawling survivors of the plague, bloated like pregnant bedbugs. Gershon spurred his helpers on to further efforts by shouting: "Forward! Forward! Always forward, comrades, never backward!" These were words from a song that used to be sung in the market square during meetings of the shoemakers' and the needleworkers' unions, when from the balcony of their joint premises was hung a red flag with a gold-lettered inscription: "Long live the Jewish Socialist Party". It was Comrade Simon, of course, who delivered the main speech at those meetings. Even educated ladies came to listen to him, so beautifully did he speak—this dark, tall man, with a fine head of hair. Not at all like Gershon, who was small and thin as a rake.

Yevdocha, the cow-girl, entered the guest hall of the inn, and although she had often seen customers drinking sour milk there, she withdrew quickly.

Minna, Tag's daughter-in-law, had time to ask her why she had brought the cows back from the pasture so early.

"They'll be here any minute now."

"Who's 'they'? Which 'they'?" asked Minna, irritated.

"The Russkis. They're going to take the cows."

"Have you eaten, Yevdocha?"

"Oh!"

"There's nothing left to eat. The milk is all gone. Lolka will bring you a piece of bread in the cow-shed. With cheese. We didn't cook any dinner today."

"Did you hear?" Soloveytchik pointed with his head to the door, which closed after Yevdocha. He got up and signalled to his large wife and daughters that it was time to move on.

23

But nobody stirred. They sat and chatted.

Lolka, now wearing her grandmother's shabby taffeta dress, was clearing the dirty milk mugs, eggshells, and gnawed chicken bones from the tables.

"Aren't you in a hurry?" asked Old Tag. "Not even after hearing what the girl said? You're right. Why hurry? How many kilometres can you cover in a day on your own two feet?"

"But the enemy is certainly in a hurry," warned Soloveytchik. "I know all about them. From over there." He meant Kishiniev, the town from which he had escaped with his wife. His wife was expecting their first daughter at the time they crossed the frontier. They gave the child the Russian name of Lena. The other children did not have Russian names. As luck would have it, they were all girls. When the fourth daughter was born, Soloveytchik escaped again. He left his wineshop, his wife and children, a trick that was unheard-of among Jews. Maybe that was the custom over there. But a week later he was back. "Why did you come back? I won't have another child, you can be sure of that. I'd get rid of it, even if I knew that it would be a son. What do you want from me? Was it my fault?" The smallest girl, now a year old, was cradled in her mother's arms. She had inherited her mother's white skin and plumpness.

"I don't get it, I just don't get it," said Apfelgrün irritably. He was the short, fat owner of a shop that sold fashionable footwear. The gold frame of his pince-nez flashed when he turned his eyes from the door, which had now been closed for some time. What red legs that barefoot girl had! He might perhaps find her a pair of old-fashioned boots in the shop.

"Well, whose fault is it that somebody doesn't understand?" Soloveytchik shook his head. "A person only understands as much as he can or as much as he has to."

Apfelgrün threw back his head to examine Soloveytchik, who was sitting opposite him, more closely. "What did you say?" he asked. After a while he turned his back to Soloveytchik.

"I wouldn't mind another glass of sour milk," he began again, after a moment's silence. "When I say that I don't understand, I know what I am talking about. All right, so there's a war, but what kind of enemy is it? On the same day that war has been declared, the enemy occupied Podwoloczyska. Who ever heard of such a thing? As far back as anyone can remember, there's never been anything like it. In a real war, as I understand it, you give battle, you say: There will be a battle at such and such a place, somewhere near a town, best of all across a river. The armies stand opposite each other, with guns, ammunition, cavalry, infantry, with a band, trumpeters, and so on and so forth. And on the hills stand the generals on horseback facing one another with binoculars, and they watch the field of battle between them and run the whole show, just like God, as it is written. If the enemy attacks on the left flank, you send in troops from your right flank; if the enemy attacks on the right, you counter with troops from the left flank. But this kind of war? To enter a town without even knocking at the door! It's barbarous, I tell you! Neither the Germans nor the French would do anything like that. But what am I getting so worked up for? What else could you expect from such an enemy? Do you think that our 'Russniaks' are any better? I mean those peasants in bast shoes or the ones who go around barefoot. Thank goodness none of them has the nerve to come into my shop. But I remember them from the days when my father, blessed be his memory, did business with them. And my father, when he felt his end was near, made a last confession like every pious Jew: 'I have sinned, I broke the faith' and so on, then he called me, I was his eldest son, the apple of his eye, and he said to me: 'Either gold or muck'. I understood right away. I threw out the peasant boots; what I mean is, I didn't throw them away, I sold them as fast as I could and never bought that kind of merchandise again, and for the front of my shop I had a signboard made reading: 'Elegant footwear'. And now there is no need to sweep the floor all the time and I have some peace."

"Where there is no muck there is no gold. Remember that for a start." It was Pritsch who spoke. He sat beside the long table, not on a bench like all the others, but on a chair with a

25

straight wooden back, with a heart cut out in the middle, country style. Like Apfelgrün, he was unmarried and had no family. He might have stayed quietly at home, but being the owner of a tobacco shop and a concessionaire for the National Lottery, he had many enemies and was afraid of informers. Not so much of Jewish as of Ruthenian informers.

"Secondly: war is a game of chess." He smiled with his thin lips and turned again toward Apfelgrün. "I make a move and wait for my opponent to make one, then he makes a move and waits for mine. And so on, and so on. . . . And as for gold, I could tell you a story. . . ."

"And what about international law?" snorted Apfelgrün. "So why drag chess into it? I make a move, you make one! What do you mean? Do you take me for a kid? What's this got to do with war? You've got to have a conscience! You've got to have some human feelings!"

"Exactly! He hit it on the nose!" Soloveytchik intervened. "He wants the Russians to observe the rules. Believe me, I know them better than I ever wanted to, and I don't wish them on anybody. Who do you expect to have a conscience? Or to have humane feelings? The pogrom-mongers of Kishiniev and other towns? The world only knows of Kishiniev, because the pogrom there was a big one. But those who were killed don't care whether it happened in a big or a little pogrom. International law, history? Ah, cut it out. Those are the kind of stories grandmas tell their grandchildren. The whole world might shout in horror, but the Tsar wouldn't lift a finger. Right, Hana?" he asked, seeking his wife's support.

Instead of replying, she shrugged her powerful shoulders slightly and kept leaning over the infant in her arms.

Kramer the bookbinder was sitting at the head of the table and gazing back and forth at the two speakers, all the while shaking his head. Then he propped his elbow on the table.

"What's so surprising about that?" he asked. "Whoever starts a war wants to get it over with as soon as possible and to win it quickly. Doesn't our Emperor want the same? But, it must be admitted—I don't know much about left flanks or right flanks, I'm no Hutzendorf, it's unimportant, Mr Apfelgrün, excuse me, Herr Apfelgrün—but it must be admitted that the enemy is in a hurry. It's a fact. But why is the Tsar in a hurry? The answer to this is simple: Because he's got to be. If I don't know something, then I say: I don't know. One thing is certain: if someone is in a hurry, it means that he's got to get a move on. Perhaps the ammunition situation isn't too rosy, but that's not the main thing. . . ."

"Rosy, not rosy," Pritsch shook his head. "They've got an answer to that: We shall cover you with our hats. . . ."

"Allow me to finish my sentence," Kramer requested politely and looked toward his wife, whose curly head towered over everybody else's at the table. She held her head high, slightly tilted back. With downcast eyes she glanced at her son, Boom, and at Asya, the photographer's daughter, who sat facing him.

"Cover with their hats?" he bowed his head. "Perhaps. Why not? Let them. No one has ever been killed by a hat yet." The bookbinder laughed at his joke. "Well?" he looked around. "Am I right or not?"

"I wanted to tell you the story about gold, which just goes to show that if there were no muck there wouldn't be any gold," intervened Pritsch. "To say nothing of the fact that gold is produced from . . ." Pritsch was smoking a fat cigar and now he swallowed some smoke. His yellowish face became red and swollen. Gershon handed him a glass of water. Everybody waited for Pritsch to stop coughing. Apfelgrün tried to help him by clearing his throat.

"Well, at last," gasped Pritsch.

"Did you want to add something?" asked Gershon politely. "Because if you didn't . . . " The lottery concessionaire waved his hand.

"Well then, allow me to take part in your discussion." Gershon combed his black hair with his fingers. Because of his hair, he was sometimes nicknamed "Tar-Brush Gershon". "All that has been said so far, if you will excuse my boldness, is inaccurate." The cobbler looked toward the rigid figure of Mrs Kramer. When she raised her eyes and caught his eye, she pulled down the corners of her mouth slightly and straightened her shoulders even more. "I think, gentlemen, that you are slightly mistaken in your views. In my opinion, to my mind no one has mentioned one very important matter, namely France. For if you say that the Tsar is in a hurry, you must also look at it from another viewpoint. From which viewpoint, then? First of all, what about France? Everybody knows the answer to that. Does the Tsar appeal to everybody in France as a business partner? Everybody knows that he doesn't. It must be as clear as daylight to everybody that the French General Staff has said: My dear partner, be so good as to occupy the city of Vienna for us within, say, two months. At most. Not a day later! A bill of exchange which is to mature in two months. I'm speaking as a businessman. But what happens then? We know that in two months it will be October, our High Holy Days will begin and, as we know, so will the rains, mud, dampness, 'all the seven things', as we say in Yiddish, and then we'll see how the Russian infantry tries to wade through our Carpathian mud. Let it occupy Vienna. For the moment the enemy is happy to have occupied Podwoloczyska and other little towns which, were it not for the war, no one would ever have heard of. Let him be pleased. But it's still a long way to Vienna. So, of course, the partner can't meet the bill of exchange. What will the French General Staff do then? Send a telegram: Partnership dissolved. The engagement is over, the fiancée is available again. Then we'll move in lickety-split and win the war. I wanted to say something else, but . . ."

The bookbinder's wife started waving her arms about.

"Max," she said very loudly, "what are we waiting for? Either we return home or we keep on walking. Either-or . . . I have no intention of listening to all these speeches!"

"Mama is right," said young Kramer, the curly-headed Boom. He was looking with wide open eyes at Asya Wilf.

Old Kramer silenced his son with a wave of his hand. "Don't you interfere." And to his wife he said: "We'll be going soon enough. Well, well," and he waved in Gershon's direction. "Pray to God it'll be as you say. This is not stupid, not stupid at all! Go on talking, go on!"

But Gershon sat down at the end of the bench and kept quiet.

Apfelgrün sighed.

"Yes, yes, France! France! A fellow comes along and talks as if he were on chummy terms with France. Has he been there? Has he lived there? It's all very well to talk!"

"Herr Apfelgrün," interrupted the lottery concessionaire, "this is an altogether different story. Who cares whether a certain person has been in a certain place or not? That's not an argument."

"Quite right," Kramer kept nodding his head. "What that young man said was not at all stupid."

"Max," Kramer's wife said in a muffled voice without lifting her eyes, "let's go back home. Sitting here doesn't make any sense."

Kramer kept looking at Gershon.

"All right, all right, we'll go in a minute. What's your trade, young man?"

"What difference does it make?" Gershon threw a sidelong glance at Kramer and lowered his eyes,

"That was not at all stupid," Kramer kept repeating.

"Why should it have been stupid?" asked Old Tag.

"I seem to remember," said Kramer, pursing his lips, "that I mentioned ammunition a bit earlier. Does Russia have ammunition or doesn't she? I've got information from a reliable source. This war won't be fought with bullets, but with bayonets. I didn't invent this. I'm not brilliant enough to invent anything. Before anybody had ever heard of Sarajevo or of mobilization, a certain high-ranking officer passed it on to my son Leon, my doctor son who as you all know is a regimental surgeon, which means that he has the rank of captain. This was when Leon went to Abbazia on his honeymoon two years ago. No bullets, just bayonets." Kramer placed his hands on the top of the table, took in all those present with his gaze, and slightly rose as if he were getting ready to leave. He waited for somebody to agree with him or ask him a question. But nobody spoke, everyone seemed to be deep in thought. Kramer slowly sat back in his chair.

*

Boom, however, got up from the table and walked over to the window. He then gestured to Asya to go out with him. Asya, wearing a white voile dress with pink flower print, sat at the table slowly sipping her sour milk, or rather pretending to sip it, because her mug had been empty for a long time. She pretended not to see Boom's signals. She pretended not to see him at all. The war had broken out, true enough, but her step-mother was sitting next to her, barefoot, with swollen toes, and tears in her eyes. Asya's father was whispering to her, while she kept turning her head away from him. Poor Father! Poor Boom! How she has suffered because of him! He had neglected his studies—he was a year ahead of her—and had to take his final exams in a year's time, but he had played truant from his afternoon classes, running over to the girls' high school, "Fiat Lux", in order to wait for Asya. She had to conceal it from her teachers and the headmistress, who might have called in her stepmother. How much worry Boom had caused her! Boom's mother knew everything and so did Asya's stepmother. Boom's mother said: As you make your bed, so you will lie in it. If you fail your exams you'll have to work in Father's workshop. Leon is a doctor, and you'll be a craftsman. Then you can marry whomever you want, even a cobbler's daughter. Asya's stepmother said that she would throw her out of the house. She would have kept her word if the war hadn't started. But the scandal had come to light earlier. Boom was expelled from the boys' high school. The scandal broke during a performance by the amateur dramatic society, "Our Stage". The town was crazy about the theatre. Whenever the troupe of Boritz and Glimmer came to town or Stadnyk's Ukrainian theatre (the Ruthenians wanted now to be called "Ukrainians"), not to speak of the guest performances by Irena Trapszo or Ludwig Solski, tickets were hard to come by. But no troupe was quite as popular as the local dramatic club, "Our Stage". And the club would have enjoyed its popularity for a long time to come were it not for a play written by Benedict Horovitz, a young local attorney, the son of a poor but respected unlicensed legal adviser. Horovitz had a part in his own play, and Asya and Boom played the roles of lovers. Asya had the stage name of Asta, like the famous film actress Asta Nielsen, who was starring just then in the film *Mother's Eyes*, and Boom the name of Alfred like the Viennese actor Alfred Gierasch. Alfred's parents were members of the born aristocracy and did not want their only son and heir to marry a poor girl from an otherwise respectable family, whose father was a postal clerk in a provincial town. The only solution to the lovers' problem was suicide! On Asta's birthday they decided to take poison. Goodness, how tragic were their death throes! The poison was burning their insides: they writhed, choked, clasped their breasts! Their suffering was terrible to see. Someone called out in sympathy: "Enough! Enough! Stop it!" Mrs Henrietta Maltz, who was sitting in the first row, covered her face with her fan. And her sister Erna hid hers in a handkerchief. Did she foresee then that Destiny was preparing a similar fate for her? But luckily, thanks to Henrietta, she had escaped that tragedy. So when the couple were dying on the stage, and Asta was whispering: "I am on fire, Alfred, but think of yourself, save yourself if you truly love me; it is too late now to save me, I can feel the kiss of death on my lips, I love you, my handsome knight, I love your deep-set eyes, your mouth, which will never again touch my longing lips, I love your hands which will never again stroke my hair, I love all of you and therefore I beg you, save yourself first!"—sobbing could be heard in the audience. The drama was entitled *Too Late*. Just then the parents of the hapless Alfred come home from some aristocratic reception in a gay mood; they turn the light on; on the floor they see two prostrate bodies. Alfred's mother lets out a shrill cry: "My son, my only child, why have you done this to me? Oh, why? Why didn't you tell me! We nursed you with a silver spoon. Ah, my husband! Donald! Hurry, fetch the best doctor! Maybe we will succeed in saving our son at least! We shall forgive him, let him marry whomever his heart desires. But make him live! Half our fortune for saving our Alfred! Hurry up, Donald! Every moment counts! Oh, woe is me, the most unhappy of mothers! What have I done to deserve this? I am like Niobe now!" Then just as Alfred's father is about to leave the house and is looking around for his hat, she

cries: "It's too late! Can't you see it's too late? Don't leave me alone with two corpses on the floor!" Then she falls in a faint, calling out, as if in warning, toward the audience: "Too late!" These were the last words of the play, and the curtain slowly began to come down. And while the last sounds of the violin, played behind the scenes, were dying away, calls from the audience rang out: "Henry Mund! Henry Mund! Bravo, bravo, encore!" And in front of the curtain a small boy, the child of an ordinary artisan, appeared, wearing long trousers and a reefer with a white collar adorned with blue anchors. He was clutching his violin to his breast, and bowing like a real virtuoso left, then right, then straight ahead. The author of the drama, Benedict Horovitz, who acted the part of Donald, Alfred's father, acknowledged the applause in a similar manner. He called out: "Curtain!" and the curtain rose again and all the actors lined up on stage, among them Asya and Boom, both very pale. Asya received a beautiful bunch of narcissi. The audience clapped and yelled "Bravo", the women shouted "Encore, encore!" and so did the men, though less loudly and with sour smiles as if they were feeling somewhat guilty. Two weeks later the play had a repeat performance. Benedict Horovitz added something to it, namely, a final scene in the form of a conversation between two gravediggers in the cemetery, one of whom blamed the rich parents; the other sympathized with the tragic young couple. But the added scene was destined never to be performed. Additional rehearsals were held; posters with an inscription apeared: "By popular demand —repeat performance featuring the child virtuoso Henry Mund, who, in the last act, will play 'Solveig's Song' on the violin." The repeat performance ended in a scandal. Seated in the audience this time were all the town's educated people who had missed the first performance. Some people were there for a second time. The men wore cutaways with striped trousers, the ladies egret feathers in high coiffures, gowns of velvet and satin, jewelled ear-rings, brooches and rings and multi-coloured silk stoles on their bare shoulders. Entering the theatre, a person was overcome by the hot air redolent of scent. All tickets were sold out a few days before the performance. The
32

gate of the "People's House" where the "Edison" cinema was located had been closed before eight o'clock. The film was cancelled, and instead of the white screen, a hand-painted curtain was lowered. It was an enormous curtain depicting a group of Ruthenian peasant boys wearing white embroidered shirts and clogs, and girls in red and green aprons and wide pleated skirts, motioning people into the "People's House". Others were pointing to a picture of a painted river, a group of trees, and the towers of a Catholic and an Orthodox church. The people could recognize their own town at once. Not only was the main chandelier in the centre of the ceiling lit, but so were all the lamps on the staircase and in the passages. The hall was brighter and more crowded than for the first performance. There was a small crowd of people waiting in the streets, and the number of firemen present had to be doubled, to make four, in order to hold back the pressure of the crowd. Some people insisted that Benedict Horovitz, author of the play and chairman of the drama club, be summoned. Some demanded standing room tickets. Everybody was willing to pay, but nothing doing! Gershon was let in as an exception. When Dr Leon Kramer, the bookbinder's son, was let in through the back door, the tailor yelled: "I protest!" Horovitz stuck his head out through an opening in the door—he was wearing a grey wig, so that he was not easily recognizable —motioned to the tailor to come in, and said to Gershon: "You may come in too. But I should like to point out that the actors' nearest relatives have the right to enter without a ticket."

The trouble occurred toward the end of the performance, when the lovers began acting out their death scene. Alfred suddenly became so excited when Asta begged him to save himself that he flung himself on his beloved and began to kiss her passionately—although the stage directions did not call for this at all—on her mouth, on her neck, wherever he could reach! At first no one wanted to believe his eyes, and thought that Boom was only play-acting, that these were only stage kisses. But then somebody hissed softly, somebody else began to giggle, and at once the hissing became bolder and louder. In the back stalls and in the standing room—where

33

the prices were the lowest, and where the worst elements had gathered—and on the balcony, usually filled with schoolboys from the higher forms (although officially schoolboys were not allowed to attend the theatre before their final exams without being accompanied by adults, except for school performances), people began to smack their lips as they did in the movies when the actors are about to kiss. Poor Asya defended herself as best she could but Boom kept squeezing her tightly and did not loosen his embrace. One might almost have thought that he had gone mad, as some actors have been known to do when they have become too engrossed in their parts. Somebody in the first row exclaimed in a high-pitched voice: "Shame! Shame!" It was Mrs Maltz, the head of the "Women's Hearth" welfare committee. She got up, extended her forearm in its long black lace glove, and banged her fan against the prompter's box, onto which Benedict Horovitz had now leapt. With one swoop of his hand he tore off his false aristocratic beard and, waving it, tried to quiet the audience. "Let us finish!" From the hall, people called: "Such behaviour on the stage is a public disgrace!" In the first two rows the spectators, mostly women, stood up screaming: "This is a scandal! There are young children present!" The folding chairs were banging and overturning in row after row. A few middle-aged ladies pushed their way forward, helping each other toward the door. The balcony shook from the stamping of feet. People in the orchestra waved at those in the balcony, imploring them to stop stamping for fear of a disaster. Amalia Diesenhoff had come to the theatre alone, because the Baroness, whom she ordinarily accompanied, was spending that part of the year in Vienna. She now got up on a chair and, holding her pince-nez in her hand, began to speak. Although she opened her mouth wide, no one could hear her. The schoolboys in the gallery kept on stamping their feet and calling: "Asya! Boomy!" Somebody was beating the seat of his chair like a drum, somebody else was shouting: "Fire! Fire!" Other voices took up the cry: "Fire! Fire!" Still others began calling for help: "Women and children first! Don't push! Open the emergency doors!" By now most of those present were getting up on their chairs to see where the fire was. "Calm yourselves! Sit down!" an elderly man exclaimed. At the exits the four firemen were shouting: "Who has seen a fire?" No one answered. "Please calm yourselves." The firemen tried to keep back the crush of people pressing toward the door. "Please go back. There is no fire. Leave the exits free. Where is the fire? Where? We would have been the first to notice it." The elderly man was helping the firemen. He spread his arms wide and called: "Ladies and gentlemen, please act like human beings! Who was the first to shout?" Gershon knew. He had a standing place and had heard a hoarse voice shouting: "Fire! Fire!" Pessa, Comrade Simon's sister, was very red in the face. She fell into a frenzy whenever the weather was hot. That year the attacks came earlier. It was a sign that some disaster was in store for the world. Mad people have premonitions. Meanwhile Amalia Diesenhoff continued to speak. Her tie was askew and she was squinting. All of a sudden everybody began to hiss: "Shh! Silence." People turned toward the stage. In front of the painted curtain, Dr Leon Kramer stood smiling, his hands held high. Behind him a few other gentlemen, all trying to smile. Benedict Horovitz was calling from the prompter's box: "As the author of the play . . . as the author of the play . . . I assume full responsibility, both legal and judicial, for the public scandal, for spreading . . ." Dr Kramer interrupted him: "I can't see that much harm has been done," he said, "but all the same my little brother will get what's coming to him from my mama. . . ." The whole audience burst out laughing, and the tension subsided at once. The firemen were now able to open the doors wide. First to leave were women with children, then the men, cracking loud jokes. But in the gallery the pupils from the boys' high school, the seventh-formers, Boom's colleagues, kept banging on their chairs, leaning over the railings, shaking their fists and shouting in unison: "On with the show! Asya! Boomy! Keep going!" But by then there were no people left. The theatre was empty.

At home Boom had to listen to a lecture from his mother, while the headmaster threatened him with expulsion. And they had ample reason to do so. That a schoolboy had performed in public without permission would have been enough—and this was the headmaster's answer to Boom's defenders. Kramer used all the influence in the town that he could muster. He went to see Mrs Maltz. Neither the Jewish religious instructor nor the school chaplain could help: the clergy did not have any influence. The headmaster was fuming: from a theatre to a dance hall was but a short step. A thing like this doesn't just appear out of thin air! It must have some source! And anyway, who was responsible for everything: the school authorities or the clergy? In the curtained-off booths of the "Vienna Café", that brothel, that den of vice, sixth-formers had been found in the company of chorus girls. And what about the house of ill-fame run by that Israelite, what was his name? Suspicion fell at once on the Royal and Imperial Boys' School. Who would be reprimanded by the school superintendent's office? The clergy or the headmaster? The school chaplain smiled ironically. Whose fault was it? How much influence did a religious person have nowadays? In an era of an ever wilder race for profit and pleasure, in an era when immortal values such as virtue, honour and even love of one's neighbour, or willingness for sacrifice, had been devalued what could one expect of the younger generation? Was there a single one among the teaching staff who regularly went to church? Example comes from above. Weren't some regrettable instances of drunkenness in public reported about the teachers? And what about certain masters who turn up drunk for their classes? And I needn't remind you, gentlemen, of the disgraceful fact that some students from the "Fiat Lux" girls' high school were invited home by one of the teachers on the pretext of coaching them before the final exams, when the reasons for the invitation were actually quite different? The chaplain bowed his head and addressed the Jewish teacher as "the Reverend" although he was not a rabbi, and motioned for him to speak in defence of his coreligionist. The Jewish instructor began with a quotation: "A foolish son is the grief of his father." He paused for a moment and continued: "Withhold not correction from a child: for if thou strike him with the rod, he shall not die." And went on: "A whip for a horse, and a snaffle for an ass, and a rod

36

for the back of fools." And on: "He that spareth the rod hateth his son: but he that loveth him correcteth him betimes." The religious instructor stroked his short beard and lifted a finger toward the ceiling. On the other hand, it has been said: "Folly is bound up in the heart of a child; but the rod of correction shall drive it away." And further: "By his inclinations a child is known, if his work be clean and right." But most important: "Say not: I will return evil. Wait for the Lord and He will deliver thee." And further: "It is no good thing to do hurt to the just: nor to strike the prince who judgeth right." But most important of all is what has been said in the Holy Books of Wisdom: "He that is patient is governed with much wisdom: but he that is impatient exalteth his folly." The chaplain coughed, covering his mouth with a handkerchief, while the headmaster blushed, blew smoke into his tobacco-stained moustache, and walked out of his study. Through the good offices of Mrs Maltz, Kramer managed to see the headmaster's wife. He offered her, as a member of the Committee of the Polish-Jewish Orphanage, a twenty-kroner bank note. The donation was received with expressions of gratitude on behalf of the poor orphans, but the money might just as well have been thrown away. The headmaster knew nothing about it and probably would never find out about Kramer's generosity. He scolded his wife for interfering when at teatime she started talking to him about young Kramer. Meanwhile, young Kramer was losing weight. If it hadn't been for Asya, curly-haired Boom would have taken poison like Alfred in the play. Mrs Kramer forbade him to see Asya. And Mrs Wilf threatened to chase Asya away from her home. It was the end of the world.

Although Asya was not expelled from school, her mark for behaviour was lowered from "excellent" to "satisfactory", which for a top pupil was sufficient punishment, as the headmistress, Miss Falk, was the first to admit. Then a miracle occurred. The Baroness, who was a very close friend of Mrs Maltz's, suddenly returned from Vienna, where she had been spending the winter. It was said that the Baroness had access to the Court at any time. Testifying to this was the fact that a whole wall in the Baroness's drawing-room was hung with photographs of the Emperor in white dress uniform, the Emperor shooting in Tyrolean costume, with leather shorts and braces and a hat with a feather brush, the Emperor at Gödöllö in Hungary with the residence of the Empress Elisabeth in the background—his hapless consort who sought a quiet refuge away from the bustle and ceremonial of the Court, the Emperor with his beloved granddaughter Elisabeth, nicknamed Erci by the people of Vienna . . . and on top of the piano a portrait of the Baroness herself, wearing a pearl necklace, by the Court painter Angeli. The Baroness's famous pearl necklace . . . She often used to tell the story of the cavalry captain in whose memory she still wore mourning and who at that time had been a very young lieutenant in the Viennese Dragoons, and who had selected her from among many hundreds of ladies and young girls at the Court ball, opened by His Most Gracious Highness. The Emperor was walking toward the rostrum followed by eighty archdukes and archduchesses. The archdukes in white full-dress Court uniforms, with decorations, and sashes, the archduchesses wearing tiaras, and jewels unmatched anywhere in the world. The Emperor walked through a double row of people, while the gentlemen stood at attention and the ladies made deep curtsies. Oh, may nothing go amiss! May no hook come undone! This is what a curtsy should look like: the face almost touching the floor, one leg stretched far to the back, the other lightly bent at the knee. Nothing could be seen, only the Emperor's red trousers and his boots, polished with ordinary shoe cream. Another moment and there would be a disaster: the thread of the necklace would break and from the string of pearls a pearl, the size of a berry, would roll under the feet of the Most Gracious Emperor. No one could lift a finger to stop the rolling, which was turning into a hailstorm. It was paralysis in the presence of Majesty. And now comes the climax, the most important moment, worthy of being entered in the chronicles of the Austro-Hungarian Empire: the Emperor stops and brings his foot back slightly so as not to crush the pearl. And what does *le premier Seigneur de l'Europe* do? He stoops to pick up—whether the pearl or the lady frozen in her deep curtsy and nearly fainting is not recorded. The Great Chamberlain in a cape lined with sable and with gold frogging is there ahead of the Emperor and picks up the pearl. A lieutenant in the Dragoons helps the lady to her feet and together with the Chamberlain escorts her to Franz Josef, who in the meantime has taken his seat on the rostrum. Amid the applause of the eighty archdukes and eighty archduchesses and other ladies and gentlemen of the highest Viennese society, she is given a handkerchief. In it are collected the pearls of her necklace. As she later confirmed, not a single one was missing. She took one step backward and curtsied deeply; following her example, all the ladies present did the same. After that incident, there was nothing the Baroness could not do in Vienna. Her good friend Mr Tralka, the land surveyor, was offered the post of mayor, the previous mayor receiving in an envelope a politely worded notice of dismissal. This was the Baroness's way of returning an insult. The ex-mayor, while still in office, had once leaned down to the subprefect, like himself wearing a gala national costume, with a *kontusz*, a fitted coat, and high boots, and whispered something into his ear, indicating the Baroness with his eyes. She had entered the church in a black silk dress and sat down in her pew, with her personal maid for company. The priest was just delivering a sermon about a harlot's conversion. . . .

One beautiful morning an open landau, driven by two grey horses, trundled along an avenue of chestnuts in bloom and stopped in front of Kramer's bookbindery. The Baroness, still quite young-looking, jumped down lithely and then helped Amalia Diesenhoff to get down. She had brought a small book to be bound, which looked like a prayerbook. She took a long time in choosing the colour of the buckram and the leather for the corners and spine and gently dismissed everything that Amalia Diesenhoff selected. Amalia asked Kramer if he had ever heard of the great Italian poet D'Annunzio. She showed the bookbinder on the flyleaf of the book, which was entitled *Alcyone*, a handwritten date—Fiume, 1913—and a signature; it was difficult to decipher the name "D'Annunzio". Kramer sighed. No, he had never heard of him. He was sure, however, that his son, Dr Leon, the staff surgeon of a regiment, with the rank of captain, had heard of D'Annunzio, perhaps even his wife, who liked reading books in Polish and German, and was educated, unlike himself. He only handled the outside of the books. But this was not why he was sighing. Maybe it wasn't right to bother the Baroness with such matters, but if he could ask for her help and support . . . Which form was his younger son in? The Baroness asked to see Boom. That afternoon Kramer took his son to the Baroness's villa. In front was a garden where magnolias bloomed in the early spring: passers-by used to stop to gaze at the pink, mauve, red, and white flowers, so strange because they grew on leafless branches at a time when melting snow still lay on the ground. The maid led the way to the orchard, where apple trees grew in straight rows and peach trees climbed the walls. Kramer introduced Boom to the Baroness. She shook her parasol at him in mock anger. She was sitting on a seat near a whitewashed wall in the full glare of the sun. She looked the boy up and down from head to foot, then told him to come nearer and tousled his hair. When he was taking his leave, she gave him her hand to be kissed, and said that the visit had exceeded her expectations. To the headmaster she sent Miss Amalia Diesenhoff (and not her chambermaid) asking him to call on her without delay; she was waiting for him. "I should not hesitate to intervene on behalf of young Kramer even with His Majesty himself," the Baroness told the headmaster, who was breathing heavily, wiping his neck and his yellow tobacco-stained moustache. "He's worth the trouble. I know what I'm talking about," she added.

"Bullets, bayonets, ammunition, the works." Soloveytchik shoved his hat back. "What's important is that the enemy is in a hurry. And if he's in a hurry, it means, I'm afraid . . . I had to escape, once before . . ." He intended to repeat once again what people already knew.

He was interrupted by Apfelgrün, owner of the store that sold fashionable shoes.

"But this is Austria, not Kishiniev. And thank goodness there won't be a Kishiniev here as long as Emperor Franz Josef is on the throne. There's no Jew in existence who wouldn't wish him a long life and good health. And the rabbis are praying that his affairs shall prosper and that all who serve him—his family, his Empress (she is no more with us, alas), his armies, his police, his Ministers—should live long as well. A pity he's not a Jew. Then again maybe it's better that he isn't; if he was a Jew he might not admit to being one. It's enough that he has a Jewish heart. The Emperor likes to dress as a simple peasant, to ride in an ordinary peasant's cart lined with straw, and to find out for himself what's happening in his Empire. Whether it's good or bad. Once he dropped in at a country inn—he was quite young then—and the owner's son, an only child, was dying. The Emperor had no inkling of this, and started asking his usual questions about what people were grumbling about, but the innkeeper brushed the questions away with a wave of his hand. Are the taxes too high? The innkeeper waved his hand in silence. Has anybody in the village been treated badly? The same gesture from the innkeeper. The civil servants for sure don't like the Jews. Why doesn't he name the ones who don't? The innkeeper waved his hand again. The Emperor ran out of questions and said: 'Are things really so bad with you?' 'Yes, only God can help me.' Only then did the Emperor learn about the tragedy that had struck the innkeeper. So he said: 'Yes, certainly the Almighty is all-powerful, but I know a man who might help you.' And right away Franz Josef had his best doctor sent to the inn, and the child was saved. The Emperor made his presence known, and the whole village came running to pay their respects. The peasants also profited from the Emperor's Jewish heart, because, thanks to the innkeeper, they each received two acres of land, while the innkeeper got a thousand guilders in cash, which in those days was worth as much as two thousand, and on top of that a licence to sell spirits. He's still alive, lives in a big city now, his old age is secure and his children are doing well, and may God, without harming them, give us all such a reward."

"I don't want to boast," said Pritsch, the tobacconist, and cleared his throat; everybody was afraid that he would start coughing again. "In 1848 my grandfather captured a Hungarian flag and was decorated with a medal. Actually, he wasn't decorated until the Emperor had learned about what he'd done, and then he got the medal. After the battle, the Emperor rode over the battlefield, the Austrian troops lined up to present arms, as is the custom in such cases, and everything was as it should be. But when the Emperor began to speak to the soldiers to thank them for their bravery, somebody in the front row fainted. As you will guess, no doubt, it was my grandfather. While he was grabbing the Hungarian flag, he was wounded with a lance. But Grandfather kept right on fighting. After the battle was over, he didn't report himself wounded, he didn't go to the hospital because he thought it was all a bunch of nonsense, and he very much wanted to see the Emperor face to face. 'This is an example,' said Franz Josef, 'of how one should love the Emperor and one's motherland. Here you have an example of that courage which they claim is missing among certain nationalities. In my empire, which embraces numerous races, all living in harmony, there are no cowards on the field of battle!'"

"Unfortunately," interrupted Apfelgrün irritably, "the Emperor was wrong. Take the Ruthenians. I heard that a Ruthenian priest was hanged in a village. I have known many priests. I know the priest from Duliby. He buys from me, and so do his wife and son. Who'd have thought that there are priests capable of spying against their own country?"

"They're not spies, they're Russophiles," corrected Pritsch. "Among the Ruthenians and the Greek Catholics you'll find lots of them. They think of Russia as their country."

"How is it possible?" exclaimed Soloveytchik. "I can't believe it!"

"They have their own way of thinking," replied Pritsch. "Their view is that they are persecuted, that they are being cheated not by the Emperor but by the Poles and Jews who are all over the place: in the judiciary, in the municipal offices,
42

in the subprefectures. Although actually there are very few Jews in the civil service."

"That's true enough," confirmed Kramer.

Apfelgrün was angry.

"What's true enough? What have they got to complain about? Why do we always have to be the ones who feel sorry for everybody? Let's face it: you've got to have servants, otherwise who is going to sweep the streets, lug the water, chop the wood? The Jews? The Jews haven't got the strength for that kind of work. How have the Ruthenians been treated badly? They've already started opening their own trading centres and co-operatives. Now the peasants shop here, but luckily prices are higher there than in Jewish shops. And as to doctors and lawyers, they've got their own. And that priest was no Russophile, just an ordinary spy. He was caught fixing telephone wires in a stable. What did he want a telephone in a stable for? And then there was the peasant who sat on the bank of the River Seret at night-time and used a lantern to show the Cossacks where there was a ford. Would you call him a Russophile? He was just a spy."

"Only a man who doesn't have any views and doesn't read the papers can talk like that," said Pritsch through clenched teeth.

"I'm not so sure whose views are better!" Apfelgrün took off his pince-nez and began to clean it with a handkerchief.

"To start with, it takes a minimum of schooling," answered Pritsch with a wry smile.

"Look at him, the learned professor!"

Kramer, the bookbinder, was drumming his fingers on the tabletop.

"Could we perhaps go now?" asked his wife.

Gershon raised two fingers.

"I apologize for taking the floor again. It's not so important that one person says one thing and another person another. What matters is how things are in reality. Everybody might be suspected. If you're a stranger all you have to do is stroll a few times round the market square. Who's that? people begin to ask. No one knows. Where did he come from? No one knows.

So he must be a spy. What's he looking for, that spy? I once saw people attacking a blind man. And who were they? I am ashamed to say that all of them were Jews. They said he was pretending to be blind. When his dark glasses were broken, they saw that the man had no eyes in his sockets. They let him go, but with his lips cut and bleeding. That's no way to behave. A person should act like a human being."

"You're right," said Kramer. "I always say: Humanity before all."

"And harmony," added Old Tag.

"Yes, yes! Harmony," Gershon said in Tag's support. "Harmony builds, as the proverb says, disharmony ruins."

"You're right again," Kramer nodded in agreement. "If you want to win a war, you've got to have harmony first of all."

"Very true, very true," said Old Tag. "The Temple of Jerusalem was destroyed because of discord."

"I didn't start the argument," said Apfelgrün with a shrug of his shoulders.

"That's neither here nor there," said Kramer waving his hand. "We need harmony to win the war. We must win the war not only for the Emperor but for ourselves. Because if we win, we shall have eternal peace. And if we don't, we'll have a war on our hands every five years. Every five years! My elder son, Leon the doctor, is already in the army. Doctors too are being sent to the front now. And my younger one, that rascal," he said, nodding his head in the direction of young Boom, who stood under the window, shifting his weight from one foot to the other, "in five years' time may have to defend the Emperor and the country. The country can do without one young scamp, but may God grant the Emperor the longest life and the best of health, not forgetting my children either."

They walked and walked, but seemed not to make any headway.

They kept to the highway, not to the footpath, but, like soldiers without a commander, each of them did what he wanted, pushing forward or falling behind.

Old Tag followed them with his eyes from the window, until the dust screened them from his view. As a matter of fact, there was a lot of dust that year.

"A leap of road," said Old Tag aloud.

How many kilometres can a man cover in a day? Plagues, like locusts for instance, can happen twice, but miracles never happen twice. Gershon the cobbler does not understand what a "leap of road" is. How could he? He imagines himself to be knowledgeable; he thinks that a *World History* in six volumes contains all one needs to know in life. Yet the only wisdom is to be found in the small print of the Holy Books. So listen here, simpleton: If God feels like helping people who escape, the road leaps toward them and distance shrinks under their feet, as it did under the feet of Jacob when he was escaping from Esau. For a long time now poor Jacob had been running from that brute Esau. And he's on the run again. "Maybe I've got it backwards," Tag sighed, watching a cloud of dust slowly settle on the ground. "The drifting and running has started, and there'll be no end to it. God Almighty, will it ever end? Never? Is this why You chose us? Many thanks! If our fore-father Abraham hadn't started wandering we might have saved ourselves a good many miles during all these years. How many volumes are there in that history? Six? And where does it stop?"

Gershon has been gone for some time. When you want some-body, he's never there.

The highway was empty now.

The column of dust still hung in the air at the turn and trailed after the refugees, as if the wind were blowing in that direction; it enveloped Axelrad's two-storey mill where Tag's only son Elo worked as a book-keeper. Where was Elo now? Maybe already at the front?

Silence. The silence of desolation; anticipation of the enemy. Soon they will come into view. Those who escaped won't see them. What will they look like? What will they threaten us with? With what interdictions will they begin their persecu-tion? With what edicts will they start their rule? For hundreds of years people have had to wind their way along a narrow

45

passage of interdicts and edicts. Such people can only be likened to mice eternally looking for a place of safety.

Panic was approaching from the General Hospital, which had been converted into a military hospital for a day or two. The rumbling was getting louder and louder.

The hospital had been evacuated so quickly that there had been no time to take down the Red Cross flag from its façade, not to mention the white sheet with a red cross on it on the roof. Wounded soldiers had been hurriedly loaded onto peasants' carts. Where could all those wounded have come from in the very first days of the war? Women and children had crowded round the gate and peered through the railings. This is what war is like. All one's life one had heard of war, and this is what it looked like. . . . Closed eyes, dirty bandages, the smell of gangrene, of carbolic acid, of iodine, a doctor in a bloodstained gown looking like a butcher at his stall. The same kind of blood, the same sickly smell . . . The orderlies with red crosses on white armbands had shouted: "Get a move on, there!" Such valuable bodies . . . So much money has been spent on them for so many years! Beautiful, fully grown, well-cared-for bodies were now hurriedly flung onto the carts and blood was seeping through the bandages. At least these men were still alive. Another man had his face covered with a blanket and the doctor ordered him to be taken away.

The rumbling noise came from the baker's cart. Wohl the baker was now approaching from the direction of the hospital. His elder son was with Elo at Horodenka, where they had stopped on their way to the front.

Instead of the Cossacks, a cart appeared, or rather two, one chock-full of Jews in caftans, the other loaded with their wives and children. One for men, the other for women, as in a house of prayer.

This was all Tag needed at the moment! All of them would sit around, not stirring, expecting to be served.

Tag went out and stood in front of the inn in his waistcoat and skullcap, like an innkeeper who had no more food or drink to offer.

The baker did not get down from his seat. A good sign; thank God for that. It meant that he did not want to stop.

"Where are you going, Jew?" asked Old Tag. "What's that freight you're hauling there? One Jew, two Jews perhaps, I might understand; but so many Jews at one time . . ."

The baker cracked his whip.

From above the caftans the perspiring, bearded, but mostly young faces turned around. Only one face did not turn, that of the tsaddik from Zydaczow. He was travelling with the ritual number of ten Hasidim, the requisite number for prayers during a journey. The holy rabbi's eyes were closed, but his lips were moving. Was he by chance one of the lesser rabbis who can recite psalms during a journey? Any water carrier or simple artisan can do that. The tsaddik was still a young-looking man, with a luxuriant black beard in which his pale, narrow face seemed submerged and lost. He sat in the shade of his own wide-brimmed hat. The ritual ten were also moving their lips. There was no doubt about it: these were the lesser Jews who recited the psalms.

"That's a long story," answered Wohl.

Two drivers, hired at Zydaczow, ordered the Hasidim to get down in the middle of the market square, and then drove away in their wagons. The tsaddik and the Hasidim with their wives and children spread themselves out in the square like Jews in the desert. And, with folded hands, waited for a miracle. They did not move from the spot. What was Wohl to do? Every year before the Days of Awe it has been his custom to visit the tsaddik at Zydaczow for at least half a day, as his father and his grandfather had done; his sons didn't go with him. Ah yes, that reminded him: his oldest son Nathan was with Elo in some small village; he has had a letter from him; and in the other wagon is his younger son, a complete ignoramus, who does not even know how to pray. So going to see the tsaddik is all right, but when it comes to giving him a lift was Wohl supposed to leave him in the lurch? So there was nothing left to do but harness the horses to his two carts—one wouldn't have been enough for the whole retinue. His wife had screamed: "You lunatic!" She grabbed him by his overcoat: "A menace to your soul!" Little did she realize at the time that their younger son was to drive the other cart. "I'll drive 'em and be back before dark." "Why of all people do you have to stick out your neck? There are plenty of other Jews around. There's the town rabbi, there's the congregation, let them take care of them!" I thought: I won't make it to Skole, but on the way I might come across some other driver . . . . I'd pay for it out of my own pocket. For a tsaddik I'd foot the bill any day. If a person only knew whom they were escaping from! And what if the rumours were true and it really was the Cossacks? Then better to escape from your own people. The market square was empty; no one in sight, neither any of our people nor any outsiders; not a policeman anywhere; everything deserted. Anybody could have a field day. The town looked as it does on the Day of Atonement: the shops are closed, the stalls all empty. A real fast day. But plenty of activity in the station yard instead: the military stores were being ransacked. The day of janitors and thieves has come. All day long they were loading barrows with flour, army-issue bread, hardtack, groats, chocolate, sugar, all sorts of goods, provisions for the whole war. You call it war? Is this what it's like? Today they're looting the military stores, tomorrow they'll turn to Jewish shops. If our soldiers are to fight Russian soldiers, let them. What business is it of mine? It's enough that my son has been mobilized. Let them fight at the front, but here I demand order! And where have the policemen disappeared to? A town without policemen! Especially now, when they're needed most. Near the town hall, papers were blowing about: whole sheaves of them, deeds of land, plans, surveys, mortgage records, receipts for taxes, birth, marriage, and death certificates! Now no one will know who owes money and who has already paid: all will be equal! All that's missing now is the Messiah! What more do you want? Before trouble has even started, my janitor came up to me and said: There will be slaughter. I didn't even ask what he meant, just took him by the scruff of his neck and threw him down the stairs. He's still counting his teeth.

Wohl's son in the other cart burst out laughing. His

shoulders shook; he blushed and pulled the peak of his cloth cap down over his eyes.

"Why're you laughing? Has foolishness got the best of you?"

"Dad," the boy said, "let's go; how long are we to hang around here?"

Wohl whipped up the horses. Then he turned round and asked the tsaddik if he would like a drink. It was hot and they wouldn't be stopping anywhere else on the way. And later on there might not be anything at all to drink.

"Leave him alone. He doesn't want anything," said a red-haired Hasid with a thin beard. His head was bare except for a skullcap while he was fanning the rabbi with his hat. "If you wish, give a drink to the poor little things."

The poor little beggars on the other cart, dirty from sweat and tears, sun-baked, in thick jackets, wrapped in shawls so as not to catch cold, were whimpering softly. Among various bundles, women in wigs were huddled together, flushed from the heat. Buttoned up to their chins, they sat with their heads thrown back, their eyelids half closed, and now and then wiped the perspiration from their faces with handkerchiefs they held in their hands. The tsaddik's wife wore a black and silver kerchief on her head, tucked behind her ears and tied under her chin. Leaning forward, she was staring at a baby laid across the knees of a wet nurse who was just changing it. This done, the nurse gave the infant her breast. It refused to suck. The nurse covered her large breast, then uncovered it again. She did so repeatedly. The other women were nursing their children, covering their bare breasts with handkerchiefs.

Old Tag's daughter-in-law, Minna, and his granddaughter, Lolka, brought some towels and water out of the house.

The women got down from the cart and washed their hands, faces, and necks, sighing with pleasure. They then lifted the children from the wagon and undressed them so that they too could wash. The men bunched together and poured water on their fingertips and on their nails, then rubbed their eyes with it. Yevdocha brought a pail full of fresh milk and poured it into mugs. The children drank greedily and cried out for more. Their shawls were taken off, their jackets unbuttoned. Unfettered now, they began to run around in the front garden, trampling the bed of mignonette. The older ones climbed on the wattle fence round the yard. Then they came back, shouting that they were hungry. From some white linen bundles their mothers brought out some white cheese and butter in earthenware pots and spread it on bread. Finally, they laid out on the grass some apples and some bruised peaches.

"Hurry up, now! We must be off," the red-haired Hasid urged. "Have you all eaten? Drunk? So off we go."

They climbed back onto the carts, the men in theirs and the women in theirs. First to climb up was the tsaddik, whom the redhead had led behind a tree and brought back again. After him climbed the remaining eight Hasidim, some on the seat and some behind him on the cart. One of them was a young boy, a child practically, with a pale face and enormous eyes that nearly filled his face. All in wide-brimmed hats, black caftans, low shoes, and white stockings: one with his right shoulder higher than the left; one tall and fair, very beautiful with golden corkscrew curls; the tallest of all, with a face white like a piece of linen with holes for the eyes and mouth; a very short and fat one; a thin man with a wiry, forward-tilting beard; a youth with down instead of hair on his face; a man on short, bandy legs; and a white-haired old man, the oldest of them all. They pushed and shoved as if each wanted to beat the others in the race toward the tsaddik. The women took their places calmly, decorously, around the tsaddik's wife, who thanked Old Tag, his granddaughter Lolka, and her mother, while the redhead thanked only Old Tag and, on the tsaddik's behalf, commended his house and family to God who never forgets to send down some calamity or other upon His chosen people. As the simple folk say: God is our papa, if He doesn't give us a hole in our shirt he'll surely give us a patch. . . .

The wet nurse stuck her nipple into the mouth of the crying infant. This time she succeeded, praise be to God! The tsaddik's baby son caught it and began to suck greedily. May he grow up to be a healthy young man!

❀

Once again there was silence. The silence of defenceless people haunting the highway now wide open to the enemy. The highway was unconcerned, so was the enemy. What did they care about Old Tag's life and kin? The enemy did not know a thing about them. They had no inkling of Minna's or Lolka's existence either, did not know their faces or their names, yet in a single moment they might become as important as God, who gives or takes life at His pleasure.

The fields on both sides of the highway were deserted, indifferent, although not a single blade of grass had changed since the previous day.

The three of them peeped through a gap in the curtains to catch sight of the first Cossacks.

Nothing to be seen.

But from the direction of the General Hospital they could hear the grating of a stick against the flagstones of the pavement, and the loud sound of approaching steps. A straggler.

On the first day of the war he began to limp and had continued to do so, although the military commission had declared him unfit for military service. He walked about jerkily and people laughed in his face. A fool. Perhaps he was afraid of informers, in whose ranks even Jews could be found. . . . One could even go so far as to say that it is not terribly difficult to find them among our beloved people. And now, although not a soul could possibly see him, he continued to limp. He got so accustomed to it that people even began worrying about what would happen to his foot after the war. He might even, God forbid, limp forever!

"Why is the cantor's son escaping?" wondered Old Tag. "It might be easier to go around with a limp here than in Vienna."

The cantor's son was walking quickly, not looking to right, or left, or behind him. He beat a short tattoo with his stick, which had an iron spike. He did not stop at the inn. He crossed the narrow bridge under which a large stream nearly the size of a river had flowed once upon a time and moved the wheel of the water mill, before it became a steam mill; now a thin ribbon of water trickled in the middle of the river bed, and in

51

front of the dam all that remained was a six-foot-deep embankment. The cantor's son receded in the distance until he disappeared around the bend of the road.

Again silence.

Old Tag, Minna, and Lolka left the window.

"What now?" asked Minna.

Old Tag went outside, latched the garden gate and closed the house gate.

"What now?" she repeated when Tag returned.

"You two will make a dash for the cellar."

"We won't go dashing anywhere," protested Lolka crossly.

"Why not?"

"First thing they'll do is ask for vodka. And then they'll find the cellar," said Minna, biting her lips.

"Sure. Mama's right," Lolka chimed in.

"All right, then: I'll hide you in the cellar. I'll close the trap door and put a piece of linoleum over it. Nobody'll guess there's a cellar under the kitchen. The first night is always the worst. And during the first night, the first hours of darkness are the worst. The later it gets, the quieter it gets. I'll move the cupboard against the kitchen door." He pointed to the one he meant. On its shelves stood earthenware mugs for milk and plates painted with red roses and blue leaves. "Don't worry, I won't let them in. I'll tell them that in the country there are no cellars, only a pit for potatoes in the back yard. Anyway, that's how it is with us, and it'll be up to them to make a liar out of me. Is it any different with them? If so, I can't help it. There aren't any women here; they've all escaped. Why? I wish I knew. Probably because they're just plain stupid."

"Stupid! Stupid!" exclaimed Minna. "That's all you hear: 'stupid', stupid'. Maybe Mrs Maltz is stupid too? Gershon told me he saw Mrs Maltz getting into a train. Together with her husband and her younger sister Erna." Minna lifted two fingers to her temple. "I would have to start getting one of my migraines now. Lolka, go get my drops, please. Wait, I'll go myself." On her way to the bedroom she kept rubbing her forehead. Then she stopped abruptly.

52

"Oh," whispered Lolka. She was the first to hear the sound and turned pale.

"What is it?" asked her mother nervously.

"Away from the window! Move away!" exclaimed Old Tag. He rushed toward it and drew the curtains.

All three stood in the middle of the room under the hanging lamp with a black tin plate for a shade.

"They're here," whispered Lolka.

"Come on, listen to me! Let me cover the trap door with linoleum." Old Tag went up to the kitchen door.

The women remained motionless.

Old Tag wrung his hands.

"For God's sake, come on!"

Both lifted their index fingers.

"Yes," sighed Minna. "They are here."

The clacking sound of horses' hoofs could be heard distinctly. And then nothing, as if the horses had suddenly been reined in. Voices sounded in front of the house. The garden gate creaked. Heavy steps and the jangling of spurs were heard. Somebody was rapping on the windowpane with one finger. Softly, unmenacingly.

"*Aufmachen!*"

In German?

"*Aufmachen Fenster!*"

What kind of German was this?

"*Aufmachen sofort Tür!*"

"German without any articles?" Minna was now more frightened than ever. "Oh, how terrible. They're pretending to be our soldiers!"

"Cossacks in disguise?" Old Tag blinked and went up to the window. "What a joke!"

"Don't open the window! Don't!" Minna backed away toward the bedroom door.

Lolka ran over to her. They clasped each other.

Tag waved his hand. He went up to the window and got ready to open it.

Minna pinched her own cheek; Lolka stuck two fingers into her mouth.

Another rap on the window.

"*Bitte keine Angst!*"

Old Tag stroked his beard with both hands, straightened up and, moving close to the window, shouted loudly:

"*Kosaken? Sind Sie vielleicht Kosaken?*"

"*Nicht Kosaken. Aufmachen! Magyar! Magyar!*"

Minna and her daughter exchanged glances.

"My God!" exclaimed Minna. "Are they on our side?"

"Open the window, Grandpa!"

"Magyar?" Old Tag drew the curtain. "Why didn't you say so in the first place?" He opened the shutters. "Elyen! Elyen! Magyar!" He held out his hand by way of greeting. "*Honved Husaren?* You should have said so right away in Hungarian. That much I can understand. Call the others. Come on in." He was pointing to two other hussars in front of the garden gate. They got off their horses and with their backs turned were relieving themselves. "Come on in. Minna, have you got the key? Open the door, or better wait here while I do it." Old Tag began to look for the key. "Ah, it's in the lock."

Minna and Lolka had their backs turned to the window. The hussar waved his leather gauntlets.

"*Nein, keine Zeit.*"

"But, Mr Honved, it won't do for the others to stand in front of the house. Make them come in. They can tie up the horses. Do you like plum brandy? What Hungarian doesn't? No? Just a drop, for good health."

"*Nein! Nicht!*"

"Just for a minute."

The hussar shook his head vehemently.

"Just for a minute: the war can wait."

Minna risked turning round; her eyes were slightly misted.

"Herr Offizier, don't refuse us!" she begged. "It would be an honour for us, it would make us happy."

The hussar stood framed by the window as in a picture. In the slanting rays of the sun his plumed shako glistened, his blue monkey jacket and red trousers shimmered with plaited braid and golden buttons.

What an army! How could one doubt the victory of one's side!

"*Wo Russen?*" The hussar knitted his brows. "Have they been here? Did they come through here? Were there a lot of them?"

"What do you mean?" Old Tag blinked. "Are you looking for them?"

"We're not looking for Russians. Myself," he said, pointing to himself, "and the others," he said pointing to his two comrades at the gate, "have lost our regiment. *Verstanden oder nicht verstanden?*"

"*Verstanden! Verstanden.* And how *verstanden!*" Old Tag was nodding his head. "He lost it? Lost a regiment just like that? Of hussars? With horses? And all the rest? With guns? How do you go about losing a regiment? It's not a pin!"

"It can happen to anyone," Minna said in the officer's defence. "Why all these questions? There's a war on!" She smiled at the Honved. "I apologize on his behalf. Please don't be upset."

"Upset?" Tag was getting angry. "Him? So you don't want to hurt his feelings? That's a fine way to begin the war! A whole regiment with guns lost. A drop in the bucket! And you want me to apologize to him. How many other regiments like that has our Emperor got to lose?"

The Honved swore aloud and blushed. He let loose a whole torrent of Hungarian words. Old Tag went red, too, and was getting ready to answer with a similar torrent in his own language. He opened his mouth and froze.

From purple the Honved's face had now turned pale.

The two other men shouted something in Hungarian and sprang into the saddle.

"Istvan! Istvan!" they called.

The third horse without a rider jerked itself free when the bullets began to hiss and bolted after the others.

The hussar cleared his throat, lunged forward to grab the horse, but three shots rang out in quick succession. The man dropped back, crouched over, and fell to the ground.

Has he been hit, God forbid? Wounded?

The soldier turned round. He started to crawl across the bed of mignonette planted by Elo. When Elo returns safe and sound, he will plant another bed.

Maybe the man has been wounded?

The hissing of bullets followed the other two riders until they rounded the bend. Real shots! The first real shots on the highway? Shots have been heard before, but fired in barracks at cardboard soldiers. And for the Emperor's birthday, with blanks. It was only a short while ago, but it was as though it had never happened. Candles in the windows, portraits of the Emperor in a white uniform with gold collar, bands, school-children marching two by two behind the soldiers, behind the civilians. Not very many schoolchildren, because the birthday fell during the summer holidays, but many trade unions with church flags and their own, along with the mayor in Polish national costume, girls and boys in costumes of the Cracow region, the "Falcon" athletic club in light-grey uniforms, the workshop owners in Polish national coats and hats. Nothing like this will ever happen again. And on every Sabbath, between the morning and the afternoon service, when the air is filled with goodness and pleasure, the rabbi, before reading a chapter from the Torah, pays tribute to the Emperor, wishing him the longest life span possible for a man. These things had never happened before and would never happen again. The Emperor, alone of all goyim, was being commended to God in the synagogues, and the hearts of all the congregation joined in the blessings with tremors of joy. No more though! The end of the world has come. How many nations are there? How many languages? But no nation venerates the Emperor more than the Jews. What will they do without Franz Josef?

The hussar pulled himself up, threw one long leg across the window sill as if it were a saddle, then the other, and, with a clinking of spurs, suddenly found himself standing in the centre of the guest hall of the inn—the same inn which he had been invited to enter through the door for a glass of plum brandy. He closed the shutters with the same gesture as anyone else and drew the curtains. He behaved as if he were at home. He knew where he was.

"*Kosaken.*" He turned round and showed his pale face.

"So I see," agreed Old Tag. "They're here."

"Who'd have guessed?" asked Minna suddenly.

"Away from the window! Away from the window!" Old Tag was gesturing to the hussar to move back. "Yes, yes, you too."

From the very start the hussar realized that Old Tag was a man to be obeyed. He made a step or two to the centre of the room and stood there, immobile, with a sabre at his side and a pistol hanging from his belt.

Tag crossed his arms behind his back, came up to the soldier and looked him straight in the eye.

"Well, Herr Honved? What next? Has the war been already won?"

The hussar nodded.

Minna was making signs at Old Tag. He should not make fun of an armed man. Doesn't the hussar understand? What if he does? What then? She smiled at the hussar. Suddenly she screamed:

"What's this, Herr Honved? Wipe it off! Where is your handkerchief? Lolka, give one to the officer. Bring a clean handkerchief from the wardrobe."

The hussar pulled a handkerchief out of his pocket and wiped his forehead. It was not blood, only traces of crushed mignonette. He looked at the green stain and smiled with relief. Clinking with his spurs, he knocked one of his heels against the other and, holding his hat to his breast, bowed his head in a short, quick gesture.

"*Danke!*"

"Not at all," replied Minna and blushed.

Old Tag was listening, his head raised and his eyes closed.

Firing could be heard again. The windowpanes were rattling, and the walls now began to shake. What was it? The ground all of a sudden felt unsafe underfoot.

They heard the heavy thumping of galloping horses and the roar of innumerable voices. What were they shouting? Urra? Urra? What does "urra" mean? Then the noise subsided slightly, and the gallop of a single horse could be heard.

The dust of the highway muffled the thudding of the hoofs.

"A patrol," exclaimed the hussar, raising one finger while holding his gauntlet with the others.

The momentary silence was broken by a thunderclap, then another and a third followed within short intervals. The walls shook, the windowpanes rattled, the milk mugs slid on the shelves of the cupboard. A whistling noise pierced the air, and the firing receded.

"Sounds as if there's a battle going on not far from here," explained the hussar. "Perhaps they'll come to rescue me."

"God willing!" sighed Minna.

"Nonsense," said Tag, looking straight in the hussar's eye.

"Nonsense, nonsense," mimicked Lolka.

"As soon as it gets dark," the hussar began in a whisper, "I'll make a run for it."

"Oh," scowled Tag, "in weather like this? With this hailstorm?"

Again a mounted detachment roared by, again the same cry of "urra" went up.

"What're they shouting for? Why? To make such a racket because of two and a half hussars! Looks as if they're still getting battle practice! Just as they practice how to cut hair with our beards. A child could win a war now. No one knows how to run it yet."

Dusk was falling.

The firing and the pounding of horses' hoofs had stopped.

Old Tag went over to the window and drew the curtain aside. The highway was empty. At the turn, not far from Axelrad's mill, the hussar's horse lay dead. The man turned away from the window and his head sank.

"Oh, dear," exclaimed Minna, "I completely forgot about supper. Lolka, let's go into the kitchen," and she took her daughter by the hand.

Lolka walked as if in a trance. She turned and from the doorway glanced at the hussar.

"*Verzeihen Sie*," she said blushing like a peony, "*Herr Offizier*."

58

Istvan stood still with his head hung low, his lips drawn tight.

"Was? Was?" he asked. "Why?" Clinking his spurs, he took a few steps toward the kitchen.

Minna quickly closed the door. Through a chink she called: "You must excuse us, Mr Officer."

The hussar turned and wiped his eyes with a handkerchief.

Tag lit the lamp hanging from the ceiling. He went up to the cupboard and opened the bottom door. On the shelves stood a glittering array of festive, red Easter wineglasses, fat bottles, silver spoons, and silver trays. From a separate compartment Tag took a black cashmere shawl with a fringe. He draped it over the hanging lamp. The room grew darker; only the very centre of it was illuminated by a bright ray of light. Perhaps this would help. He tied the corners of the shawl on the black shade of the lamp. This might do the trick. The wick must be turned down. At night, any light in a window attracts attention. Bandits have to take some risks; there's still something human about them. But those others might come without risking anything. So how are people to defend themselves? By screening the lamp with Yevdocha's shawl? A peasant's shawl? We'll pretend we're not here. When a fool shuts his eyes, he thinks he has become invisible. What do you do when the whole world is being turned upside down? This is the end of the world. Minna and Lolka—they're both like a couple of kids. And right in the middle of this whole mess who should turn up but him. . . .

"Sit down, Mr Honved."

The hussar stood in the middle of the room following Old Tag with his eyes. He smiled now.

Who is his father? Is he getting along all right? Has he got any brothers or sisters? Where is his home? In what town? Is he married, has he got a family? When you meet a stranger, you must ask him many questions so that he will no longer feel like one. Especially when he comes to your house. Why? A woman is like a small child attracted by any little trinket. And a man is like a red-hot poker which you cool in a bucket of slops. Anyway: asking questions comes from modesty, not

59

curiosity. He who does not ask is an evil man. Modesty is like a diamond. For, as King Solomon has said: "I hate arrogance and pride and every wicked way, and a mouth with a double tongue." And arrogance is worse than pride.

"You're standing there, Mr Honved, as if you were all set to shoot."

The Honved took off his coat, shako, and belt with the pistol and sabre, and sat down at the table.

Supper was still being cooked. From the kitchen came the smell of scrambled eggs. The hussar rested his head on his hand and waited.

"Make it four eggs for him." It was Lolka's voice.

"Three will do. Your father never had more than two."

Minna imagines that she will save the world with one egg. The dreamer! Old Tag took out a silk cord from his pocket, put it around his waist, and turned his face toward the cupboard, that is, toward the east. He began to sway in prayer. He put his palm against his forehead, knitted his brows, and shut his eyes tight. His lips moved quickly and regularly. He was mumbling the evening prayer in monotone. From time to time he gasped for breath, as if starting a new verse with a capital letter. When he reached the Eighteen Blessings he fell silent. Not a murmur, not a whisper, everything's still as in church. Ugh! What a comparison! Always the same! The priest's face. Who would have thought that a Jew swaying hard, bowing ever lower in silent prayer, could have such thoughts! Thoughts are like water, they seep in everywhere. No blessing can exorcize them.

Now and then a shot would crack in the distance. Whenever he heard them, the hussar would wince, glance around with fearful eyes, then again rest his head on his hand. His celluloid collar pressed into his unshaven chin. A horse neighed, its velvet lips trembled as it took the sugar, the skin of its neck contracts under the flies. The hussar was dozing; then he got to his feet with a start.

Minna and Lolka came back into the room and began bustling about the table. They asked the hussar how he liked his eggs. They had forgotten to ask him before. They have cooked some scrambled eggs for him, but perhaps he would have preferred fried or boiled eggs.

The hussar nodded his head to everything they said.

"Let's wait a minute," Minna added, "until Grandfather has finished his prayers. Lolka, d'you hear? What's going on outside?"

The wick of the lamp had been turned even lower. Minna must have done it, because the lamp was out of Lolka's reach. The flame of the lamp hissed and grew dimmer. Somebody was standing outside the house and calling in an empty voice, without words. The flame of the lamp grew brighter. Lolka ran toward the hall. The key grated in the door.

Old Tag took three steps backward, spat toward the left, and finished the prayer of Eighteen Blessings. He undid the silken cord, turned and caught sight of the open hall door and the retreating Lolka.

"What's happened?" he asked.

"Oh, God!" Minna screamed. "It's Boom."

Old Tag pulled her back.

"Get back! Both of you!"

"Oh, dear! Mummy!"

"Boom . . ." whispered Old Tag.

Boom was standing in the doorway with arms stretched out in front of him. He was carrying Asya.

"An accident!" Minna wrung her hands.

"She's alive . . . alive," Boom was mumbling.

"What's happened? What's going on?" asked Tag.

"What'll we do now?" groaned Minna.

"How did it happen? Out of the blue?" Old Tag came up to Boom, who was still standing in the door. "Come in, my son, come in!"

"She's alive . . . alive . . ."

"Oh, my God! Oh, my God!" Minna was sprinkling water on Asya's face.

"We've got to lay her down," said Tag. "Come, son, I'll help you."

"Where to put her, though?" Minna was looking round the

room. "Perhaps you can help us out?" she asked the hussar. "They must have taught you First Aid."

The hussar spread his arms. They were taught, all right. To help themselves. He might manage an arm or leg wound. But—here he pointed to his breast—he couldn't do anything there. Nobody could. Then he took out a little parcel, wrapped in paper and tied with a string.

"Gauze, cotton wool, bandage."

Minna pulled back her hand. She turned pale.

"Don't you want to use it?"

"I don't know how! Bandage! My God! It's awful!"

Old Tag showed Boom the way to the bedroom, and he helped to lay the girl on the bed. Boom sat on the edge of the bed and stroked her hair in the darkness. He wiped her forehead with a handkerchief. The handkerchief was dry.

Tag brought in some candles and put one in a brass candlestick on the bedside table.

Boom was touching Asya's forehead. He took her hand in his.

"Asya . . . Asya . . ." He was trying to wake her up.

"Where's your father?" asked Tag.

Boom was looking into the girl's face.

"She's alive . . . alive . . ."

"Should we take her to the hospital?" asked Minna. "It's not far."

"Hospital? What hospital? There hasn't been a living soul there since yesterday," said Tag irritably.

"And where is Mr Wilf?" Minna continued asking. "Does he know? Tell us, Boom! Does her father know?"

"Leave the room," said Old Tag.

Minna and Lolka obeyed.

Tag lifted the candlestick and shone the light into the girl's face. He pulled up one of her eyelids. Then he put the candlestick back on the bedside table.

"She's alive . . . she's alive . . ."

Boom looked at Old Tag.

Tag closed his eyes.

"Asya!" cried Boom. "My Asya!"

He fell to his knees, banging his forehead against the side of the bed and rolling his eyes.

"Asya! Asya! Asya! Asya!"

"The Lord giveth and the Lord taketh away. Blessed art Thou, the True Judge," whispered Tag, beating his breast. "We have trespassed . . . we have broken the faith. Thou knowest the secrets of the world and the most hidden mysteries of all living things. . . ."

Minna and Lolka peeped in through the half-open door.

Boom jumped to his feet. He rushed up to Tag, pulled him by the sleeve toward the bed. His lips were trembling but no sound came from them, only a garbled noise, the rasping voice of a village mute.

"Asya, Asya!" was all he could say.

Old Tag let himself be pulled by the sleeve. He now stood over the bed, shaking his head.

"Oy, Boom, oy, little Boom . . ."

In the doorway Lolka and Minna were sobbing.

"Asya!" shouted Boom and banged his fists against his head.

Tag's daughter-in-law rushed into the bedroom and took hold of the boy's hands.

"For heaven's sake, Boom, what are you doing? You won't do yourself any good this way. And where are your parents? Wilf, that photographer, I might understand"—she glanced at Asya's body—"but where's your father? Where's your mother? Such true parents. . . . On the road together all this time. . . ."

Boom tore himself loose from Minna and started waving his hands like a drowning man. Then he threw himself with a scream onto the bed and buried his head in the pillow. The girl's head jerked, turned to the side, and fell. Boom was now shaken by spasms of sobbing.

Minna was wringing her hands.

"What's wrong? Is he laughing?"

"Out of the room! Out of the room!" Tag tried to push her out. Minna resisted.

"I'll leave without your help."

Tag let her go.

"Stop talking, at least."

The boy sobbed like a child, then he was shaken by hiccups.

"Get him some water," said Tag to Lolka.

She returned at once with a glass of water, but Boom pushed her away. The water spilled on Asya's white voile dress printed with pink flowers.

Minna began to wipe Asya's neck with her handkerchief. Boom lifted his head and pointed to traces of dampness on the girl's arm.

"Here too . . . and there . . ." he begged, sobbing quietly.

"All right, all right, Boom."

Boom was again convulsed by sobs.

"Why? Why?" he sobbed.

"Drink the water, son," Tag tried to persuade him.

"Have a little water," said Minna.

"A drop at least," begged Lolka.

Boom directed his blurry, swollen eyes at Lolka, then, sobbing, fell on Asya's breast. In the middle of the bloodstain a paler drop appeared.

"What shall we do? We must do something!" Minna lamented. "We can't just let her lie here like this."

"Cover the mirror. Go get another candlestick and candle. Get out a white sheet. We'll lay her on the floor." Old Tag straightened his back. "And you, Lolka, get some straw from the cow-shed."

"Perhaps Gershon can find Wilf; after all, he is her father. He should take care of his own daughter. He should take her home."

"Gershon is gone, so is Wilf. D'you hear? We'll have to wait until morning. Tomorrow morning we'll see what to do next."

"The whole night! Oh, dear, this is awful! I can't stand it any longer! My head is splitting."

"I told you not to stay here. Take Lolka and go upstairs. Lie down. I'll stay down here."

"Lie down? Sleep? Now?"

Tag was silent.

Lolka put her arm around her mother. She whispered something in her ear.

Tag closed his eyes.

Blessed be the True Judge. The Lord giveth. The Lord taketh away.

Tag beat his breast.

Thou knowest the secrets of the world and the most hidden mysteries of all living things. Thou searchest the innermost recesses, and triest the kidneys and the heart. Nought is concealed from Thee or hidden from Thine eyes. May it then be Thy will, O Lord our God and God of our fathers, to forgive us all our sins, to pardon us for all our iniquities, and to grant us remission for all our transgressions. You have punished her who is as snow. Punish me for my sins. My house is a grave from now on. Let her rest here! I receive her unto my house.

For the sin which I have committed before Thee under compulsion or of my own free will.

For the sin which I have committed before Thee by unchastity.

And for the sin which I have committed before Thee knowingly and secretly.

For the sin which I have committed before Thee by association with impurity.

And for the sin I have committed before Thee by confession by mouth alone.

For the sin . . .

Spurs jangled behind the door. On the threshold stood the hussar in full uniform.

"There"—he was pointing to the guest hall.

"What's there?" asked Tag.

"Over there . . . window . . ."

Yes, somebody was knocking on the windowpane.

"Grandpa," whispered Lolka.

"Somebody's knocking," said Minna. "Who can it be?"

"Yes, yes." The hussar nodded. He lifted up his sabre slightly so as not to bump it on the floor. He saw the dead girl lying on the bed. He took off his shako, knelt down, and crossed himself.

Old Tag took a step toward the guest hall, stopped, and waited for the hussar to get to his feet.

"Mr Honved," Tag said, putting his hand on the soldier's arm. "It would be better if you left this room. Go into the kitchen, there you'll find a trap door in the floor, I'll cover it with linoleum later on; or, if you like, go through the open window out into the courtyard, the window is low; from there into the orchard and the field, the grove and off you go! . . . *Verstehen Sie mich, Herr Honved?*"

The hussar nodded and left the room. On the threshold he turned and crossed himself again.

"And what about Lolka?" asked Minna. "If he decides to go down to the cellar? And not leave by the window. Where will Lolka and I hide? We can't all hide in the cellar at the same time. . . . And when the Cossacks see Asya shot," she whispered, "what'll they think? Who has shot her and why? They'll drag us to court."

"Minna, go get everything I told you to get. War is war, but death always comes first. It's sacred. I'll go now and see who's knocking. You and Lolka go into the kitchen. And then we'll decide what to do next. Well, off you go now."

"Asya! Asya! Where's my Asya? My only child!"

They had not heard anybody's footsteps. Blanca came in first. Behind her, with her shoes in his hand, was Wilf.

Asya's stepmother was panting and trying to catch her breath; she was holding one hand on her bosom, raised up high by her tightly laced corset. Not only her shoes, everything she was wearing was too tight for her; her neck was now swollen from her whalebone collar, and the tightly drawn corset made her enormously broad in the bust and hips.

"Asya, Asya," she called, stretching her arms in front of her. In one hand she was holding a lace handkerchief, from her other wrist hung a purse embroidered with beads. Large tears appeared on her cheeks. "I'll never get over this blow! Asya, Asya! Your family's pride and joy! Your father's most precious jewel! One and only child!" She made a hissing sound and glanced over at her husband: Wilf had stepped on her foot. She lifted her skirt and showed him her swollen foot with the skin rubbed off.

Boom lifted his head. Oh, the stepmother! He again hid his

face in the pillow. Oh, the stepmother! Asya, your stepmother! Asya had whispered: "Don't, Boom! Don't! She's mean to me. She might see us." "Let's rest awhile in the forest." "No, no, not here. It's damp here. I'll ruin my nice new dress." "I'll spread my jacket on the ground." "You'll ruin your new jacket." "Come on, Asya, just a few more steps. There's a little clearing up ahead." "No, no, don't, Boom." "Don't be afraid, no one can see us." "Boom, please not here, not now, I beg you!" "Where? When? There's nothing here but trees, trees, deedle-dee-dee!" "Don't sing! Somebody might hear you! Please!" "Let them see us, let them hear us. I don't give a damn about anybody, your stepmother, my mother, the whole bunch...." "Boom, don't be so mean, or I'll get angry. I'm going!" "Wait, Asya, wait!" "Boom, I hear shooting, let's get away from here!" "Stay here, Asya, don't run away!"

"Boom, is it you?" The stepmother touched his shoulder.

Boom lifted his tear-stained face.

"Ah, Anshel! Why do you keep carrying those shoes? Boom, my dear!" She wanted to stroke his hair, but Boom flinched, hissed his disapproval. "Don't be afraid, don't be afraid! Did you see?" she turned to her husband. "What a trouble-maker! I told you, it's his fault. I told her again and again: Asya, don't wander off. But he kept pestering her until he finally got his way."

"Blanca, come here, sit down," said Wilf.

"If it weren't for him, our Asya would still be alive. Anshel, what kind of father are you? He has no business lying here! What if someone saw! On the same bed! It's ... it's ..."

"Blanca, stop it, please."

"Stop what? That's the kind of husband, the kind of father you are. Anshel, have you no eyes? Can't you see that people are looking? Have you no shame? He is lying here next to your daughter!"

"Blanca!"

"Jews are not allowed to lie next to their own wives. For all I know, it may even be a sin according to our religion. It's forbidden, I'm sure." She glanced in Old Tag's direction. "Is it a sin? I'm sure it is."

"What do these children know about sinning?" answered Tag.

Blanca turned round.

"Anshel! Oh, my God! Anshel! You don't understand anything! Get me a bowl with lukewarm water. With feet like mine it's a wonder I'm still alive. There isn't even a place to sit down here."

Wilf brought a chair for her from under the window.

Blanca asked Old Tag once again:

"Do you mean to say that it's all right for a man to lie next to a dead woman? That's all I want to know."

Tag went up to her, took her gently by the hand, and led her to the door.

"You'll find a bowl in the kitchen, and some water." He signalled to Wilf to stay behind.

Boom was crying softly.

The photographer turned the head of his dead daughter toward him.

"Boom, my boy," he whispered.

Boom began to sob.

Wilf sighed.

"How did it happen? Such a tragedy! Tell me, Boom!"

"It's not my fault."

"Oh-h-h!" Wilf sighed again.

"Why should it be his fault?" Old Tag shrugged his shoulders.

"It's not my fault."

"I know what I'm talking about. No, my boy. Neither you nor she is at fault. Her soul was pure. And you, too, are pure. But now you must get up." Old Tag laid his hand on Boom's head.

"It's not my fault."

Wilf pulled his wide-brimmed hat over his eyes. He started toward the door.

"Please don't rush off, Mr Wilf. Boom, you can give me a hand too," said Tag. "Together with her father we'll lift the girl from the bed and lay her on the floor. Boom, d'you hear? Get up and lend a hand. It'll give you strength. That's the boy, get up now!"

Boom got up. His face was swollen.

Minna came in with a sheet and Lolka with a bundle of straw.

"Spread it out on the floor!" said Old Tag to Lolka.

Lolka scattered the straw on the floor.

"Gently, gently!" Old Tag was signalling to Wilf. Minna unfolded the sheet by waving it in the air. The candles flickered for a moment, then brightened again.

"Careful!" cried Old Tag. "Boom, Boom! My dear Boom, please, leave her for a moment. Don't get in the way. Feet facing the door," he was saying to Wilf. "Yes, that's right." He sighed. "Now her soul has left this room."

"Asya!"

Boom flung himself against the tiled stove and burst into sobs again.

Asya's body was covered with a white sheet, slightly too short, from under which her feet stuck out, boots and all. At her head stood two candles in brass candlesticks.

"Asya! Asya!" Boom was banging his head against the tiles of the stove.

Wilf looked very pale in his wide-brimmed black hat, with one side of it pulled down.

"Blanca . . . Blanca . . ." he whispered. "Where is Blanca?"

"What do you mean?" asked Old Tag.

"Ah, I remember now!" said the photographer and left the bedroom.

The guest hall was empty. The way to the kitchen was covered with distinct footprints of someone's bare feet. Blanca was sitting on a stool under a wall lamp with a round mirror.

She cried out. One of her feet was still soaking in a bowl of water, while the other was being held by somebody in red trousers, who was bandaging it.

What was this hussar doing here with his strong back and boots with spurs? The town was occupied; two hussars and their horses lie killed at the edge of the forest, and one is kneeling here and holding Blanca's foot!

Blanca pulled down her skirt and her lace petticoat.

"Anshel, is it you?"

The hussar jumped to his feet and saluted, clicking his heels.

"*Frau . . . Frau . . .*" he mumbled.

"Wilf," prompted Blanca.

"*Ja . . . ja!*" The hussar saluted again.

"Anshel, why don't you say something? Say thank you. Can't you see what he's doing for me?" Blanca smiled at the hussar.

"Thank you," said Wilf in German to the hussar.

The hussar clicked his heels again.

"Blanca, get up!"

"Has anything happened?" asked Blanca, alarmed.

"We must get back."

"Now? In the middle of the night? Let's wait until morning. I can't move, don't you see? Can't you see I have become a cripple? Look at me. For the rest of my life, probably. Life's not worth living with such feet. I won't be able to wear any shoes."

"Asya must be taken home."

"Asya? What for? It's closer to the cemetery from here. Much nearer than from where we live. Why carry her there and back? And who's going to carry her? You? All by yourself? Are you strong enough to do it? Look at yourself! People in a lot better shape than you are fit for the grave."

"I'll hire a cart."

"That's right: people are just standing around waiting for you to hire their carts! And what did I escape from the Cossacks for? To run into them at night, in an empty street, sitting on a cart? Think what you are saying, Anshel! I'm scared to death! He's never heard what the Cossacks are capable of," she said in German to the hussar. "*Nicht wahr, Herr Offizier? Die Kosaken?* You must have heard. I don't even like to think about it. A whole regiment catches some poor innocent girl. . . . Oh, no! I would prefer to die than to fall into their hands! But that doesn't bother my husband. I'm not going to go anywhere now. Go alone if you wish, I'll stay here."

"Blanca, it isn't right."

"What isn't right? It's beyond me. Sometimes you say very silly things. . . ."

"It isn't right. What will people say?"

"People? What are you talking about? I don't understand. Ah, this. The bandage! What an idea! And can't a doctor be human too? What if a doctor had done it? What's the difference? Would a doctor be any better?"

"Blanca!"

"All right. Where are my shoes?"

"What do you want shoes for?"

"Bring me my shoes."

"I won't! You don't have to wear shoes."

"Oh, my God," she sighed. "Thank you, Mr Officer. Life, as somebody said, is not a romance. *Nicht wahr, Herr Offizier?*"

"*Igen!*" The hussar clicked his heels. His spurs tinkled.

Gershon the cobbler heard the clinking of spurs and stuck his head in the door.

"Where's Mr Tag?" he asked.

No one answered him. He stood around for a while, then closed the kitchen door again.

What was a dragoon in uniform and fully armed doing here? Ready to shoot any time? Now that Cossacks were galloping around the town?

"It's hard to explain," he said to Old Tag.

They were sitting at a long table in a dark corner of the guest hall that was out of range of the lamp, covered with Yevdocha's black cashmere shawl.

"Close it," Tag pointed with his eyes to the bedroom door.

Asya's boots could be seen sticking out from under the sheet.

"It's hard to understand," said Gershon. "In the course of one day, the Hapsburg dynasty has ceased to exist. It has ceased to rule, as by a wave of the hand. The armed dragoon seems a relic of the past. Poor Asya! Boom brought her here in his arms. Such a lovely girl. Earlier today, I saw her alive and healthy. And now she's gone. Dead! On the first day of the war. Like the Hapsburg dynasty. If that hussar had been killed, it would have been understandable. But an innocent girl? That's

71

hard to explain." He, Gershon, had stood at the window of the shoemakers' union. Cossacks were galloping in the market square, as if it were their right. As if it were their birthright from the beginning of time. He had raced over to the union building because he was afraid they might try to wreck the library, just as at the station they had ransacked the army depot with its supply of flour and sugar and uniform shirts. But luckily they hadn't started ransacking libraries yet. The hussar stands with his chest bulging out, armed and ready to fire. The town does not belong to Austria any more. Maybe the hussar does not know that Austria is no more, that she is dead. It's hard to imagine, it's beyond human comprehension. The Emperor had ruled for years, the dynasty had ruled for centuries, and in the space of a single day both the Emperor and the dynasty have ceased to matter. Only yesterday the Emperor could have given a person a fortune, granted a concession to whomever he liked, and today he's dropped completely out of the picture. If, for instance, Franz Josef the First wanted to come here, the Cossacks would stop him, just as they stop everybody, and ask where he is going. They don't let people into the town and don't let them out. Outrageous not to let anyone in or out! He, Gershon, had sneaked through. Through the house with two entrances onto Bolechowska Street, and from there to the main road to Duliby, along which the troops were marching. Soldiers in high boots, during the summer! With long bayonets fixed to their rifles. They did not notice him. Today, the Emperor has no right of entry. Just like a man trying to get into a cinema without a ticket. . . . The market square was deserted. Hard to believe. Strange-looking people on horses with rifles in their hands rode about as if they had known the square all their life, as if they had been born here, had lived here, had been married here. They rode in threes or fours. In front of the Ruthenian People's Co-operative they stopped for a minute to swap stories with the soldiers standing guard there, guarding their commander, perhaps the general himself. Then they would ride off again. Sometimes they would fire a shot for no apparent reason. There was no telling, either, why they rode around, back and forth, as if they were chasing ghosts, for there was no one in sight, no one to be heard. Occasionally they would pull on their reins and peer into the ground-floor windows of the houses. But curtains were drawn everywhere. The Cossacks were human, after all, like everybody else, and they were frightened by the shades in all the windows, all of them exactly alike—white linen with black stripes. One-storey houses, some higher, some lower, as in any small town; it must be the same where they come from, but blinds in every single window! All the windows screened. When there is no war, a man can live to be a hundred and never notice such things. When there is no war, nothing is very important, but during a war any little thing might save you. Who would have thought that blinds could alarm the Cossacks? Have they never seen them before? Nomadic people always live under canvas—tents are a kind of protection from the sun. Maybe this reminded them in some way of their own country. Maybe their religion forbids window shades. But what kind of religion can that be? A great scholar could perhaps account for this, one who has studied the customs and habits of savages, nomads, and so on. It was still light outside, so the windows were dark. This was normal. But blinds drawn during the day and no lamps lit inside? That's not normal. The market square deserted, streets empty, horses parading on pavements like people. And in the square known to all since childhood the sounds of a strange language. It was so quiet that one could hear every word. The Cossacks talked and laughed among themselves. One of them burst out laughing very loudly, agreeably even. He was the one who made a gesture as if he were about to smash a window with his rifle butt. He stopped just in time and burst out laughing, at the same time reining in his horse until it almost sat back on its hind legs and kicked its front legs in the air, as is sometimes seen in circus posters. The Cossack wore a lambskin hat, a *kutchma*, as our Ruthenians say, but very broad and very curly. Never in my life have I seen such a curly hat, and I'm amazed that there really are such curly-haired sheep anywhere in the world. The hat, which had a red lining and a yellow cross on it, was tilted back. The Cossack had an

73

enormous forelock, which reminded me of Comrade Simon of the needleworkers' union. Perhaps it is because of that forelock that even girls fresh out of high school fall in love with Comrade Simon. As, for example, Erna, Mrs Henrietta Maltz's sister. Yet she left him and took a train to Vienna. Henrietta once came to Crook Street, in spite of its bad name, its wooden huts and eternal mud. Simon stood at the door of his house and would not let Mrs Maltz come inside. In his unbuttoned shirt he looked like a bandit. This is what Mrs Maltz told him finally: "Where is my sister?" she asked. "How should I know?" Comrade Simon replied arrogantly. "Is this how you show your gratitude for all I've done?" That meant for her help during the strike and for teaching him Esperanto, for running a tea-room and for Toynbee Hall, for all the welfare work of the "Women's Hearth". "What's that got to do with it?" asked Comrade Simon. "My sister will never marry an ordinary tailor!" "That remains to be seen." "Please tell her to come out and say good-bye to me. Who knows if we shall ever see each other again!" When Erna heard this, she ran from Simon's house crying, wrapped her arms round her sister's neck and they both drove off in tears, leaving Simon alone. And from the other wooden shacks the thieves and drunkards, the other inhabitants of Crook Street, came out to console him with a bottle of vodka and they drank all night long, including Comrade Simon, although he had never drunk before, and they sang melancholy folk songs and prison songs. . . . To go back: the Cossack's horse danced around like a horse in a circus act; sparks flew from under its hoofs. The Cossack swung his *nahayka* in the air. So this is what a *nahayka* looks like. So much had been heard about it, you would have thought that nothing could be worse. And yet we Jews knew it from our Jewish school. This is simply our old pal from childhood days: the whip. The horse turned round. Now I had no trouble seeing the Cossack's dark face and his long, hooked nose. I could have spotted him in the dark. On his breast he wore an embroidered strip for ammunition. This looked very nice, but for the life of me I can't see what good it can be. Have you ever seen the likes of it?

"You're talking rubbish!" interrupted Tag. "Send a fool to the country fair and the peddlers rejoice. Such unheard-of things are happening here and yet you talk such rubbish. Sit down next to the girl and keep an eye on her."

"Boom is there."

"Boom doesn't count, seeing as he's not her brother or husband, relative or father."

"I saw her father, Wilf, in the kitchen. Some hussar was holding his fat wife's foot. What was he trying to prove?"

Tag waved his hand. He burst out laughing and stopped at once. There was a touch of malice in his giggle.

"D'you hear?" he asked. "Or am I just imagining things?"

"Somebody's snoring."

"Somebody? It must be Boom! She's all by herself now!"

From the kitchen Wilf and Blanca came out. They stopped Old Tag.

"Where can I find a bed," asked Wilf, "for my wife, for my Blanca? I'm ready to pay for it. Somewhere in the neighbourhood, maybe."

"Let me through. On a night like this nobody pays. There's an empty bed on the top floor of the house. Watch your step going up the stairs; the fourth step is rotten. Gershon, show them upstairs."

Tag went hurriedly to the bedroom. The candles, which had already melted in the brass candlesticks, now burned like oil. The flame was licking the blackened wick and flickering up and down before going out. What a hard death, God forbid! The white drops of wax were falling to the floor. The light, alternately yellow and red, shone on the sheet. On the bed lay Boom, snoring.

"Oh," groaned Old Tag. "I knew it! I even said so: the body is alone." He went up to the sleeping Boom and jerked his arm.

"Asya, Asya!" groaned Boom. Tag let him be, and sat on a chair between the girl's body and the bed.

He took his watch from his pocket. It was ten o'clock. The next hour or two will be the worst. Afterward it will become quieter. Midnight means midnight for everybody. For the enemy too. The hour of thieves is between four and

75

five in the morning. And between ten and eleven at night is the hour when a man sneaks up to a woman's room. The hour of sneaking to Yevdocha's bed. That's the hour of rape. The hour of sin even for the pious and the faithful.... After midnight you can relax. And worst of all is the first day and the first night, when the generals too are at their worst, those generals who think that soldiers will shoot better if they have a chance to loot and to rape. With impunity. And with the Jews you can do it with complete impunity. You can ask me, I'm going on seventy! I know all about it! Nothing in this life is free, but at the same time nothing can go unpunished: it only seems that way at first. But every act of violence ... You don't forgive it, O Lord! You don't forget! On the contrary, You write down more than there was. O generals! I fall flat on my face before you: stem the tide of violence. Save yourselves and your children! Save us and our children! I'm going on seventy and still haven't been through a war. I was born when the Cossacks were fighting against Hungary. I guess it was only in the old days that commanders let their soldiers whoop it up whenever they captured a city. What would the world be worth if human savagery didn't let up? What would the world be worth if man didn't become wiser with every century? Is there any sense in evil-doing? Aren't evil and foolishness the same thing? Did You create the world to torture man? Do You cut short his life so he won't have too much fun here on earth? So that fathers can live longer than their sons? The time has now come when hundreds and thousands of young men, the very blood and milk of life, will perish daily, a time when parents will have to bury their young. Where's my son Elo? I haven't got the nerve to ask whether he's still alive. Dear God, save him! This was brought on by my sins. Taking my wife away from me was punishment enough. Yes, yes, I know! Even so, I beat my head against the wall like young Boom when she died! The Cossacks will now rape because of my sins! But why did Asya have to perish, she who was as white as snow? The punishment is all out of proportion to the sin. In this case the Great Book-keeper has entered more than there was.

76

The photographer stood over his daughter's body and wailed like a woman:

"Such a tragedy! Such a tragedy has struck me! How kind my Blanca was to you, like a real mother! Such a calamity!" He turned to Old Tag.

Tag kept quiet.

"What could I have done to prevent it?" asked Wilf.

"Yes, a great calamity," agreed Tag.

"Beautiful, young . . ."

"The Lord giveth, the Lord taketh away. Blessed be the Truest Judge."

"What can we do?"

"We can beat our breasts: we have trespassed, we have been faithless, we have lied."

Wilf was shaking his head.

"You're right," said Tag. "Why should I enumerate? It has been written: Thou sitting in the clouds knowest all the mysteries."

"Such a tragedy."

"The end of everything."

"What am I to do?"

"Ha, if only one knew."

"My Blanca loved her, believe me."

"And even if we knew what to do . . . we'd never know enough to prevent its happening."

"How did it happen? I don't know. I don't even know how it happened. If I knew at least how my daughter died . . ."

"What difference would it make? It's a woman's business to ask such questions. Only a woman thinks that there's an answer to everything. There's no answer to anything. How else could it have happened other than the way it did? It happened, which means that it had to happen. It had to be, and it could not be different than it was. And there's no way of proving how things might have been. Things can't happen twice: once this way, once not this way; but things in this world can only take place once. And what makes the world go round is that no one can prevent anything. Such a simple thing as this: if I were in a place where I'm not, would this change something happening

77

there? Or if I find myself in a certain place, has it any bearing on what is happening there? Take me, for example: I'm in the guest hall of the inn. A couple of customers are sitting at a table, they drink a little, eat a little, and talk. They don't talk to me; they don't even notice me. And they don't know then I'm listening to what they're saying. They say, for instance: It would be nice if I won in the lottery. I would marry off my daughter and buy a house, or they say: It would be good if we had some rain, because prices would go up. If I weren't around, would they say the same thing? There's no way of telling. This is a joke, nothing, a trifle not worth wasting one's time on. Or so it seems. But what about important things where it's a matter of life and death? At first glance they, too, seem to be trifling. But afterward they make you think. Instead of this guest hall, imagine a whole town or the whole world, and instead of two men, imagine a whole community or even a whole nation. Or take life itself. If a person has done something in the world, does life change because of it, although no one may know? I don't mean God, who knows and sees all, as in the words of the deathbed confession: 'O Lord who dwellest on high, in the exalted places among the holy and pure, who knowest all the mysteries and all which is open.' That goes without saying. I mean people, about whom nothing can be proved. Is anything at all changed by the fact that a certain man has lived in the world? Even if no one knew about him? This can never be proved. So what is the sense of anything in this world? What is the sense of getting married, of having children? Does the world change because a child is born? Does the world change because somebody has died? How can you tell? How can you tell when you don't even know for certain such a simple thing, such a trifle. . . ."

"He must be wakened," said Wilf.

"Let him sleep."

"My Blanca is asleep upstairs. And here are her boots. It's already ten o'clock. I never go to bed before midnight. I used to sit up until Asya went to bed. Until she had done all her homework. Asya was a star pupil. She always had the highest marks until he came along and threw her into a

78

tizzy. This is all his fault. My Blanca always used to tell her: You . . ."

"A good thing that she's asleep upstairs. In case of trouble we'll have to wake the women and hide them in the cellar."

"My Blanca was always very kind to her. . . ."

"Why shouldn't she have been kind?"

"Before I married her, she told me herself: 'My dear, there's no need to worry, I'll be like a real mother to her'."

"That's only right."

"I'll take her shoes up. In case she wants to get up."

"She can walk barefoot."

The door opened suddenly. A gust of wind blew in, and the flame of the candle shot high and was almost blown out.

Gershon appeared on the threshold separating the guest hall from the bedroom, the business side of the house from the private quarters.

"Who's here now?" Old Tag jerked his head up and, keeping it cocked, listened intently.

He then adjusted his skullcap and left the room.

"Who can that be?" asked Wilf.

Gershon crossed the threshold and came into the bedroom.

"The Cossacks?"

"I don't know," said Gershon.

"The hussar . . . is he here?"

"I don't know. Maybe."

"Something must be done about him. Where is he now? In the kitchen? Did he stay in the kitchen? Is he still there?"

"If he stayed in the kitchen he must still be there."

"Is he sitting at the table?"

"Maybe he is or maybe he got up from the table, how do I know? And what difference does it make?"

Gershon went up to the bed.

The flame had revived again. It kept leaping up, then disappearing in the cups of the candlesticks.

Gershon looked at Boom and at the mirror covered with a black shawl. The worst way of dying is the Jewish way.

"How come he's snoring like that?" asked Wilf.

"He's worn out. He brought her here in his arms."

"My Blanca always used to tell her . . ."

"Poor boy. She died in his arms."

"My Blanca told her: 'Don't wander off, stay by my side or you're sure to get lost.' Then before you knew it she was gone." The photographer motioned Gershon to the chair next to the body.

"Sit down, please. With us Jews it is forbidden to leave a body without care. It is forbidden to leave it alone. I'll be right back. Please wait awhile. Will you wait?" He pushed down on the door handle. But before leaving he turned round and took the pair of shoes standing by the closet.

The cantor's son stood in the centre of the guest hall.

On the benches on both sides of the long table the guests all sat in the same order as before the escape. They had all been forced to turn back.

Their faces, indistinct in the twilight, gradually faded, the farther from the lamp they sat, and only the lenses of their gold-rimmed glasses fleetingly reflected the light. The centre of the room was illuminated by a spot of light from the lamp covered with Yevdocha's dark shawl. In that bright circle stood the cantor's son, his right foot crooked like a branch. Why had he started limping now, when the Emperor needed soldiers who were physically fit? asked Leon Kramer, the army surgeon and son of Kramer the bookbinder, who was now sitting at the head of the table as if he were a rabbi. "A man doesn't choose the day, the hour, or the moment when he becomes a cripple," the cantor's son answered in a loud voice so that the whole Commission could hear him. The chairman of the Mobilization Commission, Major Sakowicz, then moved that the Commission should accept this explanation as valid, to the discredit of Leon Kramer. "Instead of helping a Jew, you tried to foul him up. This wouldn't have been so bad if the punishment were not a bullet in the man's head, God forbid! And you're a Jew yourself, Doctor, while Major Sakowicz is not." The whole town had blamed Dr Kramer, the son of an ordinary bookbinder, that is to say an artisan, for forgetting his

80

origins. A Jew in a high position can sometimes be worse, God forbid, than a non-Jew. The chairman of the Commission, Major Sakowicz, used a proverb in Latin which means that music is silent when the cannons roar, music in this instance meaning singing; his point being that the cantor's son had no business being at the front, and it would be better both for the front and for the cantor if he stayed behind with his coreligionists in the synagogue where, together with his father, now of blessed memory, he had been singing since his childhood. His boyish treble had tinkled like a bell and brought tears to the eyes of the listeners. There were two very gifted children born in the town. The current child prodigy was Henry Mund, who played the violin. Henry was lucky; fortune had smiled on him, and although he was the son of very poor people (he was ashamed to admit it, but his father was a street vendor of bagels), he had been taught by a private music teacher who gave him lessons free of charge. The cantor's son had not been so lucky. Only once had it seemed that he had picked the winning ticket. On the Day of Atonement Jews and non-Jews alike had come to our synagogue, to listen to Kol Nidre, the song of the Spanish Jews condemned to the stake by the Inquisition. The Baroness came with Amalia Diesenhoff. It was a most moving scene: the Baroness wept into her handkerchief while she was listening to the cantor's son, then promised to help the young singer who had before him the future of another Caruso. But unfortunately, she had to go to Vienna the very next day. A telegram had been waiting for her at home, asking her to attend the funeral of a very close friend. It was rumoured that the man had committed suicide, but nothing certain was really known. Mrs Maltz had visited Miss Diesenhoff, a fellow member of the "Women's Hearth" welfare committee. There was talk of cards, races, even of a woman other than the Baroness. What was the truth? Amalia Diesenhoff kept silent, pretending not to know anything. Or perhaps she was pretending to pretend? The Baroness reappeared in town wearing a black dress, a black cross, and long black ear-rings, and she has never worn anything but black since then. Even to the ball, organized by the "Women's

Hearth" for the benefit of the Polish-Jewish Orphanage, the Baroness came in black. But she forgot about the cantor's young and gifted son, and fate had looked the other way. This is how the death of a stranger in a distant city can affect the course of another man's life. When you come right down to it, peace isn't much different from war, during which one complete stranger may kill another. Afterward nobody took much interest in the young singer any more although his voice became stronger and fuller, although people referred to him more often as "the cantor, the cantor's son" than just "the cantor's son". He began to sing not only in front of the Ark of the Covenant in the Central Synagogue, but also at Jewish marriage ceremonies, in front of the bride. And as there is nothing lovelier on earth than a Jewish bride, he sang in verse. He wrote the lyrics himself, sometimes sad, sometimes gay, but always in rhyme. . . .

The cantor's son had to jump into a ditch during his escape. Nothing mattered any more anyway, so he ran without limping. A bullet whizzed over his head. Never mind! I'll make believe it was a fly, an enraged fly, not a bullet. Why a fly? Because I remembered that Titus, the enemy of Israel, when he was destroying the Temple, had breathed a fly into his nose. And the fly flew inside his head, God gave it claws of iron and a beak of steel, so that it could tear at his brain day and night. This means that God will not abandon us! Even in the worst possible moments He'll find a way! Ah! Life! Life! I had already made my last confession: "For the sin I have committed before Thee . . ." Bad thoughts were already going through my head. Instead of dying in my own bed, I'll die alone in an empty field, shot by a foreign soldier or one on our side. I was lying with my face upturned so that I could see everything right up to the end: the sky, from where salvation might come, a bit of the sun, the tensed, unclean bellies of horses, first the horses of our two hussars, then the hundreds of horses of the savage hordes. I saw sweat on a horse's skin, hoofs above my head—but a kindhearted angel turned them away from my breast, to save a miserable man. I saw Cossacks' feet digging into the horses' flanks, spurs bloodying their hides. . . .

Only a horse could take that, could take such a beating. One hussar, then another, one horse then another escaped into the forest. This was just the beginning, later on hundreds of horses jumped across the ditch. I thought it would never end. God, You are a merciful God, I believe in You, save me from the faithless enemy. You are the fount of my life, my shield, and I am Your servant, Your soldier. So save my life, oh, save my life while there's still time; You gave me an immortal soul, but I don't wish to die before my time.

When the cantor finished speaking the room was silent.

The first to break the silence was Apfelgrün, the owner of the shoeshop.

"We escaped just in time and kept hidden in the forest until nightfall. But what do the Cossack horses really look like? What do such animals look like?"

"What a question!" Pritsch the tobacconist shrugged his shoulders. "One horse is like another always and everywhere."

Apfelgrün looked at Pritsch in expressive silence.

The cantor now stepped outside the circle of light. He wrinkled his nose and blinked to see who had asked the question from the dark corner of the guest hall. Shining glasses, a round face under a round bowler hat, a white collar, a black bow tie against a white stiff shirt front—he had spotted the man at once when he had entered. All of them must have been sitting here for a long time—their heads floated in the twilight like balloons; and at the head of the table, as if he were at home presiding over a Sabbath or Holy Day family meal, sat Kramer the bookbinder, sprawled out comfortably so that everybody could tell immediately that his son was a doctor. All of them have come back. No one had any luck escaping—he had been the only one, he with that "lame" foot of his. The curly-headed Mrs Kramer held her head high and sat stiffly, her arms in puffed sleeves crossed on her bosom; her daughter Rose, in similar but shorter sleeves, also sat with crossed arms. They sat in silence, all three of them. Asya's relatives were not to be seen at the table. Neither the photographer nor his wife was there. Haven't they heard? And where was Boom? But why should Boom be blamed?

What could that curly-headed boy have done? Is there anything more lovely and wholesome than an engaged couple? Sooner or later the parents would have had to sign the letter of engagement and there would have been a beautiful, big noisy wedding. The soldiers were still shooting, he was still lying in the ditch when he saw Boom carrying Asya from the forest. He will remember the forest and the ditch all his life. He would have something to tell his children and his children's children. Life had never been exactly a picnic, and now, on top of everything else, a war! His whole life, singing included, wasn't worth a cent. The whole life . . . What was left of it? Asya did not look dead; she looked tired. A bride, a Jewish bride! How little Boom loved her!

"What does a Cossack's horse look like?" repeated Apfelgrün. "I don't like horses."

"Well, well!" exclaimed Old Tag. "Who ever heard of anyone not liking horses! Have you ever seen a horse drinking water? I wish some human beings could drink so nicely."

"And where's Boom?" The cantor smiled at Mrs Kramer.

"Boom?" Mrs Kramer looked at her husband. "And whose business is that?"

"He's asleep," said Kramer.

"Asleep?" The cantor was astonished.

"He fell asleep, so now he's sleeping, simple as that," said Mrs Kramer.

"And where's his fiancée?" The cantor folded his hands on his stomach.

"His fiancée? What fiancée?" Mrs Kramer shrugged her shoulders.

Her daughter did the same while looking fixedly at the cantor.

"Asya," said the cantor. "The beautiful Asya. Poor Asya, the orphan. Great care must be taken never to harm an orphan."

"Oh God, oh God!" exclaimed Kramer. "How horrible this is!" He looked at his wife.

"Has anything happened, God forbid? I didn't know." The cantor glanced around.

All those present sat in silence, with their heads hanging.

All of a sudden Mrs Kramer jumped to her feet and, standing erect and with clenched fists pressed to her hips, she left the room. Her daughter also jumped up and followed her mother toward the bedroom.

"Stay here." Mrs Kramer pushed her daughter back and entered the bedroom alone, where she was greeted by the smell of burned-out candles. She shut the door after her.

"I'll sit here now!" she told Gershon. He got up and left the room.

Boom's mother stood over the bed and looked into her son's face. Boom was tossing from side to side.

"Boom!" She leaned over him.

The boy was groaning in his sleep.

"Boom!"

Mrs Kramer sat on the edge of the bed. She looked at Asya's shoes sticking out from under the sheet, then she pulled at her son's arm.

"Boom." She laid her hand on the boy's forehead.

Boom shivered.

"Boom, you have a temperature. Can you hear me?"

The boy hid his face in the pillow.

"Have you got a headache? Tell me!"

Boom banged his fist against the headboard.

"Get up!"

Boom did not respond.

"Get up at once!"

No answer.

"This is the second time I've come here."

Again no answer.

"I'm not going to let you stay around here any longer!"

Still no answer.

"Can you change anything by lying here?"

No answer.

"Boom, you must leave this room. You have no right to stay here! D'you hear?"

"Leave me alone!"

"I won't leave you now. You're not a child any more."

"No, I'm not."

"So you must act like an adult."

"Leave me alone!"

"Listen! Her parents aren't here!"

"Leave me alone, I tell you!"

"What will people say?"

He did not answer.

Mrs Kramer got up and began pacing back and forth.

The flame of the only candle which was still alight flickered for the last time, and then died. From the embers of the wick a white thread of smoke rose.

Mrs Kramer put a handkerchief to her nose.

"It smells here, Boom, I'm going now, d'you hear me? You can't stay here by yourself and sleep! Aren't you ashamed of yourself, sleeping in this room!"

"Oh!"

"It's shameful!"

"Leave me alone!"

"Aren't you afraid?"

"Go away!"

"How dare you speak to me like that!"

He made no reply.

"All right. I'll go now. But you'll be sorry!"

Boom was groaning softly.

"You mourn her as if she were your wife!"

"Go!"

"I bet you wouldn't grieve like this if any of us had died."

He sat up on the bed with a start.

"Would Leon act like this?"

"Go away! What do you want from me?"

"How dare you speak like that to your own mother!"

"I know! I know! You're glad now, aren't you?"

"Boom!"

"I hate you!"

Mrs Kramer covered her face with her hands.

"I hate you!" he kept shouting.

"My God! He's gone insane!"

Boom jumped off the bed.

In the darkness, Mrs Kramer saw the twisted face of her son, his swollen lips, eyes, nose.

Boom pushed his mother away with his fist.

"My God," she screamed.

"Get out! Get out!"

She slapped Boom's face.

"You . . . you . . . How dare you attack your mother?"

Boom sank down into the chair.

"My God! Oh, my God!" he was pounding his fists against his knees.

"How dare you raise your hand? Against your own mother? D'you know what you are? A monster! Have I lived so long just to see this? What have I lived to see! I would rather . . . Out of my sight! You aren't my child any more. You're not worthy of me! D'you hear?"

The door flew open. Kramer rushed in, followed by Rose.

"What's happened, Sabina?" Kramer ran to his wife.

Old Tag brought in some candles.

In the doorway were crowded Apfelgrün, Soloveytchik with his wife and daughters, the cantor, Gershon, and Pritsch.

"Sabina? What's the matter? Boom? What's happened?"

"Mama! Mama!" sobbed Rose.

"Be quiet, Rose! Let your mother speak!"

Mrs Kramer still had her face covered with her hands.

Old Tag was putting the candles into the brass candlesticks.

"What a to-do! What a to-do!" Old Tag mumbled, shaking his head. "The first day of the war, and already everything's in a mess! What'll happen tomorrow?"

"Such goings on! Such goings on!" Apfelgrün was cleaning his pince-nez.

"But nothing so terribly awful has happened," Pritsch tried to reassure them all.

"All this wasn't enough for him," said Apfelgrün irritably.

The candles in the candlesticks burst into flame. Tag was smoothing down the sheet on Asya's body.

"What's going on?" Minna barged into the room, followed by Lolka. From under their light dressing-gowns, one could see their nightdresses printed with blue and pink flowers.

"Why all this shouting? Minna, go back upstairs at once; we can manage without you. You might have found a longer sheet! My dear guests"—Old Tag turned to those huddled in the doorway—"please respect the sacredness of death. Shut the door. Gershon, go find the girl's father. He must be in the yard."

"What kind of father is he anyway?" Apfelgrün gave vent to his indignation.

"Please leave this room, and close the door!" Old Tag requested them.

Nobody moved.

"My dear Jews, you hallowed flock, as they say on Holy Days, pick up your behinds and go sit on the benches in the guest hall. Don't you understand simple language? Ever since this inn first opened its doors, I can't remember hearing such a racket or fuss. To shout in a dead person's room! One death is all we've had, and already you take it for granted? That was quick! Go upstairs: I'm speaking to you, Minna, and to you, Lolka. Herr Kramer, you're a gentleman, after all, try to set a good example. Take your wife and leave this room. Comfort her. And let Boom stay behind. Sooner or later he'll have to leave too. But now let him stay."

"Yes, yes," Kramer agreed, "you're quite right. Come, Sabina! Come, Rose! You too, Boom!"

"Let Boom stay here," repeated Old Tag. "I said: let him stay behind. Go without him. I don't know what you're all so worried about. If he doesn't want to leave, let him stay; if he wants to sit here, let him do so. What harm does it do? Is it written down anywhere that it's against the law? That's just somebody's imagination! If only people would do . . . a little less imagining," he sighed.

All the time he was gently pushing Kramer, who was walking backward, toward the door. Behind her father, Rose was backing up. Mrs Kramer, her head held high, walked stiffly straight toward the people crowding in the doorway.

"Boom, Boom, my son," Kramer was still crying.

Old Tag hushed him up.

"I want to tell him something," Kramer tried to explain.

"Not now. Not now."

"But I can't just leave him like this, for goodness' sake!"

"I'll be here the whole time."

"But I'm his father!"

"Father or mother, what does it matter now?"

Old Tag finally got the door closed.

"Well, at last! Father, mother. A person has to get along without them for the better part of his life. And always when they're least needed, they come along and interfere. Dear Boom, dear little Boom! How I wish it were already tomorrow!" Old Tag was straightening the candles. "Even the candles are bent, as on the Day of Atonement. Are you hot, Boom? What can I say to you, Boom? God has touched you with His mighty finger. He too is a Father! He knows where to strike: where the skin is thinnest. Dear God! Dear God! Because of Your doings people will stop believing in You. You must always do the opposite of what people expect. If You punish young, innocent children and spare an old sinner, You cheapen sin, and sin ceases to be sinful. All right! But people should be told about it so that they don't have to suffer in vain. You are not a good father. Boom, do you think that I believe in God? I try to. But I'm finding it harder and harder. And I'll tell you this: the harder it is for me to believe, the more I fear Him. Even Gershon tries to turn me against God. That simple little cobbler is trying to convince me that the world just happened by itself. That's silly. But that's not my affair. If somebody finds it easier to think so, let him— nobody's forcing him to believe. But if a person could just have a smattering of doubt about God, that would be fine, something to hold on to for a rainy day. Nothing in the world can happen by itself. There must be a male and a female, and there must be sin. The wisest man can explain everything as far back as original sin. And what was it like before? Nobody can explain that. There'll always be a 'before', and the further back you go, the harder it is to understand. That's why people have to believe, I don't mean believe entirely, but with a grain of doubt, in God. And as long as they can't figure out which was the original sin, they can't figure out any of the later ones

89

either. That's why I don't know what is a sin and what is not. D'you understand, Boom? Although, on the other hand . . ."

Boom was sitting with his cheek resting on his palm; his eyes were closed, and he was breathing heavily. Suddenly he lifted his red and swollen eyes and fixed them on Old Tag.

Tag got up and began stroking the boy's head.

"A little shroud must be made for Asya. Her parents should do it. Her father seems to be busy with something else and has no time. Let's not be cross with him. But who is to do it? Boom, are you afraid to stay here alone?"

Boom shook his head.

"All right, son."

The door opened quietly and Gershon's pitch-black head appeared. He did not want to come in, but beckoned to Old Tag.

"Now what's wrong?" asked Tag.

He left the bedroom and closed the door behind him.

"Two carts have pulled in. Somebody's knocking at the windowpane."

"Just what we needed! The Hasidim?"

"Yes."

"With their women and children?"

"Yes."

"I can't think of anything worse!"

"Maybe you'd rather the Cossacks had come instead?"

"Don't even mention such a thing! 'Maybe you'd rather!' How come you're so smart all of a sudden? The night isn't over yet."

"As it is written in the Holy Books: Let us not give up hope. . . ."

"In what Holy Books? I haven't seen that anywhere. In your books, maybe. When God wants to punish an ignoramus, He makes him recite from memory what's in the Book."

"I seem to remember it."

"Well, then, I'll tell you something from memory: 'Let a darksome whirlwind seize upon that night: let it not be counted in the days of the year, nor numbered in the months.' Do you understand it, Gershon?"

"Oy, Mr Tag, things are going badly for us!"

"Those people fear death which has not yet come, and don't fear the death which is among us."

"It's not the girl I'm sorry for. It's all the same to her now. It's the boy I feel sorry for. He has been stabbed right in the heart."

"True enough. But, on the other hand . . . when you get a lot older than you are now, you'll begin to see things as in a mirror—that is, in reverse. Old age is life in reverse, life from the side of the dead. Have you seen her father?"

"No."

"Gershon, come in here and stay with Boom. This is the best you can do for him. I see that you're not quite in the mood for it. Am I right?"

"I've already sat with him."

"Are you scared?"

"It's not much fun being in there."

"And do you believe in God? No. So what do you have to show for it now? At least you wouldn't be scared. If I didn't believe—it's not my lips that spoke those words—I would . . . Go in now! You won't be alone in there, you know. Sit with Boom, tell him an interesting story while I go out and welcome the tsaddik."

Gershon went into the bedroom and Old Tag walked the length of the inn to the great table.

"My dear Jews," he said, "I have some good news for you. The tsaddik from Zydaczow will be here in a moment. Receive him with the respect due to a holy Jew. Make some room for him at the table; for him and his Hasidim. Maybe one of you is among his followers? Like Wohl, the baker, who goes to visit him on Holy Days? Make room for the tsaddik. A tsaddik can't sit just anywhere."

"Now this promises to be a real Noah's ark," said Pritsch.

"And do you all know the story about the pig in Noah's ark?" asked Apfelgrün.

"Oy, Mr Apfelgrün." The cantor shook his head.

"That's not surprising," whispered Pritsch.

"No? Then listen." Apfelgrün took off his pince-nez and

began to clean them with his handkerchief. "It's a long story. Funny. I heard it from my father."

"Blessed be his memory," prompted the cantor.

"Blessed be his memory. . . . Well then, the pig . . ." Apfelgrün began to laugh.

"Everybody likes to talk about himself," whispered Pritsch.

Apfelgrün stopped laughing.

"Did you wish to say something, Herr Pritsch?"

"I did not wish to: I said it."

"What did you say? Would you mind repeating it?" Apfelgrün tossed back his head, to have Pritsch in focus when he repeated the insult.

"They're here! They're here!" exclaimed Rose Kramer.

"They're here! They're here!" the cantor took it up.

"Here they are!" Soloveytchik smiled at Apfelgrün. "Well, tell us quickly about that pig, before the tsaddik comes in."

The tsaddik appeared.

He moved slowly, like an old man, supported under one arm by Wohl, the baker, under the other by Old Tag.

The red-haired Hasid, short and slim, with a pointed beard, pushed forward and, turning his back to the guest hall, motioned the tsaddik inside.

The tsaddik blinked, although the light was dim. His black beard, now grey from dust, covered his breast. He wore a wide-brimmed hat, a grey silk caftan, white stockings, and black shoes.

Behind him the group of Hasidim quietly squeezed sideways through the open door. They burst into the room like a swarm of bumblebees, holding their hats with one hand so that they would not fall off, and with the other clutching one another as in a dance. As if each of them were afraid to be left behind.

The women with children followed at a considerable distance behind the men, like those in Jacob's trains before his meeting with Esau. The first to enter was the tsaddik's wife in a silver and black shawl tucked in behind her ears, leaning her arm against the large, fat wet nurse who carried the swaddled infant; behind her walked a short woman, her wig askew and with its strands sticking to her forehead, surrounded by six children—six, touch wood, like the six days of creation; behind her a dark-haired one with a chubby little blond baby, then a hunchback encircled by her brood like a hen surrounded by her chicks, then a woman with two small twin girls, their braids half undone; then two women with infants, one tall and skinny, the other also tall, wearing a lace shawl over a velvet dress with gold stars; and at the very end two childless women, one short with a large head and the other with a long nose and a protruding lower jaw, wearing not a wig, but a crocheted cap on her head.

"This way, this way!" The red-haired Hasid led them, waving his hands.

Old Tag let go of the tsaddik's elbow and rushed toward Kramer, the bookbinder.

"Herr Kramer," he said smiling.

"*Aber selbstverständlich!* But of course!" Kramer got up. He gave up his place at the head of the table to the tsaddik and sat down next to Apfelgrün. "Why not? Why not? Such a visitor! Blessed be the newcomer."

"Blessed be the newcomer," repeated Old Tag.

"Blessed be . . ." whispered Soloveytchik.

"Blessed! Blessed!" Apfelgrün shook his head. "It won't hurt me to say it," he mumbled to himself, at the same time throwing Pritsch a sidelong glance.

Pritsch did nothing but put on his hat, stare at the newcomers, and drum his fingers on the tabletop.

The tsaddik took Kramer's place. He immediately shut his eyes and hung his head, his face buried in his luxuriant black beard.

The redhead stooped and put his ear to the tsaddik's lips. He then began to whisper in the tsaddik's ear, after which he again put his ear to the tsaddik's lips and whispered something else in the tsaddik's ear when the other was done. Meanwhile the others had already seated themselves on either side of the long guest-hall table.

93

"The rabbi would like to wash his hands," said the redhead, standing on the tip of his toes and swaying slightly from left to right.

"Water! Water!" The Hasidim's whisper filled the room.

The bowl was still standing on the kitchen floor. Old Tag poured out Blanca's footbath, filled the bowl with fresh water, and threw a towel over his shoulder. Before leaving the kitchen he scraped the rest of the cold scrambled egg from the frying pan. The kitchen window was open. The hussar had come in through a window and had gone out through a window. Thank God for that.

The redhead was waiting by the door; he took from Tag the bowl, the pint jug, and the towel. He himself poured a few drops of water on the tsaddik's fingernails, then dried them with the towel. The other Hasidim dipped their fingers in the bowl. The redhead took out of the tsaddik's pocket a silken cord and helped him wrap it around his waist. The other Hasidim followed suit. Old Tag pointed to the sideboard with the earthenware mugs and plates: they all knew that this meant the east—that is, Jerusalem, where the Wailing Wall stands, all that is left of the Temple of Solomon the King. The men were now facing the Prayer side.

A beautiful voice rang out, although no one had expected it. It was the cantor's voice.

"Blessed be the Lord, who is to be blessed for ever and ever!"

The redhead nodded to the cantor to continue.

"Blessed art Thou, O Lord our God, King of the Universe who at Thy word bringest on the evening twilight, with wisdom openest the gates of heaven, and with understanding changest times and variest the seasons, and arrangest the stars in their watches in the sky, according to Thy will. Thou createst day and night; Thou rollest away the light from before the darkness and the darkness from before the light," chanted the cantor.

The others repeated the prayer in whispers, with the exception of the youth with down on his face who from time to time raised his voice, waved his hands, and then lapsed into silence.

The redhead, murmuring the prayers and keeping a distance from the women, motioned to them to leave the room, or at least to move away from the table.

Old Tag intervened:

"Leave that to me, leave that to me. I'll take them out." Tag winked at the women, "Come, come with me."

Kramer motioned to his wife. She rose, tall and erect as ever.

"Noo, noo, noo!" the redhead urged them on.

"Come, Rosie," said Mrs Kramer, nodding to her daughter.

Mrs Soloveytchik woke her youngest daughter when she rose from the table. The three remaining ones followed her on their own account, the eldest, Lenka, holding the two younger ones by the hand.

"Get a move on, my children, you 'Hallowed Flock'," Old Tag encouraged, thereby nicknaming them the Hasidim's wives. The whole time they kept as far away as possible from the men and gathered together by the kitchen door. "My children, numerous as grains of sand on the seashore, may no man's eye harm you."

Tag led the way to the kitchen.

"Make yourselves comfortable here. Sit wherever you like —camp wherever you want to; I'll go to the cow-shed right away—God has blessed me with a cow-shed and other earthly goods—and get some straw, spread it on the floor so that you can lie down and rest. And, God willing, may you rest in peace. Amen! One night only! We'll have to manage! And the breast-fed infants should lie in bed with their mothers." He pointed to an iron bedstead in the corner, covered with a black rug. He turned up the wick in the lamp with the round mirror on the wall, then stooped and pulled from under the bed a wire-meshed stable lantern. He shook it; the oil in it made a gurgling sound. He removed the soot-covered glass and lit the round wick.

Before going out, Tag paused for a moment in the guest room of the inn. The Hasidim were swaying, reciting their prayers in whispers. The loud singing was now followed by silence.

Kramer, Apfelgrün, and Soloveytchik were standing up,

their faces turned toward the east. Only Pritsch remained sitting at the table.

Tag put the lantern on the floor and went up to the owner of the tobacco shop and lottery concession.

"I don't think you're being very polite, Pritsch. As for me, I've said my prayers already. Nobody's asking you to pray; it's enough if you stand up. Why offend the others?"

Pritsch did not reply. He sighed and got up.

Lolka in a dressing gown over her nightdress was running down the stairs.

"Grandpa, Mama doesn't feel well!"

"Go back upstairs. I'll get her drops. Don't leave your mother alone. Has she got a headache? She always gets one at just the right time. Well, get a move on!" Tag turned back and walked toward the bedroom. He slowly opened the door.

The smell of candle wax overwhelmed him. Gershon and Boom sat on the bed, in silence. Gershon looked up.

"I was just about to leave," said Gershon and got up.

Tag waved his hand angrily and Gershon returned to his seat on the bed.

Minna's drops were in the drawer of the bedside table in a dark-coloured little bottle. Tag examined the bottle in the flickering candlelight and put it into his pocket.

"I'll be right back," he told Gershon as he shut the door.

In the hall he lifted up the lantern to light the way upstairs. The fourth step was broken; it had begun to sag right after his wife's death. After that he never got round to repairing it. Tomorrow I'll fix it. Tomorrow at the latest. Her name was Haya; Haya means Life. Actually she began feeling sick right after Elo was born. But now the step must be repaired, for it might well cause an accident. The members of the family knew about the step, but so many new people were in the house now that someone might break a leg, God forbid. But to put a light in the staircase would be worse still, because the light might shine brighter through the cracks than through the windows. Tonight is the most dangerous night. O God, cover my house with darkness or, as in Egypt, let thick darkness fall, a palpable one, so that our enemies shall be

96

unable to see us for three days and three nights. You "Hallowed Flock", you don't realize how great the danger is. And another thing, Asya's lying here, on the floor. I take this house of death upon myself. And tomorrow is Friday! When will they make a shroud? God help us if we don't manage everything by the Sabbath! A death on the Sabbath! The tsaddik never says a word himself. "No one has ever worn himself out from not talking," said the rabbi of Czortkov. But these young Hasidim, they look frisky enough to sing and dance. Old Tag has whispered in the redhead's ear in the hall: There is death in my house. She's lying in there, still unclean, I warn you! So that none of you should become stained. The redhead smacked his lips, stopped for a moment, then hissed: Hush now! and pointed to the tsaddik, being led in by Wohl, the baker. Tag took the tsaddik by his other elbow. And what if they should begin to sing, while she is still in the other room? If the tsaddik has nothing against it, then it's all right by me. It might even be a good trick to play on the Cossacks. When they hear the Jews singing they might be stunned long enough for their hot-tempered blood to become cool. "The Lord is my rock, and my fortress, and my deliverer, in whom I will trust." That hussar was the last straw: a trouserful, but a brain like a chicken's. He didn't feel like hiding in the cellar. When the wet nurse came into the kitchen she closed the window, so that the tsaddik's child wouldn't catch cold, God forbid. That means the hussar must have jumped out of the open window. Thank goodness, one worry less. And what if they catch him? One goy won't harm another. They'll take away his sabre, his pistol, and the rest of that jingle-jangle stuff. We can do without it. I shouldn't have let him in through the front-room window. First anger is the best anger. Later it is too late.

"Have you got a headache?" he asked his daughter-in-law.

Minna was lying on the bed with two damp towels, one on her head and one on her heart.

"Oh," she groaned.

Old Tag counted some drops onto a lump of sugar, while Lolka held a glass of water for her mother.

"This is the worst Mama has ever felt." Lolka's eyes were filled with tears. She wiped her nose on the sleeve of her dressing-gown.

"You're silly," murmured Old Tag.

"She's right," moaned Minna. "You can't keep calling everybody silly. Not everybody."

"All right. I'll call the doctor tomorrow. And where is that short fat woman? Isn't she asleep here? I saw her going upstairs."

"Mrs Wilf?" asked Lolka. "She stayed for just a minute or so. She didn't even feel like lying down. She just hung around waiting for her husband to leave," said Lolka with a wry grin.

"Wilf has been in and out looking for her," said Minna in her wistful voice.

"D'you feel better now, Minna?"

She shook her head with difficulty.

"You'll feel better in a moment. Lie quietly. Lolka will give you some more drops, but later on, not right away. I must get some straw for the kitchen, then I'll be back again. Just relax, you're not going to die."

"Straw? What for?" moaned Minna. "My God! My God! What will the floor look like tomorrow? And tomorrow is Friday! How will I manage everything by the Sabbath?"

"Yevdocha will scrub the floor, don't worry now."

"Ah, that Yevdocha!"

"Try to sleep now!"

Old Tag closed the door. He stopped for a moment on the broken step, listening. From the guest hall he could hear the quiet incantations of the Prayer of Eighteen Blessings. Outdoors all was quiet, too, thank goodness. If only we can get through the first night! At Dubiecko the dead had to be buried at midnight. The Cossacks, under their chief, Chmielnicki, had raped all the women and killed half the male population of the town. People were afraid to leave their homes during the day. That story had terrified people for generations. Poor Asya, the first victim! I would like so much to see her buried according to the customs and ordinances. Grandfather, blessed

98

be his memory, used to travel as far as Braclaw, to visit the great-grandson of Holy Rabbi Baal Shem-Tov,* while Grandmother, may her soul rest in peace, ran the inn. In those days no one was ashamed to call it an 'inn. Now one has to say "a tavern". When his daughter died, Grandfather forbade Grandmother to weep. A dead person laughs in secret at those who mourn him because it's as if they were saying: If only you were still alive, you would be suffering just like us and tasting the bitterness of life! We believe that another world exists. What about this one? Where is it? Because what we have here is hell. What kind of world is it where every human being hangs suspended by a fine thread over the centre of an ocean, while around him a hurricane roars to the very heart of the sky? God Himself is sorry when He looks at this world and says to Himself: For what purpose have I created it? He must be crying now and beating His breast. All this is supposed to last six thousand years: chaos reigned for two thousand years, our world will last for two thousand, and from the coming of the Messiah till the end of the world it will be another two thousand years. To think that chaos has lasted such a long time! What good has come of it? Man, who carries in himself the instruments of sin: his eyes and heart—the tools of temptation and evil. Is Evil the footstool of Good? Some people say that it is. No, it can't be. Is Evil the lowest degree of Good? No. If the seed is bad, the ear of corn cannot be good. How can man ever be good if his experience of the world is to be a bitter medicine? Then God is a bad doctor: He should have given mankind a sugar-coated pill. Miracles are the patches with which the saints have tried to mend the world, God's world, which is full of holes!

And my young Boom sits there and cries: "The adornment was taken from the daughter of Sion." Poor boy: Boom! Listen, Boom! I'll tell you a parable which I heard from my grandfather, who once travelled to Braclaw to visit Holy BEShT. There is a great mountain, and on top of the mountain there is a large rock, and from under that rock pure water

* One of the Founders of Hasidism; his name is subsequently referred to as BEShT.

gushes forth. And on the other side of the world there is a soul, longing, all its life, for the spring of pure water. But the soul can never reach that spring of pure water, can never quench its thirst. Not until the coming of the Messiah. It has to wait for the coming of the Messiah! By that time no one will care any more: and in the meantime one can die of a broken heart.

Old Tag straightened up.

He was still standing on the fourth step of the staircase. He might have fallen, but woke up just in time.

He quickly retraced his steps and went out into the back-yard. A double shaft was pointing upward, the rim of a wheel gleamed in the darkness, while the rest of the cart was in shadow.

The baker's horse was tossing its hooded head and snorting. From above its feed-bag, full of oats, only its pointed ears were showing. The white cat rubbed against Tag's legs, then it gave a sudden leap and disappeared into the orchard behind the cow-shed. Old Tag stumbled and raised the lantern to look at the ground: one of Blanca Wilf's boots was lying there.

From over the roof of the barn which also served as a cow-shed the silver light of the moon was streaming down. From the shed drifted the warm smell of fresh milk and manure. The yellow light of Tag's lantern picked out the heads and backs of the regally resting cows. Both cows, one white, one brown, were chewing the cud in their sleep. Yevdocha had not changed their straw today. She was not asleep. Tag could feel it, without seeing her, from the moment when he had entered the shed. Only now did he throw her a furtive glance. She was lying on her straw mattress on a shelf over the crib: she lay on her stomach, her head propped on her hands, in a shift which only partly covered her breasts. Her moistened teeth glistened in her wide-open mouth.

"Aren't you asleep yet?" asked Tag.

Yevdocha did not answer.

"Where's the ladder?" he asked.

"Over there. . . ."

100

"How did you climb up?"

Yevdocha did not answer.

The ladder was propped against the sheaves of threshed rye. On its upper rung stood Blanca. On the lowest, hanging on to it with one foot before jumping down, stood the hussar. He had escaped indeed, but not very far.

Wilf was keeping his distance, but when he caught sight of Tag, he ran up to him, his broad-brimmed hat slightly askew. He stopped in front of the ladder. The hussar jumped down to the ground, saluted, and made an about-face.

Blanca remained on the upper rung.

"Please move the lantern, it's blinding me," she said.

Tag screened the light with his hand.

"Is that better?" he asked.

"Thank you. Thank goodness somebody has come. Thank goodness you're here. Please tell him . . ."

"Who?" asked Tag.

"Him." Blanca pointed her finger at her husband. "Please tell him that . . ." She was catching her breath.

"The tsaddik"—Old Tag decided to help her—"is asking for the father of the girl, the one killed by the Cossacks, who might now become the redeemer of all Israel."

"Exactly! Exactly!" said Blanca with relief. "Tell him that. His daughter killed by the Cossacks . . ." She gathered the folds of her wide skirt with one hand while holding to the ladder with the other; she began to come down quickly. "His daughter is dead—and yet he keeps imagining things! What a disgrace! A father who thinks of such things at a time like this!"

"Blanca!"

"What?"

"What about the hussar?"

"Don't you even come near me, d'you hear!"

"Just tell me one thing."

"What's that?"

"That hussar?"

"The hussar? What about him? How can I tell? Do I know him? This is the first time I've ever set eyes on him. I can't speak Hungarian. I couldn't talk to him even if I wanted to."

"Blanca!"

Blanca stopped halfway down the ladder.

"Please tell him that I am not 'Blanca' for him any more. From now on, it's finished!"

"Blanca, how can you?"

"Exactly! How can I? I can't any more. I can't go on like this any longer. Never a moment's peace. Don't look here! Don't look there!"

"Did I ever say that to you? When?"

"You didn't have to say it! I could guess!"

Old Tag lifted high his stable lantern.

"Where is that crazy hussar?"

The back door of the shed was open. A breeze came from the orchard. Black trees, bushes, unmowed grass shone in the moonlight.

"Hightailed? He must have jumped over the fence again. Here today, gone tomorrow. Now everything's back to normal. There's nothing to worry about, Mr Wilf. And Blanca ought to go upstairs to bed. Only quietly, because my daughter-in-law has a headache. And Mr Wilf, you'd better go and sit down for a while by your dead daughter." Old Tag tucked his head between his shoulders. "And stop pestering your wife. There's nothing to be surprised about. For: 'Such is also the way of a woman, who eateth and wipeth her mouth and saith: I have done no evil.' There might be some truth in that, you know. And besides, what can you or I do about it? It is written: 'There is no just man on earth who would do good and not sin.' Even Aristotle, the wisest of men, said that the world is so finely balanced, that if one more grain were to fall on one of the scales, the whole earth would tip over. And Aristotle himself fell into the hands of a beautiful woman and perished. If a wise man can lose his balance, what can one expect from a stupid creature such as a woman?"

Blanca and Wilf were now standing side by side and talking. Perhaps she was not so bad after all.

102

Old Tag went up the ladder propped against the threshed sheaves and began to throw down the straw. He glanced at the cow-girl's mattress. Yevdocha had gone.

"Help me to carry the straw to the kitchen. Little children are waiting for it. Thank God you two have made it up. The most important thing is peace in the home. And thank God that hussar has escaped. One worry less. Mr Wilf, look through the little gate and see if by chance he's still in the orchard. If the Cossacks find him there, they won't do him any harm, but they might string me up."

"He might be captured!" exclaimed Blanca, drawing away from her husband.

"He might."

"You heard Mr Tag say they won't do anything to him," said Wilf.

"But he's a human being!"

"Of course he is," agreed Tag. "Please take two sheaves each."

"Gladly, gladly! Don't you carry any, Blanca. I'll carry yours too."

"Go on back to the house. I'll be right there."

Old Tag got down from the ladder. He lifted the lantern and illuminated the cow-shed.

"Don't your feet hurt any more, Blanca?"

From the ground, Blanca picked up first one, then the other of her shoes lying in the yard.

Old Tag waited until the Wilfs disappeared in the hall. He blew out the lantern.

"Yevdocha!"

No answer.

He went into the orchard through the back door.

"Yevdocha!" he called softly.

There was a rustle of branches and the girl came running. She was out of breath.

"Where did you go?"

She sneered:

"None of your business!"

"You wench!"

"Let me go, you old devil!"

"Come on and go to bed! And don't you dare go out of the shed."

"I'm not sleepy."

"If I catch you with the hussar, I'll kill you both!"

"Let me go, you old devil!"

Yevdocha shoved him aside and went into the shed. She took the ladder, stood it under the shelf, and climbed up to her mattress.

In the darkness Tag could see her fat calves moving up the rungs. It was too dark to see how red they were. They were red in winter and summer, just as when he first noticed them, as she emerged from the cold waters of the stream.

A moment later, Yevdocha jumped down from her shelf and ran out into the yard.

Old Tag called after her in a hushed voice:

"Yevdocha! Yevdocha!"

He caught up with her in the hall of the house.

"Are you crazy? Where were you running to? In your shift? Crazy girl! He's not there, I tell you!"

Suddenly the door of the guest hall opened. Mrs Kramer and her daughters came out, pressing their handkerchiefs to their noses.

"This is impossible! They won't let us open the window! An epidemic might start at any minute! Jaundice or typhus! Where can we go?"

"I'll show you," said Old Tag, pointing to the staircase, "go upstairs. My daughter-in-law's in bed, but never mind. Just watch out for the fourth step. I'll fix it tomorrow. We've been putting it off too long. My son has already fixed it once. . . . I'll fix it tomorrow for sure. This way. . . ."

The photographer stood with his wife in a corner. He was holding four sheaves of straw under his arm.

"Maybe you'd like to go upstairs too?" Old Tag asked Blanca. "There's room for one more person. Ah, Yevdocha! Please take this straw. In there, in the kitchen."

She obeyed.

"Well then, up you go," Tag encouraged the women.

"I'll try," said Mrs Kramer and took her daughter by the hand.

Blanca did not budge.

Old Tag sighed, and entered the guest hall. He peeped into the kitchen.

Yevdocha was scattering the straw on the floor. On her way out she glanced at her shawl covering the lamp, and stopped for a moment. She felt Old Tag's eyes on her, bowed her head, and left the kitchen.

The cantor was sitting on the edge of the bench; his straight leg was hidden under the table, the crooked one displayed for everybody to see.

He intoned a psalm:

"To the chief Musician. A psalm of David."

He paused, but no one took up the tune.

"I will love thee, O Lord, my strength," he continued, louder. His voice rose strongly, then scattered into trills, flourishes, and loops; it fell to a whisper, gradually rose again, flowing effortlessly from his breast and throat. Before the word "Lord" there was a slight pause, as before a leap. Every syllable of the word denoting the Highest had a different pitch; each word was interrupted with stresses, moans, and melodious sighing. The cantor lifted his head and closed his eyes; his throat vibrated like that of a singing bird. "The Lord is my rock, and my fortress, in whom I will trust." The cantor fell silent, but not for long. He started again: "Out of the depths have I cried unto thee, O Lord, hear my voice."

"Enough, enough!" The youth with down on his face instead of a beard was waving his hand in the air. "Others may not feel the same way, or maybe they do, but I for one am not a psalm-singing Jew. I am not a labourer, and none of us here are water carriers. We have our own songs."

The cantor laid his hands flat on the table. He stopped leading. He was interrupted during the most solemn of the Psalms. When on the Day of Atonement the groans and cries of all the synagogues float to heaven and prayers crowd in front of God's little window and there is a danger that no prayer will reach the Almighty's ears, that Psalm "Out of the depths have I cried . . ." is the only one that can smash the bolts and open the gates to the Creator of the World.

"We have our own songs!" the youth with down on his face repeated with some embarrassment.

"Singer, sing for us!" called the Hasidim. "Psalms have their place, but we want you to sing for us now."

"Sing, you singer with an echo." The redhead winked. "The tsaddik has said so. The tsaddik says we are to be merry."

The youth with down on his face began:

> Where dwelleth God, who knows?
> Where dwelleth God, I know.
>> Where is the open door,
>> Where dwelleth God,
>> Where is the open door,
>>> Where is the open door, who knows?
>>> Where is the open door, I know.

> Where is the house
> Where dwelleth God?
> Where is the open door?
> Where is the house?
>> Where is the house, who knows?
>> Where is the house, I know.

> Where is it clean?
> Where dwelleth God?
>> Where is the open door?
>> Where is the house?
>> Where is it clean?
>>> Where is it clean, who knows?
>>> Where is it clean, I know.

> Where a modest man abideth,
> Where dwelleth God,
> Where is the open door?

Where is the house?
Where is it clean?
Where a modest man abideth?
  Where is the house?
  Where is it clean?
  Where a modest man abideth. . . .

By now the other Hasidim had joined in.

Old Tag was staring at the floor.

The singers were clapping their hands; they were lifting their feet from the floor.

Old Tag wrung his hands.

"My dearly beloved ones!" he exclaimed. "What can this day be compared to? Who knows? To the day when the Temple was destroyed. Can one sing on a day like this? It's forbidden to sing on such a day. Wouldn't it be more seemly to lament as Jeremiah lamented over Jerusalem? Can one clap hands on a day like this? Can one, God forbid, dance? I know that none of you can be thinking of dancing. Because a day like this should be a day of mourning. I told you, I warned you that a maiden is lying dead here in this house." He pointed to the door of the bedroom.

"What's that Jew saying?" asked the redhead. "When did he tell us? Whom has he told?"

Old Tag took hold of the redhead's thin, pointed beard. He wanted to make him listen.

"When will the Death Brotherhood come?" The redhead waved his hands, determined not to let Tag get a word in edgeways. "Woe is me! Look at me!" he cried.

"And who is dead?" asked the Hasid with the lopsided shoulder.

"A girl."

"Woe is me! Look at me!" called the redhead.

"Let him speak!" said the handsome one with the golden locks. "He has something to tell us."

"What's going on?" The oldest Hasid put his hand to his ear. "I can't hear anything." He stared at the redhead's mouth.

"You are looking at a sinner now!" exclaimed the redhead. "Take a good look at me." He was violently shaking his head and closing his eyes. "Here I stand, sinning. I talk and by talking I sin. I look around, and by looking around I sin. I'm up to my neck in sin. Huh?" He suddenly opened his eyes and looked at the tsaddik. "All right," he pressed his ear against the tsaddik's lips. "Yes, yes," he exclaimed. "The danger of death is prowling the streets. I come from the line of Cohanim. I am a priest myself. . . ."

"I, too, am descended from priests," said the downy-faced youth. "The threat of death wipes away sin. On a night like this you go outside at the risk of your soul!"

"What do they know? They should ask *me*," Soloveytchik remarked aloud.

"Why didn't I leave this place when my son did?" said Wohl the baker, springing to his feet. "If you don't mind, Rabbi, I'll be on my way."

"What did he say?" asked the redhead, rousing himself. He gazed at the baker.

Wohl walked up to the tsaddik.

The holy rabbi sat with lowered head, his face engulfed in his luxuriant beard. His smooth eyelids were closed.

"Rabbi," pleaded the baker, "give me your blessing for the journey."

The redhead clapped his hands. He moved the baker away from the tsaddik.

"The great, holy rabbi has ordered me to stay here. He told me I may stay. Blessings on his head."

"Rabbi"—Wohl came up to the tsaddik from the other side —"I ask your blessing for my journey."

"If he can stay," and the beardless youth clapped his hands, "so can I. When life is in danger, a fire can be lighted even on the Sabbath; for reasons of health. And the girl over there doesn't concern us priests."

"Rabbi," said the baker, holding out his hand, "a blessing for my journey, so that I may not meet any obstacles on the way, so that I may return home safely."

The rabbi gave him his hand.

Leaning backwards, his hands pushed into the pockets of his caftan, the redhead kept his eyes fixed on the baker.

"I'm going home too." Apfelgrün rose abruptly. "Will you take me in the cart? I've had enough. This is no place for me. I have no wife, no daughter—what can they do to me?"

The redhead lifted both his hands, spun around, and found himself between the tsaddik and the baker.

"Wait a minute! Wait a minute! Easy does it! Mr Jew—what are you: a wise man? Get a load of this know-it-all." The redhead got hold of the baker's beard. "Going home, are you? Turning your back on us and going, eh? How? Why? What is it? Is there no one else in the world? And what about the tsaddik? Don't you care about him? Does the tsaddik count for nothing?"

"The tsaddik gave me his hand in farewell," said Wohl in a plaintive voice. "Help, you rogues! What do you want from me?"

"His hand, you say. Two fingers, maybe. The tsaddik is special all right. But I'm the one you should ask. He's got more important things on his mind. Who knows where he is now? You see him sitting here, but in fact he is somewhere high above. Catching angels. A lot he knows about what's going on around him! He doesn't give a moment's thought to whether the baker should go or not go. He can't tell the difference between a cart and a horse. He had to knock himself out to lift from me the sin of being under one roof with that girl. Did you hear what he said to me? The danger of death is prowling the streets. At the risk of your soul. And you make a big hullabaloo and yell 'Help'? For shame! Shame on you. Such a refined Jew as you! Sit still and don't move. You, too, have a wife and children, yet you want, God forbid, to bring upon yourself and your house the greatest misfortune? Ugh! It was not my lips that said it."

"Ugh! Ugh! Ugh!" The Hasidim were spitting.

"Nothing will happen to me," insisted the baker. "Nothing has happened to my son, thank goodness, so nothing will happen to me, God willing. . . ."

"And how do you know for sure that nothing has happened to your son?" asked the redhead.

Wohl looked first at him, then at the others.

"Has anything happened?"

"No, nothing. Not that I know of, anyway. I mean it just as a manner of speaking. Anyway, that's not what we were talking about. What matters is that you haven't thought what would happen to us, or to our wives. Have you ever thought about that? No? Well, then . . ."

"I'll come back tomorrow to take you all. My son and I will be back with another cart."

"Tomorrow? Tomorrow? Listen, Jew: I order you, in the tsaddik's name, to sit down and not to move. And let this be the end of it!"

"It's beyond me," Apfelgrün said indignantly, "how a man can be stopped from taking his horse and cart wherever and whenever he has a mind to."

Pritsch coughed and covered his mouth with a handkerchief.

"For once I agree with you," he said, turning his head toward Apfelgrün. "It's his cart and his right."

"If he wants to go, let him," said Soloveytchik. "He has a right to go, but he doesn't know what he's up against. They may ask him for a pass."

"A pass? What d'you mean by that?" asked the baker.

"You'll soon find out, all of you."

"Why try to scare me? I don't scare so easily," answered Wohl. "A pass? All right then, a pass. God has provided for other things, he will provide for a pass too."

"I don't want to scare anybody, but I remember Kishiniev. About ten years ago. My wife was pregnant with my eldest daughter, Lenka."

"The same old story all over again," groaned Apfelgrün.

"I remember Kishiniev, listen, just listen, I don't mind, I'm not offended. It was the day before the pogrom. A drunken Cossack came barging into my in-laws' house. He threw himself on my sister-in-law. But my father-in-law came running with an axe in his hand. The Cossack got scared and

110

took to his heels. But what if my father-in-law had killed him, God forbid? That's why I keep saying, time and again: escape from them or else. As far as possible!"

"What would have happened? Just what did happen. The next day there was a pogrom, you said so yourself. So you'd have been better off killing that Cossack, wouldn't you?" said Wohl.

"And spill more blood, you mean?" Soloveytchik became purple with indignation. "It's disgraceful to speak like that! Really disgraceful! Ugh!"

"Disgraceful? Maybe. But why should anybody teach me what to do? I'm not a kid any more and won't be taught by just anybody."

"Just anybody! Look who's talking! Over in my shop I have lots of people like you. A baker of flat loaves!"

"What? Say that again!" Wohl leapt to the centre of the room.

Soloveytchik stayed silent and sat down again on the bench.

"Oh, you Jews, you Jews!" Kramer, the bookbinder, was shaking his head. "Why do you quarrel about nothing? Haven't you had enough trouble?"

"Be quiet." The redhead slammed his palm down on the tabletop. "The tsaddik is coming round." He put his ear to the tsaddik's lips.

"The rabbi would like a little snack. Is there anything?" he asked, turning to Old Tag.

"We're all out of food and drink," said Tag, spreading his arms.

From his pocket the redhead produced a roll wrapped in a white cloth and laid it on the table. The tsaddik whispered over it the blessing of the bread.

". . . 'and you pull the bread from the earth'," he concluded out loud.

"Amen," responded the Hasidim, looking at the tsaddik's fingers.

The tsaddik broke off the roll a piece no larger than an olive, put it into his mouth, and chewed it slowly.

111

"Finished?" asked the redhead and put the wrapped roll back into his pocket.

The tsaddik stopped chewing.

The redhead turned to the Hasidim and exclaimed:

"Worthy brethren, let us now praise God."

"Worthy brethren, let us now praise God," they responded.

The tsaddik was whispering prayers, the rest of them prayed a little louder. From time to time a word leapt to the surface, like a fish from a stream.

Suddenly the beardless youth began to sing his song again:

"Where dwelleth God, who knows," and the others took it up, "Where dwelleth God, who knows," after which the youth continued to sing alone, while the others clapped their hands and repeated the last words: "who knows, who knows, who knows?"

The youth got up and took two of the Hasidim sitting next to him by the hand, the handsome one with golden forelocks and the tallest one with the ashen face.

Old Tag started toward them:

"Is this seemly? Think about it, dear ones. I've told you already. The maiden is in the house, yet you want to dance? Now, when every day could be our last?"

"The end of the world, you mean?" The beardless youth turned his head sideways and partly closed his eyes.

"Yes, that's what I mean!" exclaimed Old Tag.

"Well, so what?" He slid his hands under the lapels of his caftan. "So we shall hear the Messiah's horn. I can hear His steps now." He dropped his hands and sat again on the bench. "Dancing lifts a man three feet above the ground. And the Messiah makes Himself known in singing."

The cantor was sitting at the end of the table, right behind the boy with the enormous eyes that almost filled his face; he shoved his crooked leg forward.

"Oh yes," he exclaimed, "singing reveals everything! Deliverance will come in song. For man, a good deed is what music is for an angel. And the halo round the sun turns like a music box and fills the heavens with sound. My father, blessed be his memory, told me how once a Jewish teacher was taking some boys to the synagogue for prayer practice, so what did Satan do? He disguised himself as a werewolf, the cunning deceiver, he started barking like a dog, frightening the children, hitting them with a stick, with a leather thong, marking them with charcoal and tar. One, two, three—and the children were gone. And what did the Jewish teacher do? First he cried with compassion. And the werewolf said: I must kill (barking and jumping) so that the children shall not pray. 'Don't kill them, they are innocent little lambs.' The werewolf only laughed. 'I'll light three candles for your soul.' 'And will you stop the children from praying?' The teacher was running out of strength and on the verge of fainting. He felt himself losing faith and hope. Suddenly a last song rose from his throat, a confession which every Jew must make before his death. And right away the werewolf started cringing, whining, shaking, pissing, apologizing . . . and then, sure as a village clod stinks, he said: 'I promise I won't do anything to the children, I promise I won't hurt them.' He pleaded and cried, but it was too late for him to repent his sins. So that's how the Jewish teacher saved his pupils. And he heard a voice from heaven promising him that as a reward he would live long enough to see the Messiah."

"The Messiah? What do you know about the Messiah! I shall tell you a story about the Messiah!" The youth with down on his face jumped to his feet. "The story that happened with BEShT was as follows:

"Story of the Holy BEShT, who was about to call the Messiah," began the youth. . . .

"Oy, oy, oy." All those present shivered in anticipation.

"Messiah! Listen . . . Messiah!"

The youth lifted his hand.

"It was neither a Sabbath nor a Holy Day, Pentecost was just a few days away when Holy BEShT fell deep into thought. He sat and thought. 'What is the matter?' his disciples asked one another. 'What is the matter?' they asked. 'Before the day is over I shall bring down the Messiah into your midst. And woe to anyone who laughs.' The holy tsaddik BEShT put

the silken cord round his waist and summoned Abraham.
And Abraham came, read a passage from the Torah, and went
his way. BEShT then summoned Isaac, and Jacob, and finally
Moses. And each of them read a passage from the Torah and
went away, happy and blessed. And then a shudder ran
through the synagogue, and the shudder turned into a strong
wind, and the Holy BEShT swayed on his feet and with both
hands grabbed the platform where there was a table, and on
this table there was a scroll of the Pentateuch, and it was
from this scroll that they each had read a passage from the
Torah. BEShT shouted as loud as he could: 'Messiah!
Messiah! Do You hear me?' And in the synagogue only the
echo of his voice could be heard, and nothing more. 'Don't
play games with me! I order You to appear at once, just as our
holy forefathers Abraham, Isaac, and Jacob, also Moses, our
teacher, appeared. Do You think that You are better than they
are? And don't tell me that the time is not come. I'm down
here below and know better than You. See how my dear little
Jews suffer and what they have to endure. I, Baal Shem-Tov,
the son of Eleazar, can no longer bear the sight of our people's
misery!' And then an even stronger wind sprang up, with
thunderbolts and hail, and darkness fell, and amid the storm
and darkness there was a moment of silence and the Messiah
was about to appear and to bring an end to all our worries and
troubles, diseases and death. And just then BEShT's favourite
disciple burst out laughing. Satan had got a grip on him.
That disciple, whose name no one knows nor will ever know,
became a priest somewhere in the world. Any priest in any
city might be that accursed disciple of BEShT. And Holy
BEShT died of grief."

"Oy, oy, oy," groaned the Hasidim.

"May his name and his memory be erased forever," whispered Old Tag and closed his eyes.

"All ills and plagues of Egypt on his head!"

"May so cruel a death strike him that not even the smallest
bone of him shall remain, and let us say Amen!" The redhead
concluded the curses.

"Amen! Amen! Amen!"

"Such a calamity! Yet BEShT's soul is in paradise," sighed one.

"A step from deliverance," sighed another.

"Two hundred years have gone by since that day," interrupted Old Tag, "and the Messiah has not come, and is still nowhere in sight."

"Ah, Messiah! Messiah!" chanted the beardless one and raised one of his hands.

"His day will come," intoned the Hasid with the lopsided shoulder, "His day will come, don't fear. The Messiah is waiting before the gates of Rome. First there will be a war and seven young stars will destroy a large star, and for forty days a column of fire will wander over the earth beside the Messiah, and God will put on the Messiah's head the crown He had been wearing Himself when the Jews were crossing the Red Sea, then the column of fire will fade away and darkness will fall and all the bad Jews will die, just as they died in the desert after they had left Egypt, then brightness will come and a great mystery will be revealed. And that will at last be the deliverance." The Hasid sighed.

"That large star is the enemy," explained Apfelgrün.

"So deliverance is near!" exclaimed the beardless one. "Let's sing, then! Sing 'Hallowed Flock'." He grabbed by the hands the handsome one with the golden forelocks and the very tall one with the ashen face. "Get up! Get up! Sing!"

"There's still time, there's still time!" Old Tag tried to calm them down. "God is still weeping. He's roaring like a wounded lion and asking why He let the enemy, Titus, destroy the Temple."

"God isn't weeping!" cried the youth. "God is saying prayers to Himself and pleading with Himself to have mercy on His own creatures. Why should He weep? If God had only created the Sabbath, the most beautiful princess, it would have been enough. But God has also created the Torah, the most holy of books. If God had created only the Torah and only the Sabbath, this would have been enough. But God created not only the most beautiful princess, the Sabbath, not only the most Holy Book, the Torah, but He also created the most pious of bridegrooms, the Jewish people. And had He created only the Jewish people, that would have been enough. But God created not only the most beautiful princess, the Sabbath, not only the most Holy Book, the Torah, not only the most pious bridegroom, the Jewish people, but He also arranged the wedding of the most pious people, the Jewish people, with the most beautiful princess, the Sabbath, and on Mount Sinai gave them the most precious wedding gift—the most Holy Book—the Torah."

"That was the greatest miracle!" A shiver ran through all those present.

"A miracle of miracles!"

"A miracle! A miracle! A miracle! What do you know about miracles!" said the handsome one with golden forelocks. "I know of a real miracle. The miracle God performed with the Torah and the Sabbath was nothing! I will tell you of a miracle performed on a simple shepherd. With the tsaddik's permission."

The redhead nodded.

"Tell us!"

"Tell us! Tell us!" the others prompted him. "This is the profundity of profundities. Not everybody is worthy to hear it."

"It is a beautiful parable indeed, the one about the shepherd," the redhead conceded.

"It was once said," began the handsome one, fondling one of his own golden forelocks, " 'don't ever leave the Temple.' An allusion to what? you might ask. 'The Temple' means the world, 'don't leave' means don't die. For it is written that 'not the dead will praise God', only the living. What use are the dead to God? None. A new question arises. How to praise God? By eating and drinking one can also praise the Almighty. The delight of the body heals the soul. When a husband and wife, cleansed from gross impurities, come together on Friday night or on Holy Days, they are praising God. Why did BEShT lead his disciples out into the mountains and forests? Because by breathing the scented air you can also praise God. Each tree, each blade of grass helps us by its scent to praise God. Each blade of grass
116

has its song, said the holy BEShT, and belongs in prayer. And prayer brings up another question. Prayer is the last resort. That's why it has been said: When you're praying, wave your arms and legs around like a man drowning in a river who is trying to save himself. It is said that the Almighty likes most of all prayers in the fields, where there's no ceiling. Why did BEShT pray in the open? Because of this. Not only that, but he danced in the fields and ordered his disciples to sing and dance there too. Because by rejoicing you also praise God. Once upon a time—this story is told by people who heard it from their parents, who in turn heard it from their parents, and so on—an innkeeper was on his way back from town when he saw BEShT and his disciples dancing in the field from which the corn had just been gathered. They danced and danced. They had neither eyes nor ears for anything, their dancing was all. The innkeeper came up and asked: 'Isn't it a sin to dance like that? You've already torn the soles off your shoes.' And BEShT himself answered: 'These soles are the important thing. In the morning the angels come out to tidy up in heaven. While they're sweeping they come across the torn soles. They fly to Archangel Michael and ask: What are these? And Archangel Michael answers: These were torn in praise of God. Make a crown for the Almighty from these worn-out soles.' Deep? Eh? Ha, ha, ha!

"*But the event—*

"But the event, about which I wanted to tell you and which took place, was as follows. It so happened that BEShT went out into a field, because God let him know that there was a shepherd whom He had come to like.

"*And that shepherd—*

"And that shepherd was tending a flock on a tall mountain. He had just blown his horn and rounded up his sheep by a stream. 'Creator of the world,' said the shepherd, 'You have created heaven and earth, mountains and sheep, the sheep's owner and the Jewish people. But I am a simpleton and don't know how to praise You.'

"*And he took the horn—*

"And he took the horn and said: 'I have only this horn, this
117

hollowed-out ram's horn, I blow it with all my strength and say: You are our God.' The shepherd blew the horn for so long that he grew weak and he fainted, and he lay on the ground unconscious, quite still, until he finally came to his senses.

"*And when he regained his senses—*

"And when he regained his senses, he repeated the same words again. 'Creator of the world, You have created this world, the whole world, but only one small people, the Jewish people, is Yours. Just as You are One, so the Jewish people is one, and that people is learned and can read Your Holy Books; but I am a simpleton and don't even know which blessing to say before breaking bread and which before drinking water. But I can sing for You.'

"*And the shepherd sang—*

"And the shepherd sang, he sang with all his might until he fainted and fell on the ground and lay unconscious, quite still, until he recovered. And when he did, he repeated loudly the same words: 'Creator of the world, it is of little worth to You that I blow a hollowed-out ram's horn, that I sing You a song. If I could read and explain at least one column of the Talmud, You would be more pleased with me. And You would give me a handful of nuts and a baked apple, but how can I serve you, Father in heaven, simple as I am now?'

"*The shepherd looked—*

"The shepherd looked at the meadow and cheered up. 'Well, I might be able to turn a few somersaults for you.' And the shepherd stood on his head and turned a few somersaults and went on turning them until he fainted and fell to the ground unconscious, and lay quite still until he regained his senses. And when he did, he repeated the same again: 'Creator of the world, You must be laughing at me, a simple shepherd. This is all I know.'

"*And then he remembered—*

"And then he remembered something and said: 'Last night the landlord was giving his only daughter in marriage, and he prepared a great feast for his guests and said to his servants: Enjoy yourselves at my only daughter's wedding, eat and

118

drink, and he gave everybody a silver penny as a keepsake. That silver penny which I am now holding in my hand I give you, Creator of the world. You created heaven and earth, mountains and sheep, the sheep's owner and the Jewish people. Don't make a simple shepherd feel ashamed; accept this silver penny from me.' The shepherd stuck out his hand toward heaven. And he stood like that for a moment, waiting.

"*And from behind a cloud—*

"And from behind a cloud a hand came out and took the silver penny. The little shepherd fell to the ground unconscious, and when he recovered he sang aloud Hallelu-jah! Hallelu-jah! Hallelu-jah!"

"Ay, ay, ay," chanted the Hasidim.

"I'm shaking all over."

"Ay, ay," mimicked the Hasid with the lopsided shoulder. "Did you at least understand the allusion?"

"We did! We did!"

"I bet that none of you can see the deepest depth." The Hasid with the lopsided shoulder got up. "Who can tell me why there was a horn in the story? A simple shepherd would only have a whistle. No one knows? Then I will tell you. Because it was a horn borrowed from the Messiah. And one day the Messiah must come back for His horn, otherwise He won't have anything to blow on for the resurrection of the dead. The dead are waiting for the sound of the horn to rise from their graves in time for the feast the Messiah will give for all the just. And why did the shepherd sing? This is a hint that the High Priest Aaron, the brother of Moses our teacher, will come to the Messiah's feast and will sing the Psalms of Solomon the King. But one may ask why Aaron? This is a hint that the Temple in Jerusalem will rise from the ashes along with the people, the Temple where priests used to sing and play various instruments. And why did the shepherd turn somersaults? This is a hint that the Prophetess Miriam, the sister of Moses our teacher, will come to the feast and will dance there. It is a hint that henceforth joy and mirth will reign among the sons of Israel forever. And now let us say Amen!"

"Amen. Amen. Amen."

"Joy and mirth! Joy and mirth!" sang the beardless youth, lifting his feet from the floor under the table.

Suddenly the young boy with sunken cheeks and enormous eyes got up. His voice trembled as he stammered:

"Will the tsaddik mind? He won't get upset with me, will he?"

"What's on your mind?" asked the redhead, moving closer to him. "What is it you'd like to say?"

"Don't be angry with me. . . . Don't be angry with me. . . ."

"Well, speak up, then we'll see!"

The boy lifted his forearm and screened his face from the redhead:

"When . . . when Miriam . . . dances . . . this . . . this . . . this means," the boy grew even paler and stopped. He was gasping for breath.

"Here we go again," said the redhead. "You've dreamed about a woman again, a naked one, ugh, a harlot! Ugh! To all four winds. Ugh! Come, let me slap you on the back so you won't choke. Be gone, wicked one! Be gone! Has she gone?"

Yevdocha appeared.

"What do you want?" asked Old Tag.

"The priest is here. He's waiting."

"My God!" Old Tag left the room at a trot.

The school chaplain was waiting in the yard.

"Good evening," he said, holding out his hand.

"What's happened?" asked Old Tag.

"And what's going on here?"

"There's a dead girl inside."

"Yes, I know. But that's not what I mean. That shouting, Tag. Are those your weeping women?"

"There are no weeping women here. How can you believe such tales, Father?"

"What is it, then? A Jewish parliament?"

"I don't understand."

"Who's that inside?"

"Father, you'd better ask who's not inside. A Noah's ark, no less."

"Beautifully put. But who *are* those people anyway?"

"The worst thing is that there are women and children in the house. What am I to do with them?"

"But do they have to make so much noise?"

"It's not the women or the children who are making it. There are some very religious people in there who are chasing bad thoughts away with noise."

"A fine time, Tag, for exorcisms."

"Yes."

"What do you mean by 'Yes'? Innocent people might suffer because of these fools."

"Do you mean to say that these fools are not innocent?"

"Don't misinterpret my words. I am older than you. I deserve some respect. If only because of my age, Tag."

"I do respect you, Father. What's the difference in age between us? Two years?"

"Never mind how many! It's not something you forget."

"I don't forget; I don't forget. Once upon a time it had some importance. But now?"

"Especially now."

"Oh, you've always looked younger than me, and still do. And you've been much healthier than any of us. We Jewish kids were sickly, we didn't live very long. With Jews there's no such thing as children—we're Jewish men and women right from the start."

"What a philosopher!"

"Do you remember how big our family was?"

"Who could keep count?"

"Exactly. And only two of us survived: myself and my sister. But even she died soon after getting married, blessed be her memory."

"Blessed? Wasn't she baptized before her death?"

Old Tag made no reply.

"All right. Forgive me. She was a lovely girl, God rest her soul. She wanted to invite me to her wedding, I remember. And I told her: 'Forget it, Maria, forget it! A priest at a Jewish wedding!' I was still young then. It was just after I'd taken holy orders."

"Exactly. You weren't yet a priest then. That came later."

"Possibly so . . . I can't keep anything straight any more."

"But why are you standing, Father? Wouldn't you like to sit down?"

"I haven't got time. I've come to take you with me. D'you understand? Together with your daughter-in-law and grand-daughter."

"What's happened? Is there any danger?"

"Go back inside, tell them to get dressed and to take only the most necessary things with them, d'you understand? I came in my trap. There is a terrible uproar in the town."

"What do you mean by that?"

"I mean that our Jews are going to get hurt."

"By whom? And for what?"

"You know where the People's Co-operative is, don't you? The Russian commandant has set up his headquarters there. For all I know he may even be a general. At the entrance there are two soldiers standing guard with fixed bayonets. It wasn't me they summoned, but the parish priest and the Greek Catholic priest, along with the subprefect, and Mr Tralka the mayor. The town rabbi wasn't summoned either. What does it mean? Now d'you see what I'm driving at?"

"Where do you want to take us, Father?"

"To my place."

"Are things really as bad as that?"

"As I told you before: the town is in an uproar."

"I had a hunch it was like that. If the chaplain comes to see me in person, then you know something is wrong."

"I must go now. I left the trap next to Axelrad's mill, so it would not be noticed. The Ruthenians are also waiting for a signal."

"What about the others?"

"What others?"

"The children. The small children. The innocent ones?"

"They won't do anything to the children."

"All right, but what about the women?"

The priest spread his arms wide.

"How can I leave them?"

"I have come to get you and your family."

"How can I leave my own house?"

"You will come back."

"How can I leave those other people in my own house? With us a guest is sacred. What if any of them should turn out to be Elijah's prophet?"

"Nothing can happen to a prophet. Don't worry about that."

"And she, too, is under my roof. The dead maiden. Her body has to be cleaned; a shroud has to be made for her. With us a dead person is . . ."

"She has a father, hasn't she? And a mother. Let her parents take care of it."

"She has no mother. And the father still doesn't quite realize that his daughter is dead. He's a sick man himself."

"You've got to save what you can."

"Are things as bad as that?"

"At the moment, they're drinking vodka. They've broken into the distillery and the beer tavern, also into the wine store in the market square. They broke the windows with their rifle butts, Tag. The prostitutes from all over town are there as well. . . ."

"They're drinking vodka. That's not the worst."

"For the time being."

"What do you mean: for the time being?"

"Don't you understand Polish?"

"Better a drunken Cossack than a sober one, if you ask me."

"*Ambo meliores*, as the Latin proverb has it."

"I think that before a drunk manages to hit once, a sober man can hit twice."

"You've got it all nicely figured out, haven't you? God Almighty! Can I trust my ears? What's all that stamping?"

"I hear it! They've begun! Please, Father! I'll be right back. Or, if you have no time . . ."

"I shan't wait long. I cannot wait."

"I understand."

Both straightened up and listened.

Inside the tavern, the Hasidim were dancing.

❋

Gershon left Boom alone in the bedroom when he heard the wordless chanting and moaning. The moaning gradually took the form of a melody, soft at first, then ever louder and faster: Oy, yoy, yoy, yoy, yoy, yoy, yoy, oy oy, yoooy yoy oy, oy, oy, oy, oy, yooy, yoo yoy!

The Hasidim were dancing: all together at first, blurry shapes in the dim light of the lamp, shaded by the cow-girl's cashmere shawl.

A circle was formed: black caftans, flapping tails, wide-brimmed hats, white stockings.

The circle broke against the corner of the cupboard, against the long table of the guest hall, against the benches; fell apart.

The dancers joined hands again, like children, found one another, clung together, following the singing like sightless people. Indeed, their eyes were shut.

They stamped hard first the left foot, then the right, threw into the air first the left arm, then the right, all the while clapping their hands. They bent down, then abruptly tossed their heads like horses. They turned their faces and their torsoes to the left, then to the right. They laid their palms stiffly on the shoulders of one another and moved forward angularly like Egyptian figures in illustrations in the *World History*.

Moses had learned various tricks at the Pharaoh's court and thus obtained power over the Jews: the passage through the Red Sea was not a miracle at all. Moses knew from the Egyptian priests that the sea was tidal. Hence the miracle. He waited until the tide was low and ordered the Jews to cross quickly; then when the tide rose, Pharaoh's hosts were drowned. The Bible is nothing but a legend. And to be quite honest, I don't believe in Moses' existence. There is no trace of him in any history. The first trace to be found concerns King David. The tsaddik also performs miracles. Let him perform one now and bring Asya back to life. I'll open the door wide and let him see her. She's lying on the floor, covered with a white sheet.

The Hasidim were putting their hands to their left ears, then to their right. They were vigorously throwing their heads to the left, then to the right. They were snapping their fingers in the air, pulling up the skirts of their caftans, throwing forward their left, then their right feet. They were shuffling slowly forward with their eyes closed and their beards sticking out. They were smacking their lips and sucking in their tongues. All the time they were humming softly through their noses.

Are they some kind of savages? What have we cobblers in common with them? We are marching forward with the world, united; fighting for the equality of all human beings so that there shall be no difference between the rich and the poor; there has even been a strike of tailors in the town, organized by Simon. The first strike ever. The shoemakers didn't go on strike—who was there left to strike? The two and a half apprentices? All the same, they passed the hat for the tailoring apprentices. The owners of the workshops didn't even show up for the meeting in the union building on the square. Mrs Maltz, even the Baroness, had helped the strikers, a free soup kitchen was installed in Toynbee Hall for the strikers' children. At the meeting, Comrade Simon said: "Our slogan, the slogan of all true Socialists, is: 'Live and let live, solidarity and unity! One for all, and all for one'." Then Miss Amalia Diesenhoff made a speech, calling for progress, that is, for the study of Esperanto above all.

The faces of the dancers were clearly visible now. Perspiration was trickling from their brows onto their closed eyelids, dripping from their noses the way it does with small children.

They were forming a snake now, at a walking pace, one lifted leg bent at the knee. The man with the lopsided shoulder was leading. He had bags under his eyes, purple as plums, and brick-coloured patches on his cheeks. He was the only one with his eyes open. He was turning the human snake left, then right, dancing ever more quickly and pulling the others after him. They passed by Gershon, who was pressed against the door, without noticing him. Over all of them towered the face of the tallest man, white as a piece of linen from which holes for the eyes and mouth had been cut. Behind him the shortest man, agile as a cat, was floating above the floor, holding on to the sleeves of the youth with the golden forelocks. He looked bright as day, only his eyelids were dark from the shadow cast by his long lashes. Joseph might have looked like that, had he ever really existed. And what about the one with the wiry, protruding beard who was showing the whites of his eyes! He looked atrocious: a skeleton, thin and drooling. His beard was shaking, head reeling; his legs started to give way at the knees, he stumbled, but gripped tightly the arm of the fattest Hasid, who had short legs, broad shoulders, and a broad smiling face. His large pink head shone greasily under his skullcap; his hat was tilted way back. The beardless youth was biting his lips and gathering up his caftan. He was making knee-bends, throwing his right foot, then his left, toward his outstretched hands. The grey-haired, deaf old man was chomping out his own tune with toothless jaws. He had been pushed out of line and was trotting alongside the dancers. The shortest one found himself now at the end of the file, thrown hither and thither, but still clinging to the beardless youth. When the latter bent down, the little man fell on the floor, but he got up at once, calling aloud: "Let's make it lively! Let's make it gay!" The snake came apart, but the dancers clasped one another's hands and formed a circle. They stamped, clapped, bent, and tossed their heads sharply, all the time chanting the same wailing tune:

"Oy, yoy yoy yooh yo yoy! Oyyoy! Oyoyoyoyoy!"

Old Tag stood in the doorway wringing his hands.

Gershon began to elbow his way toward him through the dancers.

"Gershon, help!"

"What am I to do?"

"If only I knew!"

Tag tried to squeeze through to the tsaddik.

The tsaddik was still sitting at the head of the long guest-hall table, his face buried in his luxuriant beard.

Tag touched his sleeve.

The tsaddik lifted his head.

"Rabbi, see what they're doing!"

"Huh?"

"Make them stop, Rabbi!"

"What do you want, my son?"

"Rabbi! Dear Rabbi! Beloved Rabbi! They must stop dancing! They are in danger of death! Their souls are in danger! On a night like this! They're rioting in town! Drunken Cossacks are on a rampage, murdering and raping!"

"Write it down, write it down!"

"Rabbi! Please listen to me!"

"What is it, my son?"

"There is death in my house."

"Ugh!"

"There's a dead woman in my house! A dead woman!"

"She'll get well, she'll get well!"

"Rabbi!"

"Yosele must give me the chit!"

"Rabbi!"

"What name? What name?"

"Rabbi, I did not give you any chit. None at all. Tell your Hasidim to stop dancing; they're in danger of death! Their souls are in danger!"

"Your son?"

"God forbid. May God protect him from all evil."

"Write the name down! The name!"

"Rabbi! Listen to what I'm saying!"

"Yosele will pass the chit."

The redhead came running.

"Yosele! Yosele!" The tsaddik smiled with relief.

"What's going on around here?" The redhead waved his hands in front of Tag's face.

"Stop it, for goodness' sake!"

"Can't you leave him alone for a second! What d'you think he is, anyway? A man of iron? He's a human being too, you know! Can't he have a moment's peace? What's the matter with you, anyway?" The redhead was waving his arms encased in the wide sleeves of his caftan. "The only way you can reach him is through me. His channel is straight to heaven. For ordinary people, I'm the person to see."

"For goodness' sake stop dancing! For the plain fear of God!"

The redhead was already putting his ear to the tsaddik's lips.

"How can you? It's unheard of! On a night like this! Is this the night of the Feast of Torah or what?" Old Tag persisted.

"In what way is this night different from any other night of the year?" The redhead was still holding his ear to the tsaddik's lips.

"Don't you know? What kind of people are you? Don't you realize what's going on in the world? What world are you living in? Do you wish to bring misfortune upon my house?"

"No misfortune can come to a house where I and the tsaddik have stopped," said the redhead, without looking up.

"Do you know what the Cossacks are now doing in town?"

"The Cossacks will share the same fate, by the Almighty's will, as all the enemies of the sons of Israel. They will drown like the Egyptians, they will hang from the gallows like Aman and his sons."

"Life! Life!" a shout was heard.

The redhead looked up.

Tag turned his head.

The boy with the sunken cheeks and enormous eyes was lying on the bench. He was the only one who did not dance. He lay with his head tucked down between his shoulders.

"You! You!" scowled the redhead.

"Life! O life!" groaned the boy.

"Tell me what you see; is it a naked woman again? Her bottom sticking out? Tell me! Tell me what you see." The redhead was shaking his fist in the air. "Everything you see! You! You!"

"No! No!"

The cantor was stroking the boy's head:

"Don't be afraid!"

The redhead pulled a red handkerchief from his pocket and wiped his face:

"Enough! That's enough for today! Can you hear me?"

The Hasidim stopped dancing.

"What's happened?" asked the beardless youth.

"The rabbi saw a great cloud."

"Almost! Almost! We were almost there," panted the golden-haired one.

"And now you'd better take a good look at him." The redhead pointed to the boy on the bench. "The evil spirit won't leave him alone. Meat! Meat! All he wants is a plateful of meat! Like a goy! Of pork! From the arse! Ugh!"

The boy leapt up from the bench, staggered, and cried:

"Hear, O Israel: the Lord our God is One!"

"For all He cares. For all He cares!" The redhead was pulling the boy's forelocks. "Whoever wants can now get at us! Beastliness has got hold of him. May God guard us and protect us!"

"May God guard us!"

"God will prevent it!"

"Away! Ugh! Ugh!"

"Quiet." The redhead ran up to the tsaddik and laid his hands on the arms of his chair. He closed his eyes and began to sway violently.

There was silence.

"No! No!" The boy retreated to the door.

The Hasid with the lopsided shoulder barred his way.

"Where to, little fellow? Where, you cute boy?" He grabbed him by the collar and pushed him toward the table.

"No! No!" the boy shouted again.

"Quiet!" The redhead winked at the Hasid to leave the boy alone. He stooped and put his mouth to the tsaddik's ear:

"Rabbi? What am I to do with the little sinner? Ah, yes! All right! Buy his way out. All right, I have nothing against it. Let this scum buy his way out. Huh? Rabbi?"

The tsaddik kept quiet.

"What do they want from this boy?" asked Apfelgrün.

"Don't interfere. This is their business," said Pritsch.

"Is that you who's talking? Such a . . . a . . . modern man?" began Apfelgrün. "They're going to torture this boy."

"Yes." Gershon looked at Old Tag.

Tag spread his arms.

"Let's wait awhile and see; we'll see."

"Real savages!" hissed Gershon.

The beardless youth walked to the centre of the guest hall.

"May it please the rabbi to say something out loud for once.

We all wish for it very much. Am I right, brothers, sons of Israel?"

No one said anything.

The tsaddik was silent.

The redhead raised his arm:

"Be quiet! And you, sit down," he ordered the beardless one. "Rabbi, I am asking you. Deem me worthy of a reply. Is it to be a money ransom? His father is rich. What does ten or twenty florins mean to such a man?"

The tsaddik said nothing.

All was quiet in the guest hall.

Only the deaf old man with his eyes closed continued to stamp his feet in his solitary dance and to sing a prayer to accompany his dance, a prayer with a melody all its own:

> And let your will be done, O God.
> Have mercy upon me,
> That I should be worthy,
> That I should be happy,
> That I should be able to lift my feet in joy,
> That I should be worthy to dance,
> That I should dance for great joy,
> That by Your mercy Your commands should become
>   sweeter and Your orders easier to bear,
> That I should be worthy,
> That I should be happy,
> That I should be worthy . . .

"What's he doing there?" scowled the redhead.

The beardless youth waited for the old man to say the last Amen, then pulled him by the sleeve of his caftan.

"Uncle! Excuse me, Uncle . . ."

The deaf man opened his eyes. He stopped dancing and looked around:

"Are we leaving now? Well, let's go, then, or it'll be too late! We should have gone a long time ago. I told you so! I told you so!"

The youth led the old man to the bench and helped him to sit down.

130

"Rabbi," the redhead began again. "What should the ransom be? A naked woman is haunting this boy. Ugh, ugh, ugh! We must exorcise her from inside him."

"No! No!" The boy blocked his ears with his hands.

Old Tag went up to him.

"What wrong has he done?" he asked. "I don't understand it. What wrong have you done?" Tag tried to lift the boy's chin.

The boy gave a jerk and shrank back.

"What is this, some Tartar you've caught?" Tag asked the redhead. "What kind of sin can he have committed? None. Take a good look at him! Look at that Samson, that hero! You should be ashamed, you Jews! If you don't like him, don't keep him with you, send him back to his father. Let his father take him into his business, if he has a business, or turn him over to a tailor as an apprentice. Either way, that's his affair. But to say that this boy is a sinner? Well then, you'd better listen to a parable."

"We've had enough stories for one day," cried the Hasid with the lopsided shoulder.

"Let the Jew have his say," said the handsome one with the golden locks, "let the landlord have his fun."

Silence ensued, and Tag began:

"On the Day of Atonement, a Jew showed up in the market square with a piece of pork. And the Jew shouted for all to hear: 'See what I'm going to eat!' There was no one in the square, everybody was in the synagogue dizzy from fasting and praying. Only the rabbi went out to speak to the godless man. He bowed low and said: 'My son, I'm sure you don't know what you're holding there.' And the godless Jew laughed: 'Why shouldn't I know? Of course I know. It's a piece of pork.' And he laughed again. 'I'm sure you don't know that today is fast day.' 'Why not? I know very well that today is the Day of Atonement.' 'Then I'm sure you don't know that on the Day of Atonement the Almighty enters in the Book of Life the names of those who are to live for another year, until the next Day of Atonement, and those who, God forbid, won't live.' 'Why shouldn't I know? I know perfectly well, but I don't care.' 'Tell me, my son, maybe it's not pork

you're holding in your hand, maybe you're just pretending.'
'No, this is a piece of pork. And, if you like, I can eat it right
here and now.' And the godless man held up the hand with
the pork and started to stick it, God forbid, into his mouth.
But the rabbi stretched his arms out to Heaven and said:
'D'You see, Almighty God, how good Your people are?
Even the worst Jew does not want to dirty his lips with a lie
on the Day of Atonement. O Lord, look at this man. He did not
want to offend You with a lie on the Day of Atonement.'
And the rabbi burst into tears and threw himself on the
ground. And the godless man wept, too. 'I wanted to make
God angry, because I had a grievance, but I see now how
stupid I was: if I couldn't make a rabbi angry, how can I make
the Almighty so?' The rabbi blew the horn. Everybody heard
the echo coming from above. It was a sign from God that He
had forgiven the sinner. And it was a sign, too, that during
the following year no one would die in the village. So leave
this boy alone. Let there be peace among the Jews. And let us
say: Amen."

"Amen," said the redhead.

"Amen," repeated all those present.

"A good parable," said the handsome Hasid with the golden
locks.

"If you think that was a good parable," said the beardless
youth, smiling, "allow me to tell you an even better one.
About the king and the wicked heir to the throne."

"Some other time," said the redhead, passing his hand over
his moustache and sparse beard. "The time has come for the
Nightly Calling of the Name. 'Hear, O Israel: the Lord our
God, the Lord is One.' "

"Hear, O Israel," whispered the Hasidim.

Boom suddenly began to look like both his father and his
mother. Similar furrows now ran from his nose to his mouth;
similar wrinkles appeared between his eyebrows; and his
whole face, tear-smudged, with swollen eyelids, a pudgy nose,
and feeble lips, seemed to be covered with grey dust. The

poor boy. Gershon laid his hand on his. Boom opened his eyes.

Gershon shuddered with joy. He saw the reflection of the mourning candles in Boom's eyes. What a good thing that the touch of a hand, like a magnet, can extract a little pain from the human heart.

"Boom, I want to talk to you. Will you listen?"

Boom nodded.

"Do you want to hear a story about Napoleon?"

Boom did not answer.

"How Napoleon said to his troops: Two thousand years of history are looking at you. Do you want to hear it? I like Napoleon best of all."

"What's going on in there?" asked Boom.

"They're praying. The Nightly Calling of the Name."

"Where's my mother?"

"I don't know."

"And my father?"

"In there."

"Will they be sitting in there much longer?"

"I don't know. Why do you ask?"

"What time is it?"

"I have no watch."

"Will it stay dark much longer?"

"Why do you ask?"

"Will you help me?"

"Sure. To do what?"

"To take her away."

"Boom!"

"I must take her away from here."

"Where?"

"To the cemetery."

"Now?"

"Yes. While it's dark."

"But it's against the rules."

"Help me."

"You can't do it, Boom! You must understand! She must be washed and dressed! Taken away in a hearse. The

133

Brotherhood must go around with money boxes and call: 'Alms save from death!' You may think it funny, but that's the way it has to be done."

"I won't have it!"

"She can't have a funeral any other way."

"I don't want a funeral."

"Oh, Boom! What is it, then, you want?"

"I'll carry her myself."

"That's not allowed."

"Just help me to carry her out into the yard."

"Let's wait until the morning, then we'll see."

"Not in the morning. Now! Who'll know the difference?"

"The inn is full of people. They're bound to see. They won't let you . . ."

"We can take her out through the window."

"No! No! I won't!"

Gershon went up to the window.

"Please help me. Help me. Help . . ."

"It won't work. See how light it is here."

Moonlight flooded the yard.

The shaft of the baker's cart was sticking upward. The horse was tossing its head in the bag of oats.

Gershon pushed the shutter open, and a gust of wind burst into the room.

"Look, Boom, it's as bright as day. There hasn't been so clear a night for a long time. Somebody's coming."

It was the Catholic chaplain.

"What's going on here?" he asked.

"Good evening, Father," said Gershon. "You must be looking for Mr Tag. I'll call him if you like. Shall I?"

"Yes, please," said the chaplain.

Gershon quickly left the bedroom.

"Kramer? Is that you?"

Boom was silent for a moment.

"Yes, it's me," he said.

"Come over to the window."

Boom did so.

"Do you want to tell me how it happened?"

Boom burst out crying.

"It wasn't my fault!"

"May God comfort you!"

Boom was trying to fight back his tears.

"Calm yourself, it was God's will."

"Please, Father . . . please, Father," stammered Boom.

"Come on, out with it, out with it."

Boom stopped crying.

"Please, Father. Come over here . . . In a second I'll . . ."

Boom went up to Asya's body. He lifted it in his arms and came back to the window.

"What are you doing?" asked the chaplain, alarmed.

"Help me with the body, Father. Then I'll take it from there."

"You must be crazy, my boy!"

"Please help me, Father. Then I'll take it from there."

"Crazy boy!" whispered the priest and held out his arms.

Boom slowly turned and holding Asya's body, covered with the sheet, slid it sideways through the open window.

Gershon was looking for Old Tag but was unable to find him anywhere, either in the guest hall, or in the kitchen, or in Minna's room on the first floor.

He stopped for a moment in the kitchen.

The faint flame of the kitchen lamp hanging on the wall threw a thin ray of light in the corner, where a slim woman in a bright-coloured dress was standing. She was trying to quiet a crying baby. Next to her the long-nosed childless woman was swaying in prayer.

"When a child, God forbid, has a fever either from stomach-ache or the evil eye, you should take an eggshell and wrap it round the little finger of its right hand; it'll hurt quite a bit, but within an hour the shell will drop off, and with it the fever will drop," the long-nosed woman was saying in a rough voice.

On the iron bedstead lay the tsaddik's wife, with the wet nurse and the baby.

Huddled in the centre of the kitchen were the rest of the women and children. And against the wall the tall woman in

135

a velvet dress embossed with gold stars was standing, a lace shawl on her head, humming to her infant. Somebody was snoring.

The windows were shut and there was a heavy stench in the air. Outside, a pale moon shed its light in a broad circle.

Against another wall sat the hunchbacked woman, hugging her children like chicks in her arms. They were asleep. She was speaking slowly, and the dark-haired mother of the blond fat boy and the mother of two little twin girls were listening to her, nodding their heads and dozing off from time to time.

Gershon wanted to go back out, but he stayed in the room. The woman's voice reminded him of his mother's voice as she used to read stories about holy women from a large shabby book entitled *Come Out and Look*. The Sabbath dusk would burst through the small low window and his mother usually finished the story from memory.

"... she sat under a tree that came from a warm land and bore dates, and judged the sons of Israel. Why was she judging them? Because they had sinned and were overcome with bitterness. And when was life ever sweet for our brothers, you might ask, Jewish daughters? And you might ask, too, why life was never sweet for our Jews. Because they never listened to what the Almighty, hallowed be His name, told them to do, and so they sinned. You ask, Jewish daughters, when had they sinned? I shall answer you this moment. They sinned in the desert. They sinned in the land of Israel. No matter what God did, nothing was right. Everything He did was wrong. Even the manna from Heaven was bad. And yet the manna was made in all the different flavours and no Jewish woman has ever been able to make such a meal. Because to the man who thought of fish and craved a piece of fish, the manna tasted like fish, and to him who thought of meat and craved a piece of fat meat, the manna tasted like fat meat braised in gravy and flavoured with garlic. To the person who thought about a Purim roll with raisins, the manna tasted like Purim cake. To the person who thought of the Sabbath spice cake with almonds, the manna tasted like it. And to him who

136

thought of potatoes cooked with goose crackling, the manna tasted like it, and whoever wanted it could imagine the most expensive and the best dishes worthy of a royal feast. And yet the Jews complained and quarrelled with Moses: Why did you lead us out of Egypt? Did we ask you to? Did we send for you? We were better off there! We could eat our fill. Our bowls were full of onions and garlic. So what did God do? He got very angry and sent down fiery snakes. And those fiery snakes burned the sinners. And why did God, hallowed be His name, send down snakes, you may ask, Jewish daughters? Because the snake had also committed a sin with its tongue. And a snake has a forked tongue, which means that it sinned twice: once when it persuaded Eve to eat the apple from the forbidden tree, and the second time when it spoke against God in general, and that's why it was punished very heavily. God cursed it, so that its tongue would only know one taste—the taste of dust upon the ground. And since that time, the snake may eat the finest delicacies, but still they taste of dust to it. . . . So Deborah sat under a tree from the warm land. . . ."

Sabbath in winter usually seems shorter than a weekday. Pretty soon Gershon's mother would ask his youngest sister to light a candle. Pretty soon his father would return from the cobblers' house of prayer and would bless the candles and chant Hawdalah over them, taking leave of the princess Sabbath until the following Friday. . . . Deborah, the prophetess, sang to God so that He would save the Jewish people when they were attacked by the hateful Sisera and driven out of their tents. Deborah pleaded that an army be called and then she vanquished Sisera with his soldiers, his horses and chariots. Then she came out and sang before God: "Hear, O ye kings; give ear, O ye princes. I will sing unto the Lord, the Lord God of Israel. The villages stood empty until I Deborah arose: a mother of Jews arose. Fierce was the war, and the stars in their courses fought against Sisera. The hoofs of the horses were broken, and the water swelled in the rivers and even the sea joined the battle, engulfing the enemy soldiers of Sisera. All perished except Sisera, who leapt down from his chariot and fled on foot. He came to a tent at the entrance to which stood a modest Jewish daughter, the wife of a pious Jew, blessed among the women in the tents. Sisera asked her for a drink of milk, and Jael gave it to him so that he would fall asleep, also butter in a little dish fit for the princes. Jael waited and prayed to God to make the enemy of Israel fall asleep. She was saying the prayer of redemption, the same that is said over a rooster before the Day of Atonement, so that the rooster should take all the sins upon itself and take them with it after its death. And when Sisera fell asleep, she took a nail in her left hand, and an iron hammer in her right, and drove the nail into his temple. Sisera fell dead between her knees. He lay dead, like the Pharaoh whom God threw into the Red Sea, like Aman, who wanted to hang all the Jews and was hanged himself instead, because the wife of Ahasuerus, the beautiful Esther, persuaded her husband to hang him, for such was the will of God, who had chosen us so that He could aid us in every misfortune and not leave us to be tortured by our enemies, whose name will be erased, for the Lord our God is merciful and . . ."

"Have you seen my daddy?"

Gershon looked down. A small girl was pulling him by his sleeve.

"And who is your daddy?"

"My name is Lenka Soloveytchik. My daddy is Ephraim Soloveytchik, and my mummy is Mrs Hana Soloveytchik. We live on the market square. My daddy is a wine merchant. Do you know him?"

"Yes, I do."

"What'll happen next?"

"What do you mean?"

"Don't you understand?"

"How old are you?"

"My mummy is asleep, and so are my three little sisters. I'm the oldest and I'm not asleep. Oh, there's my mother, the one who's snoring. I don't like it when people snore. Neither does my daddy."

"You speak Polish very nicely. I bet you get good marks at school."

138

"Ah, let's not talk about it. Those things aren't worth talking about. Don't you agree? But if you really want to know, I don't get just good, but excellent, marks. But that doesn't count, does it?"

"That means that you must be the best pupil in your form."

"I certainly am!"

"And do you learn history?"

"We haven't taken that subject yet."

"But you must know about some historical figures?"

"They're a great nuisance."

"Why?"

"I don't care much about them."

"That's funny. . . ."

"I have other worries."

"What kind of worries? A child like you?"

"I'm not a child any more."

"And what are your real worries?"

"I can't sleep at night and keep seeing various things."

"What things?"

"I won't tell."

"Go on, tell me."

"I won't, because you may not believe me."

"I will."

"You must know that we're not from here. We've escaped from Kishiniev."

"I know, but you can't possibly remember that."

"I don't remember it myself, but I know all about it. I even know that if it weren't for Daddy, my mummy wouldn't be alive today. Daddy grabbed an axe and the Cossack got scared. Daddy told him he would kill him."

"And did he?"

"I don't know. I'll ask Daddy."

"Better not ask."

"Why?"

"Because children shouldn't ask such questions."

"So why did you ask me?"

"Lie down and try to sleep."

"I won't sleep."

"Why?"

"Because somebody around here has to keep awake."

"Why you especially?"

"You don't know my mummy. She snores. She even talks in her sleep. Father wakes up and gets angry. Once Mummy said to my little sister: Sasha, put your trousers on, it's freezing. I laughed and laughed at that. You see, I don't have any brother. And I can't sleep because I'm a very nervous child. I even went with Mummy to see a doctor."

"Lie down and try to get some sleep."

"Are you going now?"

"Yes. Time for me to go."

"That's too bad. I was hoping you would stay with me a little longer. Will you come back when you have time?"

"Yes, I will. And what am I to tell your daddy?"

"Nothing. Please tell him that I'm sound asleep."

"Lie down. I'll wait until you're in bed."

Lenka lay down and leaned her head against her mother's bovine shoulder.

Yevdocha was standing in the door of the cow-shed, her red legs wide apart.

"Have you seen the old man?" Gershon asked her.

"No."

"Where can he be?"

"I don't know."

"The chaplain is looking for him."

Yevdocha shrugged her shoulders.

Gershon looked around the yard. It was empty; only the baker's horse was shaking its now empty bag.

Gershon headed in the direction of the orchard and collided with Blanca Wilf.

"Have you seen my husband? He's been trailing after me. And now I don't know . . ."

"Is Mr Tag there?" asked Gershon.

Blanca did not answer and scurried toward the cow-shed.

"Anybody here?" she asked.

Yevdocha did not answer.

Blanca made a step forward, only to have her way barred by Yevdocha.

"Let me in," said Blanca crossly.

"I won't!"

"Please let me in," said Blanca softly.

"No."

"Why?"

"I won't!"

"I've got to get in there!"

Yevdocha kept silent.

Gershon returned from the orchard.

"There's no one out here. Only your husband . . ."

"Tell her not to be silly!" said Blanca angrily.

"Let her in, Yevdocha."

Yevdocha shook her head.

"I must hide."

"Who from?"

"Don't ask me any questions, or I'll jump into the stream."

"The stream has been dry for months. Won't you let me in either, Yevdocha? Who have you got hidden in there? Why are you in such a bad mood? Is there anybody in the shed or not?"

The cow-girl was silent, so Gershon tried to get past her in the doorway.

"I'll see for myself."

Yevdocha spread out her arms:

"I won't let you in!"

"You won't? Ah, well. Let's go. I can't fight her."

"Where shall we go?" asked Blanca.

"And whom are you hiding from?"

"Never mind."

"Has anybody frightened you?"

"Yes."

"Who? A Cossack?"

"Yes."

"Only one?"

"I didn't bother to count."

"That's too bad. Maybe what you saw was a hussar and thought it was a Cossack? Better admit it."

"It wasn't a hussar I saw. But ... Have you seen him, by any chance?"

"No, I haven't."

"Oh, my aching feet!"

"That's because you're barefoot. Feet are mighty delicate things."

"I can hardly move them."

"I could carry you. I could make believe you're a child. How about it?"

"No, thank you. I'll manage somehow, I guess."

Wilf came running up from the direction of the orchard. Blanca quickly entered the house, followed by Gershon.

"Where have you been? I was looking for you in the orchard."

"Nowhere."

"Walking barefoot on wet grass! You may catch a cold!"

"Leave me alone! I won't catch a cold!"

"Go upstairs and try to sleep."

"I don't want to sleep."

"And what do you want?"

"Nothing. Leave me alone!"

"Maybe you'd both like to join me," Gershon said, pointing at the door of his room, facing the guest hall.

Yevdocha peeked out into the yard. It was empty, except for the horse and cart.

She turned her face toward the town and crossed herself.

"Fire!" she whispered.

A Jew in an unbuttoned coat rushed from the inn.

"Is Boom here by any chance?" he asked.

"I don't know."

"Is he in there perhaps?" He pointed to the cow-shed.

"No! No!" exclaimed Yevdocha.

"What is it?" She heard Tag's whisper.

The Jew was looking round. He went up to the baker's cart.

142

He circled the house from the left, then the right. Then he disappeared.

"What is it?" whispered Tag again.

Yevdocha went into the cow-shed.

"Climb down now!"

The straw in the loft began to rustle. Tag came down the ladder.

"Who was that?" he asked.

"Hurry! Hurry!" the girl urged him.

She looked out of the shed again.

"Come out now!"

But Old Tag sat down on the threshold and closed his eyes.

The Lord be praised: no one has seen me.

A cock crowed in a farmyard; it was the loudest one of all. The last, darkest hour of the night is the one when the nocturnal creatures in the waters, in the trees, and in the crevices of the walls fall silent. The cock chases the evil spirits away with its crowing. It must crow seven times before daybreak.

"Blessed art Thou, O Lord our God, King of the universe, who hast given to the cock intelligence to distinguish between day and night."

Silence again.

There is no war. No Yevdocha. No dead girl.

O Lord, at a moment like this, when peace has filled me at last, take my soul away. Thank You. You are deserving of praise for everything.

Maybe a person like me shouldn't give thanks? Maybe I should just say, as it is written: "Cleanse me!" Also: "Wash me yet more from my iniquity, and cleanse me from my sin." And: "Purge me with hyssop, and I shall be clean: wash me, and I shall be whiter than snow." As it was written by King David. King David, to warm himself, took a young girl into his bed. How poor is the human blood which You gave us! Thank You. Modesty has been recommended to us: God lives within a modest man. Yet the Psalms are a Red Sea of flattery. The prayerbook for all the days of the year and all the feast

143

days which starts with the words: "Blessed are those who sit in Thy house and praise Thee," and ends with the word "Amen", is full of nothing but praise for You: You are the Greatest, the Mightiest, the Only One! So You, too, thrive on flattery? Thus, as You seem to be greedy for sweet words, I can oblige and say as follows: Your judgement is not like human judgements, because You don't have to abide by rules, like a rabbi, concerning what is kosher and what is not. You don't obey regulations, for You are Boundless, and the rules for mankind are measured by the ell. And if this is not so, may Your angels cover their calves' feet and their faces with their wings in shame. If my thinking is wrong, forgive me, it's not my fault that I think this way, because each one of my thoughts comes from You. Forgive me, for if You are no wiser than a man who casts stones what has mankind to lose? Perhaps You think that I'm just quibbling? You don't have to be told what the truth is. You know that my thoughts do not arise from a desire to quibble, yet who can tell me where the body ends which You have given us, and where the spirit begins which You have given us too? At what point does the joy of the spirit cease and that of the body begin? At what point does joy begin to be a sin? No one can tell me this, for no one knows. Just as no one knows at what point life comes to an end and death begins. Just as the living do not know death, so joy does not know sin. And if You consider all this as quibbling, I will tell You, to conclude: You are Immortal, You are pure Spirit, so what can You know about a mortal body? Acquire some human body, acquire some human fluids, and maybe then You will understand that to carry around inside oneself death and old age throughout one's life, means a person has nothing to lose.

Old Tag opened his eyes. Yevdocha was standing over him and tugging at his sleeve.

"Fire," she said, pointing to the east.

Tag saw a big cloud over the town.

"Is it burning?"

"Yes," she said.

Old Tag got up slowly from the doorstep.

"Some Jew is coming!" said Yevdocha and hid in the cow-shed, bolting the door from inside.

Kramer, the bookbinder, was panting for breath.

"The town is on fire," said Old Tag.

"Where's Boom? I've been looking all over for him!" said Kramer.

"Why?"

"He's gone."

"What d'you mean, he's gone?"

"I've been looking high and low for him."

"Let me look now. Has he left the girl alone?"

"She's gone too."

"When? How?"

"Nobody has seen hide nor hair of either of them."

Old Tag reeled. Kramer was wringing his hands like an old woman.

"God knows what he may have done! I wouldn't put anything past him! He's crazy!"

"You mean nobody noticed anything? Somebody must have seen him."

"Just look at that, will you!" said Kramer, pointing to the cloud over the town.

"Maybe Gershon knows something. He was sitting in the bedroom."

"As soon as I saw through the window that the town was on fire, I ran into the bedroom. The sheet was lying on the floor, and that's all!"

"Where's Gershon? I'll go and look. Maybe he's in his bedroom."

"The town's on fire, and that mad man is gone! May what I dreamed of tonight and the night before come crashing down on the heads of my enemies! I wouldn't put anything past that kid!"

"At night, especially on a night like this, all kinds of thoughts can come into one's head. Our own thoughts are our worst enemy."

"Let's hope the whole thing will turn out to be a bad dream."

"Our God is kind. He will protect us. He has saved us so many times before. . . ."

"Where can he be?" Kramer was looking around. "A lucky thing my wife is asleep. I'll go look over there," said Kramer and scudded off in the direction of the orchard.

A disaster! A real disaster!

Tag started toward the house. In the doorway he collided with Gershon, and Wohl, the baker, was following close behind him.

"The town's on fire!" shouted Gershon.

"Where are you running? Where have you been all this time? Have you seen Boom?"

Gershon did not hear him.

Apfelgrün and Pritsch appeared together in the yard.

"Where exactly is the fire?" Apfelgrün stood with his head tilted back.

Gershon ran out on the highway.

"Where are you going? Wait a minute!" Tag called after him.

Gershon was pointing to the cloud of smoke with its tongues of flame.

"Have you seen Boom? Answer me!" shouted Tag.

"I'll go have a look, then I'll be right back."

Old Tag traipsed after him onto the road.

"Have you seen Boom?"

Gershon was gesticulating that he did not hear.

A paved sidewalk ran in front of the evacuated General Hospital. Gershon's footsteps quickly faded into the distance.

Tag trudged back to the yard.

Soloveytchik was standing in front of the house.

"I recognize the sign! I've seen it before!"

Apfelgrün was pounding his temples with his clenched fists. "This is the end!"

"I knew it all along," said Soloveytchik.

Pritsch kept silent.

Wohl was unstrapping the empty bag from the horse's head.

"I'll hitch it up to the cart. I won't ask anybody's permission!"

146

"A disaster! All his life my father saved every penny. All my life I have been saving." Apfelgrün had tears in his eyes.

"It's no use now," said Soloveytchik. "I knew it all along."

"And then the devil comes and ..." Apfelgrün blew on his palm as into a handful of ashes.

"I'll hitch up the cart." The baker was straightening the shafts.

"I'll never live to see the end of this!" groaned Apfelgrün. "People! Let's do something! Let's get moving! Come on! Let's not just stand here and do nothing!"

"I'm not going to budge," said Soloveytchik.

"Where is the fire? On what street?" asked Apfelgrün.

"The market square," said Pritsch.

"What makes you think so?" asked Apfelgrün angrily.

"My wineshop, my flat ..." sighed Soloveytchik.

"What are we waiting for?" Apfelgrün looked at Pritsch.

"I told you before: I am not going back," said Soloveytchik.

"Come on." Apfelgrün pulled at Pritsch's arm.

Pritsch pushed him away.

The baker was leading the horse by the bridle.

"Who wants to get in?"

Apfelgrün climbed onto the cart.

"Come on, there's still time! There is still time!" he summoned Pritsch.

The cart was on the road now.

Kramer emerged from behind the cow-shed.

"Wait for me! I'm coming with you!"

Wohl braked and helped Kramer onto the cart. He cracked the whip and the horse started.

Pritsch went running after the cart.

"Hey! Wait! I'm coming, too!" Pritsch's voice became high-pitched. "If it's come to that," he called.

Wohl halted again. He helped Pritsch up and sat him on the box. A cloud of dust rose from the road as the cart went off, and dulled the rattle of the wheels.

A moment later, all was quiet again.

The yard was empty, except for Soloveytchik and Old Tag, who were gazing up at the sky.

Luckily, there was no wind, the trees did not even rustle. The smoke was rising higher and higher like the Tower of Babel.

"Nobody asked for my advice. I would have told them not to go," said Soloveytchik.

"How can you know what's best?"

"Why can't you?"

"I, for one, don't know."

"That's bad. People should know. Otherwise they're like little kids. And then you get your head clobbered."

"You're exaggerating. You haven't seen little Boom anywhere, have you?"

"No."

"I must go. I must try to find him."

Two young boys came into view on the road, walking toward town from the direction of Duliby. Ossip, the son of a Ruthenian priest, was talking loudly. He was wearing high boots and a military belt with an Austrian bayonet. A peasant's cart caught up with them, and both boys climbed on. Ossip lifted his fist and shook it at the inn.

"They're on their way to do some looting," said Soloveytchik.

"Oh, I don't think so," said Tag. "That priest's son is only a little older than Lolka. He used to come here once in a while to play with her."

"Why should he be heading for town tonight in a cart?"

"Maybe somebody's sick and they're going to get some medicine."

"They're going to town because the fire is a signal." Soloveytchik looked up again.

The reddish cloud was now spreading out in all directions, like spilled paint, and spitting fire. The smoke subsided and flattened out, enveloping the sky. Black flakes of soot fell like small birds, then a column of fire shot up high, showering sparks. The flames were climbing higher than the mass of smoke.

"It's tough to get out of such a furnace. I can smell burning. It must be the eiderdowns. I remember that smell from Kishiniev...."

"I can't smell anything."

"You've got to get as far away as possible from a furnace like that."

"Where?"

"As far away as possible. As from a herd of wild animals."

"But they're human beings like us."

"That's just our trouble! Treating our enemies as human beings! That's what's so terrible!"

"You're exaggerating!"

"Whoever comes at you with a knife can't be human."

"Don't talk like that!"

"This is the only way you can defend yourself."

"How?"

"To kill a Jew for them means as much as killing a fly."

"I don't believe it. Look at me, I've been around for quite a while."

"At Kishiniev, they killed little children. I ask you: Why? I'm a strong man, I'm as healthy—touch wood—as a drayman. I can handle one man, even two. But not a hundred. I could kill one, but not a hundred."

"A Jew doesn't kill."

"What if he has to? If he has to defend himself?"

"Everybody who wants to kill might say: I am defending myself."

"But it is they who came at me—I didn't attack anybody."

"Killing's wrong, no doubt about it. Everything else is doubtful."

"What do you mean: doubtful? Jew! D'you know what you're talking about? They murder us, burn our shops, rape our women! And along comes a Jew who says it's doubtful!"

"That's not what I was talking about. We can't communicate with each other."

"I know . . . I know . . . I'm not so dumb. I know what you're thinking. Pet a leopard, and he'll purr like a kitten. A Jew can't afford to think like that. That's not the Jewish way of thinking."

"I shall go and see . . ."

Old Tag took a few steps forward, then stopped.

"What did you say? I don't understand. This is not Jewish thinking. What did you mean?"

"The world has been divided ever since Creation into Jews and goyim."

"Maybe so . . . But nowadays that's neither here nor there."

Bells began to ring in the town. In the Catholic church and, much nearer, in the Orthodox one. Each of them had a different tone: the one in the Catholic church was muted, the one in the Orthodox church was clear.

Soloveytchik and Old Tag were straining their ears.

"I don't like that ringing." Tag covered his ears with his hands.

The dogs woke up in the hamlet.

"A funeral, a fire, or an epidemic," said Old Tag.

The dogs were barking now. The first to start barking was the mastiff, then all the smaller ones joined in.

"Take a roundabout way," said Old Tag as if to himself, "so as not to pass by the church. That's what my father taught me, blessed be his memory."

"Why do you bring it up now?"

Old Tag did not answer. Soloveytchik was walking beside him toward the house.

"People say that your sister left her husband and children and got herself baptized. Is that true?"

Old Tag did not reply.

"I don't believe it." Soloveytchik touched Tag's shoulder.

"Yes, it's true."

From the dark hall Mrs Kramer and her daughter emerged. Mrs Kramer was holding her arms out in front of her like a blind person.

"Where's my husband?" she asked, shaking.

"Mummy! Mummy!" Rose was sobbing.

"Where is my husband?"

"He's gone to town," said Old Tag.

Mrs Kramer covered her face with her hands.

"Where is my husband?" she repeated, swaying her head.

"Mummy! Mummy!"

"Where is Boom? Where is my son? Where is my child?"

She suddenly ran out into the road.

"Mummy! Mummy!" her daughter kept calling.

Mrs Kramer was running toward the town.

Minna appeared in the first-floor window.

"Is there a fire? Where?"

Lolka was standing behind her.

"Grandfather! Where is the fire?"

"What are we to do?" asked Minna.

"Go back to bed," said Tag.

From the hall little Lenka came running.

"Daddy!" she called.

"What is it?" asked Soloveytchik, alarmed.

"Is there a fire? I saw you through the window, and that's why I came out. I saw the beginning of the fire."

"What's Mama doing?"

"She's asleep. There's such a smell in the kitchen that I had to stand by the window."

"Instead of going to sleep."

"You know I'm nervous and can't get to sleep."

Shots could now be heard from the town. The Orthodox church bell, the nearer one, stopped ringing. The other one continued to boom. Then a distant peel of bells was heard.

From out of the dark hall stepped Mrs Soloveytchik, wearing only a shift, with the infant in her arms; her neck and large white arms shone in the twilight.

"Put something on," said Soloveytchik angrily.

Mrs Soloveytchik yawned.

"Did you leave Ruchla and Mena behind?"

Mrs Soloveytchik passed her hand over her face.

"They're all right. They're asleep."

"Why have you left the children alone?"

"Nothing will happen to them."

"There's a fire!"

"Is there? Oh well, they'll put it out."

In the hall Tag bumped into Blanca and Wilf coming out of Gershon's room.

"Is there a fire?" asked Blanca.

"Yes," answered Tag.

"Let there be a fire, I don't mind. Let everything burn down for all I care."

"Blanca!"

"Let everything burn down!"

"Blanca!"

Old Tag sat down on a step for a moment, then, clutching the creaking banisters, he got to his feet and went upstairs.

"Grandpa!" Lolka cried happily.

"What'll we do now?" asked his daughter-in-law.

"There's a fire, but far away, in the town. There's no reason to be afraid. It'll be daylight pretty soon. Go back to bed for a while. Later on there'll be the dough to make. We'll have to get everything ready for the Sabbath. And when it gets lighter I'll go into town."

"What for?" Minna was alarmed.

"We must act as if nothing had happened. The Sabbath is still the Sabbath, regardless. I'll buy meat, fish, and wine."

"We won't be able to feed everybody."

"Where will you shop?" asked Lolka. "Who will open his shop today?"

"Exactly! Lolka's right. There's a fire in town."

"Do you know that Boom's gone? So is Asya."

"Gone?" said Minna, astounded. "Maybe it's better that way."

"Beats me how a thing like that could happen."

"What difference does it make?"

"No one has seen them."

"Everybody has been asleep, that's why."

"And weren't you asleep, Grandpa?"

"I must go downstairs, to the bedroom. I've got to see for myself."

In the guest hall, the Hasidim were asleep, sitting at the table with their heads on one another's shoulders. The tsaddik sat with his face hidden in his beard. The redhead slept with wide-open eyes.

The cantor was not asleep.

"They must be waked up," he said to Old Tag.

152

"What for? The quieter it is, the better."

"But there's a fire."

"What can they do about it?"

"There's a prayer for everything, for a thunderstorm, a rainbow, for hail and so on, but there's none for a fire. 'The creator of the lights of fire.' Just this one."

"Oh, don't bother me with that stuff!"

Tag went into the bedroom. The window was open; the sheet was lying on the floor; the candles in the brass candlesticks had gone out. He walked up to the window; straw crunched under his feet. He understood.

He stooped and picked up a few bits of straw, then folded the sheet and placed it next to the candlesticks. He covered up the straw that was left in the room, then opened the wardrobe and looked into it. In a separate compartment lay a velvet bag with a Star of David embroidered on it, the Sabbath adornment. He took it out, looked at it, and put it back again. Then he sat down on the unmade bed.

For adultery in the desert, through which the Jews wandered for forty years, God killed twenty-four thousand people. I have lived to see the end of the world. What greater joy can there be for an old man! Samson said: Let me die with the Philistines. May the Philistines perish when I give up my soul! They will all perish! No one will be left. Nothing will survive me, not even my house, my orchard, or the girl. It was I who set fire to the town. It was I who sinned before You, O Lord. The sin of the astonished heart. The sin of the forsworn mouth. The sin of adultery. The sin of swift feet on their way to evil.

Boom has carried Asya to the cemetery. Gershon must have helped him to get her out. Under the window Jews from the Death Brotherhood are walking, coins clinking in their tins. "Alms save from death! Alms save from death!" I am lying naked on the floor, my feet turned toward the door, on the straw that has been left by Asya. The Jews are washing me, wrapping me in a linen shroud, they put on my eyelids the earthenware shards of a broken pot. And then throw me out through the window. Yevdocha throws my body over the wattle fence. My wife throws it into the stream. The body has

153

been desecrated and I will never enter the grave of peace. The glass hearse is driven empty to the cemetery. In the coffin lies a scroll of the Torah. I begin to run and my feet sink in the soft ground.

Old Tag wiped his forehead and got up from the bed. I have seen my own burial, refused by the earth.

He fell on his knees, pounded his head against the side of the bed, like Boom. Then he rose to his feet.

"Praised be the Lord who supports those who falter."

In the guest hall the tsaddik and his Hasidim were asleep. The redhead and the cantor were not among them. In the yard large flakes of soot swirled about.

The cantor was staring at the sky and chanting: "Smoke was spurting from his nostrils and setting fire to the coals."

The redhead was running around the yard.

"What's going on? What is it?" he called. "Is it the end of the world? A fire? Where? Out of nowhere: a fire! Today everything's done on purpose! Out of spite! Suddenly there's a fire! Tell me at least where, so that I know!"

"There's a prayer for everything, but not for a fire," the cantor complained. "Should we wake up the tsaddik perhaps?"

"No!" The redhead clasped his head with his hands. "No!"

"Why not?"

"He has no peace even at night. To do business with the angels is not an easy job."

"He should be told that there's a fire. Make him say a holy sentence, if there's no prayer for stopping a fire."

"The tsaddik knows there's a fire. You may be quite sure of that. Right now he's haggling with the angels. The angels demand so and so much, and the tsaddik gives them so much. But I'm not worried. They'll come to terms in the end. And the pious will be saved and the impious will be left to save themselves as best they can."

"So and so much? Of what?" asked the cantor.

"Fleas!" said the redhead crossly.

"I only asked," said the cantor apologetically.

154

"A disaster," whispered the redhead.

The tsaddik's wife came out of the hall, followed by the wet nurse with the infant. Her silver and black kerchief shone in the moonlight. The nurse sat against the wall of the house and uncovered her breast. The infant turned away its head; its mother leaned over it and clacked her tongue. The wet nurse pushed her away with her elbow:

"Leave the baby alone, Mrs Tsaddik," she said in Ruthenian.

The redhead went up to the women, wringing his hands.

"What's wrong? What's wrong? Why isn't the jewel asleep? Why isn't our Mrs Tsaddik asleep?"

"Is there a fire?" The tsaddik's wife raised her eyebrows and lowered her lids.

"A little one."

"Where is it?"

"In town."

"How far is it from here?"

"Very far."

The tsaddik's wife blinked.

"Tell such stories to somebody else."

"But all the same, it's not very close, thank goodness."

"Go and wake up the tsaddik."

"Why should I wake him up? He'll wake up by himself. Why disturb him? Don't start anything now. As long as things are quiet, let them be quiet."

"Go and wake up the tsaddik!"

"The tsaddik is tired, let him sleep awhile."

"We shouldn't have tried to escape. That was your idea!"

"And the fire—was that my idea too? Was I the one who started the fire?"

"Wake up the tsaddik and let's go back!"

"How? On a broomstick?"

"On a cart."

"Which cart? The only cart is gone. The baker took it."

"There must be a cart, for me, for the child, and for the wet nurse."

"Where will I get a cart from?"

"From under the earth."

"Oh! Just look, Mrs Tsaddik: the jewel is sucking! May it be for health!"

The tsaddik's wife swung round instantly. She stooped and with her finger lightly tickled the baby's chin.

"Leave him alone, Mrs Tsaddik!"

"God bless you! God bless you!" exclaimed the redhead.

"Amen!" sighed the tsaddik's wife.

The redhead slipped away.

Worst of all is a woman who wants to manage a kingdom herself. What does a male person see in a woman? Stupidity, from start to finish. If the Lord had only consulted me. But He doesn't ask anybody's advice. He knows the score best of all. "It is not good for man to be alone." And am I any better off the way things are now? If I had been alone I would have to worry only about myself, but now I have to worry, touch wood, about six people. For Himself, God did not create a wife from a rib. But, joking apart, a fire's a fire. Thank goodness, the bells are ringing, that means they're alerting the fire brigade. For the moment firebrands leap from the clouds as they did on Mount Sinai. The sky is the colour of copper as in God's curse. The copper is reflected in the windows, only the hall is black as the grave.

The redhead clutched his breast and coughed. Smoke was drifting over from the town. He wiped his perspiring face with his red handkerchief. And when he opened his eyes, he sighed again, but this time more than once and loudly.

Women were rushing out of the hall.

The first one he saw was the childless one with the long nose —the wife of the Hasid with the golden locks. May God guard us and preserve us from a nose like this! How wise are our customs which forbid the Hasidim to look at women. How must the handsome one have felt when he removed the kerchief from the face of the woman he betrothed according to the laws of Moses and Israel? Huh! It's none of my business! It's his affair!

And now his own wife! With all six of them, touch wood, as God has decreed: six days of creation. On the seventh day even God Himself took a rest.

His wife spotted him at once. She rushed at him with all her flock.

"Why are you running?" He spoke first. "What's the hurry?"

"What? Can't you see there's a fire?"

"What's on fire? Where is the fire? Jewess, stop and think: the fire's in town and we're out here!"

"Is that so? Then why don't you look at yourself. You look like a carrot. You'd think you yourself were about to catch fire, God forbid."

"And even if there *was* a little fire, God knows where, why do you and the kids have to make such a fuss?"

"It's all over now! There'll be nothing left of us any more."

The redhead tapped his forehead with a finger.

"You must be crazy! Take the children back into the house. They'll catch cold."

"The world's caving in! And you! Have you thought about me? About the children? My breadwinner! The tsaddik's arse!"

"Have I thought? I don't have to think! I know. The night is dark. The whole neighbourhood's asleep, and all you can do is yell! See what the other mothers are doing. Go on now and let my little pets relieve themselves."

The yard suddenly became crowded: the mothers were bringing out the children. The little ones were squatting with their shirts pulled up to the navel. The place was filled with noise. The fat fair-haired boy had broken away from his tall, dark mother and, laughing, was chasing the white cat. The small twin girls, their braids undone, were pulling at their mother's skirt and calling out that they were thirsty. The thin woman in a bright-coloured dress was soothing her child, which was breathless with screaming, by first tossing it into the air and then breathing into its mouth. The long-nosed childless woman took the child, gave it a pat on its backside, and the infant regained its breath. In the very centre of the yard the tall woman in the velvet dress and a lace shawl was rocking her baby in her arms, humming softly to it. The short childless woman scurried from one small group to another.

The redhead's wife, her wig askew, took her six children

and began to wander round the yard, unable to find a suitable place for them.

The redhead was also bustling about the yard.

"Lost little lambs! Finish up now! Go back to the kitchen," he called to them. "The night is still dark. I'll tell you when to get up, when to get ready, I'll tell you everything."

No one was listening to him. Only his own children began to run behind him, calling:

"Daddy, Daddy! What d'you think you're doing?"

"Has your mother put you up to this?" The redhead tried to wipe the youngest child's nose. "Blow! Blow hard!"

His wife came up to him, her wig askew.

"So you think I put them up to something? Nowadays the kids are smart enough on their own; they don't have to be told anything. With a father like you!"

"What is it now? A father like me? What should I have done?"

"Let's go back home."

"Daddy, Daddy! What d'you think you're doing?" called the children.

"Go back now? In the middle of the night?" argued the redhead.

They were now surrounded by a group of women.

"Yes, yes!" The short woman was crying. "We must go back."

"The poor woman is right, you know," the mother of the fair-haired boy chimed in.

The mother of twin girls came forward.

"Dear Jew! If you don't bring my husband here this instant, the father of my two little chicks, I'll drown myself and the children in the river. They're hungry and cranky, and now, on top of everything else, there's a fire."

"And my husband!" The hunchbacked woman was embracing her children, two girls on the right, two boys on the left. "Not a bite to eat since yesterday. His face is white as a sheet, not a drop of blood in it. I peeped in last night. He spent the whole night sitting at the table, a sick man like him. He must drink camomile first thing in the morning! He won't be able to stand this, God forbid. Did we need to escape? I didn't take anything with me, except the camomile."

"And a certain little bag between your breasts." The long-nosed woman reached out, her long fingers pulling at the frills and bows. "What have you got there? Silver crowns?"

"It's all I have," the hunchbacked woman said in self-defence. "The peasants won't take paper money any more. They say it's worthless."

"Have you seen what the tsaddik's wife has?" The long-nosed woman was rubbing the corners of her mouth with two fingers. "She's carrying a small fortune in her handkerchief."

"You bet she is!" The redhead's wife smacked her smallest child, which had begun to cry. No sooner did one begin to cry than all the others joined in. "Look at my husband! Have you ever seen such a fool! Anybody else in his place would have made a bundle on the chits alone. But have a look, my dear sisters, at me and my children, this is all our fortune, my husband's and mine."

"Do you mean to say that he's losing money in the deal?" asked the long-nosed woman.

"Oh, women, women!" The redhead shook his head, stepping back toward the door of the inn.

"Listen to me, Jewesses!" The long-nosed woman was adjusting her wig, made of real Persian lamb, and disclosing a part of her shaved head. "We must do something. The best thing would be to wake the tsaddik up and to go back home."

"Let's wake him up! Let him show us what he's worth!" The mother of the twin girls clapped her hands. "Let him perform a miracle! It doesn't have to be a big miracle, a small one will do. Now, before dawn, a person is lightest in weight and it should be easiest to perform a miracle. My brother's wife used to pour wax and tell fortunes for peasant women. She told me that before dawn the wind can lift up a person, and that's why people should stick something heavy in their pockets, a piece of iron, for instance."

"Come off it!" The long-nosed woman waved her hand with contempt. "A miracle, my foot! It's already a miracle that he got himself an heir!"

"Maybe we could ask for milk for the children?" the fat boy's mother asked softly.

"Maybe we could buy something from the peasants?" added the slim woman in the bright-coloured dress. She was still holding her baby in her arms and still breathing in its mouth each time it woke up.

"Shh!" The long-nosed woman cast a sidelong glance. "The tsaddik's wife is coming."

The woman in the silver and black kerchief, which was tucked behind her ears, was approaching slowly, followed by the wet nurse with the baby.

"What were you saying and why are you suddenly so quiet?" The tsaddik's wife looked straight into the long-nosed woman's eyes.

"We weren't talking about anything in particular. Just chatting." The redhead's wife was adjusting her wig. "It's not even daybreak yet, and all six of my children—may God keep them in good health—are already awake. And as soon as they open their eyes they open their mouths. How'll I feed them? Do I own a business? Has my husband got a rich father-in-law?" The redhead's wife glanced first at the hunchback and then at the long-nosed woman. "The children, thank goodness, have a father, long may he live, but he's looking after somebody else's business, not his own. Meanwhile the children go hungry."

"Somebody else's business?" The tsaddik's wife lifted her eyes to Heaven.

"Ah, my lovely one," said the long-nosed woman, stroking the tsaddik's wife's arm, "I don't much like this fire."

"Do you think I do?" answered the tsaddik's wife.

"But there is a difference! When one has a husband like yours! If only he would wake up, not a hair would fall from his wife's or his baby's head."

"If that's so, then everybody's safe." The tsaddik's wife looked at all the women in turn.

"We must wake up all our husbands!" said the short woman with the large head.

"And I say we must wake up the tsaddik first!" The redhead's wife was trying to undo the back of her high whale-boned collar. She was moving her head from side to side. "I told my husband so already."

"Maybe he'll perform a miracle? What do you think?" The long-nosed woman turned to the tsaddik's wife, her lips pressed tightly together.

"Before you wake up the men, we must find some food for them. They're worse than children. At least you can yell at children," said the short woman.

"What do you know about children?" The hunchback waved her hand.

"Look at her!" The other woman pointed a finger at the hunchback. "Look who's talking!" She slapped herself on the mouth a couple of times. "I must not sin with words. And when you come right down to it, my husband has been with me for only five years. We still have time: five years only. And meanwhile God might take pity on us. I've seen married couples, may God prevent it and save us from it, who haven't had any kids for ten years yet didn't get divorced."

"Don't be angry with me," apologized the hunchbacked woman. "I'll tell you what to do. You must keep your husband well fed. What do you give him to eat? A lot of eggs! A lot of eggs! With chicken broth, and with noodles!"

"That doesn't help." The long-nosed woman stroked her chin like a man. "I had a tip from a tsaddik, Rabbi Mechel of Zloczov. He told me to wait for my period, put a piece of black wool you know where, get a small fish out of the belly of a larger one that had swallowed it, chop it with the liver of a hare—you can buy it from a goy, it doesn't matter if it's not kosher, when it comes to a person's health anything's permitted—fry it all in a frying pan until it's almost black, then pound it in a mortar with some bread crumbs, pour the mixture into a glass of water and drink it. . . ."

"Well, and did it do the trick?" asked the tsaddik's wife.

"No, but the remedy is a good one."

"I know a better one," the mother of twins blurted out. "A childless woman, God forbid, should not get down in the mouth. That's all. She must always be cheerful and laugh a lot. Doctors advise you to laugh. And as soon as a husband notices that his wife is in a good mood, then everything'll go the way it should. I heard this from my mother-in-law, blessed be her soul in paradise. 'Rejoice, childless woman who hath not given birth!' so it is written in the Holy Books, my mother-in-law told me, blessed be her memory."

"Women! We're talking about trifles. Let's stop now!" The long-nosed woman looked at the tsaddik's wife. "My lovely one! You shine like the moon, you stand here among us like a Jewish queen after her bath on Sabbath night waiting for her husband to come to her. . . . Be so kind as to go to see him now. You go to him and wake him up."

"What are you talking about?" The tsaddik's wife was smiling. "How do you know what a husband does on Sabbath night?"

"Listen to what I'm saying," the long-nosed woman chanted as if reciting a page of the Talmud: "A husband who walks alone knows his business, but a husband who has to be led around doesn't. . . ."

"Well? Well? Go on!" the tsaddik's wife said, looking toward the wet nurse. "You are always trying to pick a fight with me. What are you insinuating now?"

"Nothing! Nothing. I can see that the baby is undernourished and isn't strong enough to suck," the long-nosed woman said, trying to stroke the baby.

The wet nurse turned her back to her and pushed her away with her elbow.

"The wet nurse must be changed. Her milk is probably bad," the long-nosed woman said, folding her hands on her flat breasts.

"A mother's milk is the bone marrow for a person's whole life," sighed the short woman with a large head. "When God gives me a child, I'll feed it myself."

"Whatever for? If you can afford not to . . ." said the redhead's wife. "I'd have hired a wet nurse too if I could. To nurse six children, imagine! In the end they suck your blood instead of milk!"

"You should have tried compresses of soured milk," said the mother of twin girls.

"That one knows everything." The long-nosed woman wagged a finger at her. "She has a cure for everything!"

"Look! Look at this!" exclaimed the short woman and turned up her face, which now seemed bright as a copper coin.

From the clouds a shower of sparks shot up. All the women lifted their faces to the sky.

"Such a disaster," sighed the mother of the fat boy.

"The sky is on fire," whispered the thin woman in the bright-coloured dress.

"And the fire is spreading toward us," added the mother of twins.

"Fire and water are the worst of all." The thin woman was rocking her infant, pressing it against her breast so that it would not wake up again.

"And I tell you there's nothing to fear," the long-nosed woman said, looking at the tsaddik's wife.

"May words from your lips reach the ears of the Almighty," said the mother of the fat boy, smiling.

The tsaddik's wife turned to the nurse.

"Go over there," she said, pointing to the orchard illumined by the fiery glow, "the air will be better there. It'll give my child an appetite."

"My little pigeon-doves could stand some fresh air too," said the hunchbacked woman, gently pushing first her two boys, then the two girls, toward the orchard. "Off you go, off you go, but don't touch any unripe apples."

"You go over there too, my little sweet peas," the mother of twin girls said, stroking their heads. "Come on, my precious little jewels!"

"She understands everything, every word we say." The tsaddik's wife winked toward the nurse. "She mustn't find out what we say among ourselves. The worst thing is when a goy understands Yiddish."

"You can say that again," grimaced the long-nosed woman, "but when you need a hanged man, you must cut him down

163

from the rope first. Right?" She turned toward the red-head's wife. "Why don't you take your kids over to the orchard?"

"What for? They don't need good air to have an appetite. What they need is something to have an appetite for," answered the redhead's wife.

"Yes, that's true," agreed the mother of twin girls. "Now it's time to think about getting some food for our husbands, and for the kids too."

"When there's no flour, there's no time for the Torah," the tsaddik's wife quoted.

"Mind telling us how?" asked the redhead's wife. "It's easy to talk, but what are we to buy it with?"

"We'll manage somehow," said the hunchbacked woman.

"We'd better hurry before it's too late," said the mother of twins. "Come on! The peasants must be up by now, any minute they'll be driving the cows into the fields, and they won't be back till dark."

"I'm with her," said the hunchbacked woman, nodding. "We're just wasting time."

"Let's get going," urged the redhead's wife.

"Don't all go together," warned the tsaddik's wife. "Let one group go to one village, and another group to another. Otherwise there might not be enough for everybody."

"There'll be enough!"

The tall woman in the velvet dress had been standing to one side all the time. She now wrapped her lace shawl around her shoulders, turned to the tsaddik's wife, and repeated:

"There'll be enough."

Her baby woke up and cried softly. She rocked it in her arms a few times, then leaned over it and pressed her cheek to its head.

The long-nosed woman tried to stroke the baby.

"Don't cry, little lamb," she said.

The tall woman wandered off to the side and began to sing softly:

Sleep, little boy, sleep:
A-a-a-a-a-a-a-a-a-a-a.
Listen, I'll sing you a song:
A-a-a-a-a-a-a-a-a-a-a.
When you grow up, you'll be a Jew:
A-a-a-a-a-a-a-a-a-a-a.
Almonds and raisins, you'll have a stall:
A-a-a-a-a-a-a-a-a-a-a.
Honey and milk, you'll have a shop.
When you grow up, you'll be a rich man:
A-a-a-a-a-a-a-a-a-a-a.
You won't be ashamed of your daddy or mummy.

"As long as you turn out healthy," she added in a speaking voice.

"Exactly, exactly," the mother of twin girls added. "Health is the most important thing."

"Take my husband, for instance," the hunchbacked woman said. "His stomach's as sensitive as a baby's. He must drink camomile tea the first thing in the morning."

"Why camomile?" asked the twin's mother.

"What else?"

"Are we or aren't we going?" asked the redhead's wife.

"Go, go!" said the hunchback. "I'll join you later."

"Later? What do you mean by later?" The redhead's wife shrugged her shoulders. "Later! Later!" she began to call at the top of her voice.

The tsaddik's wife lifted her head.

"Shh!" she tried to quiet her.

The women were straining their eyes and turning their faces toward the highway.

"Can you hear anything?" asked the tsaddik's wife.

"Shh!" hissed the hunchbacked woman. "Someone's running and shouting."

"A girl," whispered another, "a young girl."

The voice was coming from the direction of the General Hospital.

"Help! Help!"

Silence filled the yard. The women stood speechless.

"Help! I'm on fire!" The voice was growing more and more distinct.

"Let's go inside." The long-nosed woman began shepherding the others toward the house. She took the tall woman in the velvet dress by the arm. "Let's not stand here in the middle of the yard. Somebody must be chasing her. Up against the wall! Up against the wall."

"Help me! I'm on fire! Hel-p, I'm-on-fi-re!"

And again softly:

"Help!"

Old Tag went out into the road.

"Pessa! Pessa!"

It was Gershon's voice.

"Is that you, Gershon?"

Two columns of dust were rolling along the road, illuminated like two spectres by the red glow of the fire and the light of the moon.

The moon had moved to the far side of the sky and was on the wane, but its light was still strong. The smoke over the city was settling down now, revealing a large patch of blue sky. Dawn was breaking in the east; a distinct line now separated the sky from the earth.

It was the hour when wolves look like dogs and blue looks white. It was that most sinister hour when strength ebbs from the body and death is at the doorstep, when the young wake up with a start and the old do not live to see the sunrise. God hung on Abraham's neck a hunk of sunlight like a diamond with healing properties. Dying man, hold out until sunrise and you shall live!

I come from a line of thin and tall Jews. "Thou hast clothed me with skin and flesh. Thou hast put me together with bones and sinews." But tough is that skin and hard are those bones! I could live for a long time, if the length of a man's life were measured by passion. I did not take a girl to rejuvenate myself, like King David. I had rolled naked in the
166

snow, I bathed in air holes in the stream as I had been taught by my father, who learned it from his father, who had learned it from his father, to the greater glory of God. Through the delight of the body one can achieve the delight of the soul. This was what Holy BEShT said. God Himself wishes man to rejoice. Joy, like Jacob's ladder, leads from pettiness to greatness. Man presses an image on coins and each coin is like another, while God has impressed man with His image and one man is unlike another. Which means that every human being must say to himself: The world has been created for me alone.

In the village the cocks have already crowed for the seventh time. Thanks be to Thee, O Lord! The dogs barked; the gate creaked. Blessed art Thou, O Lord, King of the Universe. With Thy word Thou changest times, dividest the seasons, placeth the stars on guard in heaven by Thy will, createth day and night, rollest the light before darkness and darkness before light. . . . I shall bear fruit in my old age, shall be full of juices and freshness . . . the world stands erect and will not falter. . . . Blessed be the new day! Another day has been given me!

Tag raised his eyes. Standing in front of him was Gershon.

"Gershon!" Tag exclaimed. Gershon rested his head on Tag's shoulder.

"Come, sit down and rest awhile."

Gershon shook his head.

"I heard your voice," said Old Tag.

"Yes. I was calling Simon's sister."

"Come, sit down and rest awhile."

Tag opened the gate.

"Let's go inside. I'll get you a drink of water."

Gershon kept shaking his head.

"What's wrong with you?"

"Nothing. I don't want anything. Simon has killed a Cossack."

"Oh, my God!"

"The Cossack attacked his sister."

"Come. Don't breathe a word to anyone."

"The whole town knows about it. All the Jews have been herded into the market square. Simon is to be hanged."

"Have you seen him?"

Gershon replied negatively.

"I could hardly get through. All of Crook Street was blazing away, from one end to the other, like straw. The fire is all because of Simon."

"Have you seen Boom?"

"I could hardly reach Crook Street. I saw a Cossack, galloping on a horse. It was the same Cossack . . ."

"I asked you: have you seen Boom?"

"The wooden houses were on fire; so were the wooden stalls: burning as if they were made of paper. The Ruthenians were drunk: they were smashing the windows and the street lamps."

"It's the end of everything."

"They were looting the shops, loading stuff onto barrows, carrying sacks away on their backs."

"You saw all this? Yourself? With your own eyes?"

"I saw everything! I saw it! I saw Ossip, the son of the Ruthenian priest from Duliby. He knows Simon, and was helping the Cossacks to look for him. In high boots, where he got them I don't know; with an Austrian bayonet on an Austrian army belt. He was leading the Cossack's horse by its bridle. It was the same Cossack with a forelock, the one who galloped round the market square in the morning."

"Let's go inside, Gershon."

Gershon nodded assent.

"You look very tired."

Old Tag opened the gate and then closed it behind them. They crossed the small garden. The mignonette lay trampled in the flower bed. They stepped into the hall.

"Troops were marching along the main road from Duliby, they kept marching and marching the whole time I was walking to Crook Street, and on my way back they were still at it: cavalry, infantry, soldiers riding on guns, on wagons, on boats turned upside down. What does an army need boats for? Such strength, Mr Tag! Such strength! We've lost this war, Mr Tag, we've lost it."

"Have they found Simon?"

"I don't know."

"Have you seen old Kramer, by any chance? He drove to town to look for Boom. His wife went too, on foot. No one knows what's happened to the girl's body."

"It was the same Cossack with the forelock. The same one who was scared yesterday by the window shades with black and white stripes."

Gershon leaned against the wobbly banister of the staircase, then sat down. The same Cossack with the forelock. Time and again he had charged with his horse into the crowd and cracked his whip. People had covered their heads with their hands. Shoemakers intermingled with furriers, tailors with plumbers, carpenters with merchants. Bearded men became intermingled with clean-shaven men, women in wigs with women who wore their own hair. And what about that woman with the pince-nez? How did the first woman Esperantist in the town, the Baroness's companion, Miss Amalia Diesenhoff, get in there? He must try to speak to her. He had been introduced to her at the union. The crowd suddenly pushed him back, it retreated, then surged forward again toward the gallows. Amalia Diesenhoff disappeared, not to be seen either on the right or on the left. In the centre stood the gallows: for Simon. When did they have the time to build it? What kind of state is it which, together with an army, with guns, trains, and supplies, sends in ready-made gallows? The gallows waited, the people waited, but Simon was nowhere to be seen. The crowd stood there transfixed, staring intently at the gallows in silence. From its crossbar a thick rope dangled. Had the inhabitants of our town all died yesterday, they would not have known what a gallows looks like. The older ones had never seen one. A person can learn something new every day, provided he lives long enough. Silence. One man in danger thinks hard how to save himself, two people in danger consult one another, a crowd in danger does not think and cannot consult each other. Ossip, the son of the priest from Duliby, also wears his hair with a forelock. There must be a reason why our religion makes us cut our hair short over the forehead. Has anybody ever seen a Jew with a forelock? Apart from Simon? He is the only one. Where is he now? When Gershon was on his way back, he met Pessa. She ran out of the gateway in Bolechowska Street, the one which leads out to the main road, and grabbed him by the hand. "Pessa, where's Simon?" Pessa was tearing at his coat: "I love you! I love you! I love you!" "Pessa, has Simon got away?" Pessa began to run, then stopped, but just as Gershon was about to catch up with her she broke loose again.

The Cossack circled the market square rounding up the scattering people like a flock of sheep. Someone was being led forward under a pair of drawn bayonets. The crowd parted. The town rabbi had put on his Sabbath attire, a long silk caftan and a high sable hat. Alongside him walked several rich Jews, owners of the largest shops in the square: Walder the watchmaker, Rechter the grocer, Seeman the wholesale flour merchant, Lenz the stationer. The soldiers made an about turn, and an officer in a tight-fitting uniform with golden epaulets, short, with a long sabre, asked the rabbi who had killed the Cossack. Did he know where the man was hiding? Where could Simon be hiding? In the union building? With Erna, the younger sister of Mrs Henrietta Maltz? He would have been safe there, had not the Maltzes gone away. Do you want us to burn down the town because of one man? the officer asked. Wouldn't it be fairer if one man were justly punished and the town left in peace until the end of the war?

The rich Jews sighed, the crowd was silent, and the rabbi nodded his head for a long while, because he could not find his voice. Then he said that Jews were not allowed to kill. A Jew cannot kill, just as a bird cannot swim and a fish cannot fly. When would a Jew have time to kill, even if there had ever been a Jew with a single drop of murderer's blood in his veins? The rabbi knew everybody in town. From their birth to their death. No sooner is a Jewish boy born than he must be circumcised on the eighth day of his life. No sooner has he reached his thirteenth year than he must take upon himself a heavy burden. From then on he is on his own in the eyes of the Almighty and must pay for his sins, in this world or the next. Hardly has he reached his eighteenth year when he must lead a bride under the canopy and take upon himself another heavy burden. From morning to night he has to rush round the world trying to earn his keep and that of his family. And so he keeps on racing round for the rest of his life, from dawn to dusk, and he never rests until the day when his eyes are covered with earthenware shards and he is carried off to the burial ground. If you give a man like that a knife and tell him to kill, he won't know how to do it. And now you come to me and say: A Jew has killed. I've been living here, in this town, for seventy years, and I've never heard of anything like it. Even if a Cossack had actually tried to abuse a girl, a Jew would not lift a hand against the rapist—even if the girl were his own sister. In a certain country a Jew was put into prison for allegedly having killed a non-Jewish child. Because, so people said, its blood was needed for the baking of unleavened bread, that is matzoth. Such are the slanders against the Jews. Blood is considered by the Jews to be impure and they are forbidden to taste it, just as they are forbidden to eat pork or the meat of any prohibited animal. When a Jewish woman prepares meat for the Sabbath, she must first soak it in water for two hours, so that not a single drop of blood is left in it. At the time of the slander a lot of innocent Jewish blood was spilled. But God helped us and even the most severe judges had to free the innocent man. Rejoicing filled the world, Jews and non-Jews alike rejoiced. For there is no man alive who does not rejoice in justice. A bull's hide would not be sufficient to write down all our misfortunes. But truth will always out. The world stands on three things: truth, justice, and peace. And it is only because other nations don't know our rules and prohibitions that they slander us, accuse us of evil deeds which they have invented themselves. One of our wise men said that if a stranger wrongs you, you must not be angry with him, for he is only God's messenger and one must pray for him. Another of our wise men said that a Jew must pray for his enemies, because they represent his own soul from an earlier incarnation. Our prophets (may their souls rest in paradise, footstools of God's throne) saved from destruction and death both Jews and non-Jews. The Prophet Jonas learned from the Lord that the great city of Nineveh would be burned down within forty days, just as the godless city of Sodom had been burned. Sins are the same everywhere: homicide, fraud, treason, just as virtues are the same everywhere: kindness, justice, loyalty, almsgiving. Thus the Prophet Jonas spent one whole day walking through the city of Nineveh—a thing which would have taken an ordinary man at least three days—and summoning in a loud voice the inhabitants to do penance. When the King heard this, he removed his crown, took off his golden robes and put on sackcloth, then he left his throne and sat in an ash heap, although he was not a Jew. And the secret of it was that the King used to be an Egyptian Pharaoh at the time of the crossing of the Red Sea by the Jews. God gave him a long life, so that he could tell the future generations about God's miracles. The King ordered a fast, separated the men from the women, and the mothers from their children. A tremendous wailing arose. Look at these small children, they cry out to God, they are innocent; why should they suffer for sins they did not commit? And Prophet Jonas was pleased that a strange people did penance, although deep down in his soul he wondered why God worried so much about them. All of a sudden a leaf large as a tent grew over Jonas's head. His joy was short-lived. During the night a worm ate the leaf and Jonas began to worry lest he should not be able to shade his head from the sun. "You are worrying about a leaf," the Almighty said to him, "yet how important is a leaf? So now you see that I had to worry about the fate of thousands of men and women, and of small innocent children." Mr Officer, I'm sure you know it already, and there's probably no need for me to tell you this, you have been to school and are an educated man, but I'll remind you all the same, Mr Officer: Jewishness rests on one column as if on one foot—on the precept that you must love your neighbour as yourself. This is our whole wisdom, which anyone can learn standing on one foot. All through our history we have been faced by false judgements spread by our enemies: slander, lies, calumny, jeering, hatred. Enemies surround us the way wolves surround an innocent lamb. And what can an innocent lamb have for its defence? A pure heart. So now, as I am standing here in front of the tree of death, I have nothing but a pure heart for my defence. For who is to perish on this terrible tree? No one knows. Someone. How can someone perish? How can someone be guilty? How can someone have killed? Who knows him? Who has seen him? Who has tried to stay his hand? Where is that someone? Is a man like a pin? Yes indeed, my soul is weeping because one of your soldiers perished. How? Only God knows. Because he wanted to dishonour a girl? I don't believe it. Just that particular girl? And just the sister of a brother capable of killing living people? That soldier was born hundreds of miles from our town and yet he is supposed to have found his way to a narrow well here. Can it really be that that soldier had nothing else to do? Didn't he have enough worries of his own? First they take him away from his mother, his wife, his children, then hot blazing bullets start flying from all directions, every step his soul's in danger, every moment of survival a miracle! And what about the food, the sleep, all the hardships on the way here? How could such a man have any time? I don't believe it. Tell your general, please, that I, the town rabbi, don't believe it! The general must know his troops, and he will understand me. I know my community. I have known everybody in this town from birth. I know their sorrows, their joys, their good deeds and their minor transgressions. I know their souls and their conscience. I can vouch for every one of them. Tell it to your general. He will agree with me, and if he doesn't, take me away if you must, and put me before your judges . . . and may my soul . . . The rabbi's lips trembled. He whispered a prayer and sighed softly: "Creator of the world, Creator of the world, look upon our shame!"

Women began to cry, and so did men. Only the children did not cry. The officer grimaced and called out that they should stop crying at once. A rich Jew, Rechter the grocer, exclaimed: "Hush! Stop crying. Mr Officer does not like it when people cry." The weeping stopped. The women's chins still wobbled, they hugged and kissed their small ones. The men who wore glasses now took them off and wiped them. Only the thickset cattle merchant could be heard sniffing loudly: "God, dearest God, help us or make us numb!"

The chairman of the Jewish Community Council now thrust his way forward: he had a short trimmed beard and was wearing a bowler hat and morning coat, and he held a walking stick in his hand. He bowed, wiped his moustache with a handkerchief, put it in the inner pocket of his coat, and said: "We Jews believe in justice, because we were the first to give the world the principles of humanity. And the world accepted them and owes its existence to them. My address will be short. I shall only tell you what contribution Judaism has made to mankind. What have we given the world? The Bible, the Book of Books. Just as Eden or Paradise was the source of the four rivers flowing across the world, so our Bible is the source of the four greatest world religions. What else have we given the world? Many scholars, whom I won't name now, but who are known and highly regarded not only in Europe—that is, in Germany, France, and England—but also in America and Australia. We gave the world a man such as Heinrich Heine, and many, many others. Our community is not rich. We don't know what your customs are, but we shall respect them and try to do everything you order. I assure you, as chairman of the Jewish Community Council, we shall do our best to satisfy you as long as you are among us. That is all I wanted to say." He looked around and bowed. The officer smiled. Yes, he really did. He even gave an order, and the soldiers who held their rifles with bayonets fixed at the breasts of the rabbi and the rich Jews turned them toward the ground. Our God is kind, sighed the Jews with relief. As always in our history, disaster hangs over us and is about to strike, but it ends with our just having had a fright. Let this be our only offering! You aren't doing it for us, O Lord, but for Yourself! For who will adore You as much as the people whom You have chosen? Around a youth in a black velvet hat ten Jews assembled while he sang loudly: "Blessed art Thou, O Lord our God, King of the Universe who looseth the fetters of those who are bound!"

"Amen." The rabbi nodded, and after him the whole crowd repeated: "Amen, amen, amen, amen, for ever amen!" "Blessed art Thou, O Lord . . ." continued the youth, his eyes tightly shut. "Enough, enough!" said the rabbi. "The officer does not understand our prayers."

The thickset cattle merchant, with a red face and neck— there were others whose faces were red but from the heat of the burning market stalls, while he was red from high blood pressure—pushed through to the rabbi, pulled out a bulging wallet, counted out a few notes, and started to hand them to the officer. The rabbi held his hand back. Why? The cattle merchant looked at him with a puzzled expression. The soldiers now allowed individuals to come up to the rabbi. They shook him by the hand, wished him health, thanked him as they might after a sermon in the synagogue with the words: "May your strength increase!"

But the feeling of relief ended abruptly. The Jews from the crowd were beaten back from the hostages, the crowd parted, and the Cossack with the forelock rode his horse into the centre of the square. He reeked of petrol. He reined up in front of the officer, saluted, straightened to attention in the saddle, and said something. His teeth flashed, and when he had finished shouting to the officer the message from the commandant who had now come out onto the balcony—the message must have been very important, perhaps that Simon had been caught—he leaned down and with the wide sleeve of his green coat, his blue coat, his red coat, wiped the sweat from his brow. The stains on his coat were from petrol. The same Cossack had thrown a burning rag on the wooden house where Simon lived. The flames had blazed through the windows and doors, but Simon had disappeared long before the fire. The Cossack had galloped round dipping the rag into a barrel which had been rolled out from the corner shop and held it to the shingles on the roof. The flames leapt from house to house. The inhabitants of Crook Street, thieves and drunkards, looked on with their hands in their pockets. Their wives threw a few buckets of water onto the flames and dragged some bedding and clothes out in bed sheets. The smoke, oily from the petrol, crept along the narrow street as along a canal, toward the town, while firemen in helmets stood about smoking in the market square by their red engine not far from the Ruthenian Co-operative shop, in case of an emergency. The Cossack dispersed the women, urged his horse into groups of men, and kept looking for Simon. He asked if anybody had seen him. "We don't know anything," said the Ruthenians. "We haven't seen anything." One of them added: "We are your brothers, we would have told you." The Cossack did not believe them, although they talked in a language not much different from his own. The dead Cossack's body lay on the ground, wet. And his horse—if it were not for his horse no one would have suspected anything—was grazing nearby. Its rump and legs bore purple weals. The neighbours who had looked out of the windows saw how Simon had chased the horse away from his house with a stick. But the horse came back and stood forlornly at the gate. "Whose horse is that? Where is its rider?" They began to search, and a short while later they found the body of the Cossack inside the well. And Pessa? She sneaked out of the house when Simon was shooing the horse down the street to the old orchards. She screamed and pulled her brother by his sleeve. They would catch Simon, because of her! The messenger of evil was waiting. What did he say? That they have found Simon? Where? The officer seemed to knit his brows. What would he do now? Will he again order bayonets to be drawn against the hostages? The rabbi waited calmly, while the rich Jews stared into the officer's eyes. What will he say? What order will he give to his soldiers? The officer seemed to be debating it with himself. The crowd stirred. Somebody was jostling his way through it. Was it Amalia Diesenhoff? What did she want? She began an address in Esperanto. She was waving her hands toward the balcony where the commandant was standing hatless. A glaring electric light fell on his bald head from behind. "*Tuta mondo parolas esperanton. Esperanto estas linguo de la estonteco.*" The shoemakers and tailors knew these phrases from their union, where Miss Diesenhoff gave lessons: "Esperanto is the language of brotherhood. Esperanto teaches us to

176

love everyone without exception; if all the people in the world understood one another there would be no hatred, which leads to wars." The officer coughed and screened his mouth with his hand. But Amalia had just warmed up. Her mannish hat was askew, her pince-nez dangling from its ribbon; she was waving her arms, pointing to the stalls on fire, to the smoke slowly streaming down from the roofs, to the black and red windows of the houses. And when she pointed her finger at the gallows, at a given sign two soldiers took her under the arms and thrust her back into the crowd. Other soldiers quickly surrounded the hostages. The rabbi's wife forced her way through the crowd and fell screaming at the officer's feet. The man stepped back. He gave an order and moved away, holding up his sabre to avoid dragging it on the stones. The rabbi and the rich Jews were now walking between two rows of bayonets. Women stretched out their arms: "God's hostages! Sacrificed to God!" they called after them. The rabbi was praying in a murmur: "Hear, O Israel: the Lord our God, the Lord is one!" In the doorway of the Ruthenian Co-operative, Ossip in high boots stood at attention and a few young Ruthenians burst out singing under the balcony: "The Ukraine has not perished yet. . . ." The commandant must have gone in. Quietly, on rubber-covered wheels, a carriage drawn by two grey horses appeared. The Baroness alighted from it, and with her, the school chaplain. Kramer, the bookbinder, ran up to them, took the Baroness's hand, and kissed it. On the box sat the coachman with side whiskers like the Emperor's. The guard at first refused to let the Baroness in; it was the officer who invited her in with a gesture and then led in the hostages. Our God is kind, sighed the crowd. The Baroness herself has come to see the commandant. . . . Once, before he had become a shoemaker and was a child like any other, Gershon went to her villa. In a cage, two parrots were chattering. On the black piano stood a photograph of the Baroness in a tight-waisted dress, holding a fan in her hand, and next to it the photograph of an officer, holding a shako against his bemedalled breast. On the wall hung a photograph of the Emperor and of the Empress wearing long tresses. There were other photographs, too, of lesser-known persons. One was of Crown Prince Rudolf, about whom a little book was published after his death. Gershon saw it in the union's library. It had a photograph of him, riding on horseback along Third of May Avenue. After the army manoeuvres he had stopped at the Baroness's house and the whole town had crowded around her villa. A military band played all day long and the townspeople shouted: *"Es lebe unser Tronfolger!"* People came to the villa and handed in petitions in white envelopes. One civil servant asked for a rise. "What's this, you come here wearing such a beautiful frock coat and at the same time asking for a rise?" asked the Archduke's aide-de-camp. "I lent it to him," said the Baroness. There was a ball held in Falcon Hall. Gentlemen in national Polish costumes, ladies in coloured stoles with feathers in their hair and fans in their hands, drove up in their carriages. Confetti was thrown from the pavement, fireworks exploded in the sky, lighted candles were placed in windows, as on the Emperor's birthday. . . . The Baroness had stroked Gershon's head. She asked him something, but he did not understand. *"Wie heisst du?"* she asked, trying to communicate with him in German. He still remembers this. Also the flowers, climbing up the wire fence. He pushed open the gate and entered a long walk, overgrown with vines, like a green tunnel. The tunnel, the cinema, world history, and Comrade Simon. The Baroness knew Simon. She used to give him old gowns to be remodelled and even new things to make up for her. She once said to Mrs Maltz: "Young Simon has an excellent feeling for a woman's figure."

The crowd sighed with relief: things cannot be too bad yet! It began to thin out. Some people tried to leave and return to the houses which were not on fire. The Cossack with the forelock whirled round cracking his whip. The cartridges in the loops sewn on the front of his uniform glinted, the red wings on his shoulders flapped. Wasn't he worried that someone stronger than himself might turn up? Why? By what right? Did he believe in God? Are men animals? And has one the right to mistreat an animal? I have no bone to pick with you.
178

I might come to like you, just as I like Simon. All men are brothers, as Amalia Diesenhoff just said a moment ago. We are progressing and soon there won't be any rich or poor people. "All men are brothers. All men are equal. . . ." Ossip, with the group of young Ruthenians, appeared again. He was helping the Cossacks. "Stay together," he said in Ruthenian. Always in history there is one country which must be destroyed in order to save mankind. Poor Napoleon! He had even taken Moscow! He might have saved the world! It was easier in his time. And now where can one find another Napoleon? Not only that, but one would have to start from scratch. It's hard to see how Austria could do it. So this is how things are going to be from now on? What kind of country is it anyway that starts things off with a hanging?

There was a commotion in the very thick of the crowd. The Cossack with the forelock let his horse have its head. He went into a canter with his revolver in one hand and his whip in the other. He fired once, twice, three times. The hefty cattle merchant began to run. He broke away from the crowd and ran across the empty space of the market square. It was awful. But oddly enough, when something awful is witnessed it stops being sickening, and even seems quite harmless. The cattle merchant kicked Ossip in the stomach. Why? What for? The son of the Orthodox priest fell to the ground; if he gets up, fine, if he doesn't, no one, not even the Baroness, will be able to save Simon. Nor will it end with Simon. They might dynamite the brick houses, they might start a dance of death, a real slaughter, a bloodbath as in the times of the accursed enemy, Hetman Chmielnicki, or a black pogrom like the one at Kishiniev. But our God is kind, people sighed again with relief. That short officer with a sabre was a messenger from heaven. He rushed out onto the balcony of the Ruthenian National House and shouted something very loudly. The Cossack at once stopped firing his pistol and a good thing he did. He stopped urging his horse into the crowd—another good sign—turned, and pulled up in front of the balcony. He saluted and sat stiffly at attention in his saddle. "Who gave you an order to fire?" shouted the officer in Russian. We

could understand that much. During a war it sometimes happens that an army has to hang one of its own soldiers. The louder the officer shouted at the Cossack, the more jubilant the crowd became. All the while, people were choking and coughing from the smoke drifting from the stalls. They looked for a possible means of escape, to get as far away from the gallows as possible, for a sight like this is no pleasure for a Jew, not even if it was a Cossack who was about to be hanged instead of Simon. The crowd scattered; no one was stopping them any more. Ossip was helped to his feet by some young Ruthenians and taken away on a cart. Clusters of men and women disappeared in the gateways of houses, into the streets with unlit gas lamps, leading from the market square to the four points of the compass. Only one side of the square was blocked by a copper-coloured wall of fire and smoke. Behind that wall of burning stalls was the building of the needle-workers' union, "Star", and of the shoemakers' union, "Future", where Simon might have been hiding. The watchmaker's shop was wrecked, and so were the grocer's shop, the shoeshop, the tobacconist's; the carts had moved away, and the pavement now was littered with glass, paper, cardboard boxes, flour. A pool of olive oil surrounded a large damaged demijohn. People had to circle around it in order to avoid leaving any tracks behind. A married couple with a child turned quickly into a side street. Were they going to the same house? Perhaps to get in from the back, from the back yard? The yard reeked of urine and spilled wine. Soldiers stood near the fence, with servant girls from all over the town giggling in the arms of drunken men. The stairs were wet, the axed door of the wine-shop barred the way. Two soldiers were rolling out a small cask. A candle was burning in the store. From large upturned flasks in wicker baskets, rivulets of fragrant wine trickled away. The soldiers were buzzing like flies on flypaper. On the first-floor landing a couple were calmly fornicating. The union building was not closed. The bookcase did not stand in its usual place, it looked as if someone had tried to barricade the entrance with it. "Simon!" he called. No one answered. "It's me, Gershon!" No one replied. Simon could not stand it
180

there, obviously, and had left. It was difficult to stand it there for more than five minutes, the windowpanes were broken from the heat and a cloud of smoke filled the room. Gershon's eyes were watering. As he was wiping them he knocked his head against the door frame. A large figure loomed up and disappeared behind the window on the staircase. He called out again: "Simon, it's me, Gershon!" The buckle of an army belt clanked, the soldier on the landing was pulling his trousers up, but he drew back to let Gershon pass. In the passage leading to the plundered wineshop a few cigarette ends glowed. And in the yard of the next house soldiers were lined up in silence in front of a wooden outbuilding where the janitor's wife and her two daughters lived—the elder, a tall blonde, the younger, short and thin. Every now and again the door would open and either one or the other of the girls would throw out water from a basin. Only one side of the street was lined with houses; on the other side were moist meadows covered with tall grass. There, a few steps from the market square, people were quietly sleeping! The gas lamps were alight. Next to the small town park there came the smell of freshly baked bread. The bakers had not interrupted their work. In the yard of the State school stood a monument to Kilinski—a national hero, who was also a shoemaker—on short legs, with a sabre in his hand. Now both the sabre and one of his arms were missing. They had been lopped off. And his nose as well. A peasant's cart rumbled past and disappeared round the bend of the main road to Duliby. In a deserted street some Ruthenians were drunkenly singing a patriotic song: "Hey, in the mountains the Cossacks are marching, hey, in the hills the Cossacks are marching, our famous company. . . ." They, too, are a nation. They, too, want to have their own country, their own army, their own generals. On the cart lay Ossip, the son of the Orthodox priest from Duliby. His friends were singing, which meant that he would get well, that he had not been seriously hurt. Although with them nothing is ever certain, everything is possible. With them it is the custom to drink vodka after a funeral and sing merrily as if it were a wedding. The town was asleep. Black windows; here and there, occasionally, a flicker of light, where somebody was ill or dying.

"And where is Simon's sister?" asked Old Tag.

"I don't know."

"Poor soul. She must be wandering in the forest now."

"The soldiers will catch her. She'll die of hunger."

"And Simon?"

"If they haven't caught him . . ."

It was quieter now in the yard. The wives of the Hasidim were sitting on a low wall, perched there like birds before the rain. Only the tall woman in the velvet dress was walking up and down rocking her baby, singing softly:

> And when you grow up, you'll be a Jew:
> A-a-a-a-a-a-a-a-a-a-a-a-a.
> Almonds and raisins, you'll have a stall:
> A-a-a-a-a-a-a-a-a-a-a-a-a.
> Honey and milk, you'll have a shop:
> A-a-a-a-a . . .

She stopped suddenly.

From the inn the Hasidim came rushing out, all together like a swarm of bumblebees. They clung to one another as in a dance, in wide-open caftans, round hats, and white stockings, two white tapes flapping in front. Their eyes were half open from interrupted sleep and their dark mouths were ready to shout, to sing, or to pray.

The tallest one, straight as a lamp post, his face white as a linen sheet with holes cut out for the mouth and eyes, and the handsome one with golden corkscrew locks were leading the tsaddik, holding him under the arms. The redhead clapped his hands. He darted up to the threshold of the hall, then drew back and waved his hands, spreading an invisible carpet under the tsaddik's feet, which were barely touching the ground.

The tsaddik, his head bowed, his face hidden in his ample beard, did not open his eyes.

"Easy, easy does it!" called the redhead. "What's the hurry? Why did you wake him up? The tsaddik must be made of iron

182

to stand it all. Look at him, he's hardly alive. Who woke him up?"

"What's the difference? I did, he did, we all did," said the tallest Hasid.

"But what for?" persisted the redhead.

"What a silly question to ask. The town is on fire."

"So what?"

"There's a blessing for everything, there's a prayer for everything," started the cantor.

"You keep out of it," said the redhead, pushing him away with his elbow.

"I wonder whether the fire is near or far away," said the tallest one.

"And if it's near—let's say it's near, even though it isn't— is that any reason to go and wake up the tsaddik right away? Is he a fireman? And what about me? Don't I count any more? Don't I have to be asked? Not any more? Finished?"

The beardless youth came forward.

"Why shouldn't we have wakened our tsaddik? And when should we wake him up if not at a time when our souls are in danger? It is clearly written . . ."

"You!" The redhead jammed his finger into the other's chest. "You were running around with a yellow flag in your flies long after I knew what is written there. Now you want to teach me, maybe?"

"I don't want to, I have no intention, I have no desire to teach you. . . ."

"Come, come, no harm done," interposed the Hasid with the wiry beard. "No harm in asking why. Anybody can ask a question."

"Why?" The handsome one began to blink. "Soon as a person starts asking why, there's trouble ahead."

"Never mind." The redhead nodded his head. "I'll manage by myself. Why, you ask? I could give you seventy-seven answers, but I'll give you only one. It won't be the answer that the tsaddik is a human being, nor the answer that after such a day as yesterday any ordinary mortal needs a proper rest, not to mention when, as in his case, it is a mortal of pure

183

spirituality; nor will the answer be that his strength is our strength and that as long as God gives him strength, we have got strength, nor will it be the answer that what, in fact, can our tsaddik do . . . In short"—the redhead stroked his whiskers and the corners of his mouth with his fingers—"'The fear of God is the beginning of wisdom,' to start with, and secondly" —he turned to the beardless youth—"bring me a chair immediately!"

The Hasidim exchanged glances.

"I'll get it!" whined the young boy, the one who had dreamed of a naked woman.

"Go on! Go on!" The beardless youth nudged him.

The tsaddik sighed. The redhead put his ear to his lips.

"What? What? What?"

The tsaddik's lips moved.

The redhead took the tsaddik under his arm and led him away. The other Hasidim also dispersed. The cantor hesitated for a moment, then followed them, limping, toward the orchard.

The young boy with the sunken cheeks was dragging a chair.

"Come." Little Lenka Soloveytchik ran after him. "Let me help you."

"Go away! Go away!" the panic-stricken boy shouted, shaking with fear.

Soloveytchik called to Gershon from a distance.

"Ah, blessed be the new arrival!"

"He has come back," exclaimed Old Tag.

"You might almost say: from the other world," and Soloveytchik patted Gershon on the shoulder.

"You might say it," Gershon assented.

"And what did you see there?" Soloveytchik joked.

"What didn't I see. . . ."

"Are the Cossacks there?"

"Yes."

"Are they riding around?"

"And how!"

"May the earth swallow them up!"

❖

The Hasidim were returning now from the orchard, saying the prayer of hand-washing and wiping their hands, which were damp with dew, on the skirts of their caftans.

"Here's a chair! Here's a chair!" The boy rushed toward the redhead.

"Aren't you clever," said the redhead, pinching the boy's cheek.

The tsaddik was waving his hands about as if he were trying to beat the air.

"All right, all right!" The redhead calmed him.

He reached into the tsaddik's pocket and pulled out a large red kerchief. The tsaddik sneezed.

"Good health and much strength," said the redhead.

"A ripe old age," chimed the Hasidim.

The tsaddik blew his nose in the kerchief, then sat on the chair.

"It's time for the morning Calling of the Name," said the redhead, leaning over the chair.

"The Lord our God is great!" the Hasidim rejoiced.

"May this day not be worse than yesterday!" said the handsome one with golden locks.

"Amen!"

The tsaddik's moustache was moving.

"Hush!" The redhead pressed his lids tight and shook his head. "The tsaddik is about to say something. With God's help we may be worthy of hearing his voice. . . ."

The tsaddik wriggled on his chair.

"It's a delight to be a Jew."

The redhead clapped his hands.

"Ay!"

"A delight! A delight! A delight!" the Hasidim repeated.

"Look! Can you see his smooth brow? Can you see it?"

The redhead adjusted the hat on the tsaddik's head.

"There's a fire," murmured the cantor. "There's a blessing for everything, for bread, for water, for thunder, for the rainbow, only not for fire. Rabbi, please invent a prayer for fire. 'Blood, fire, columns of smoke', as it is written in the Holy Book. Everything has been foretold."

"Hush! Stop trying to scare everyone! Soon everything will take a turn for the better. A new day is about to begin." The redhead shoved aside the beardless youth, who was standing nearest to him. "Don't push. Can't you see that on him reposes the strength of his great-grandfather, blessed be his memory, may his soul live in paradise, may his merits support us today. Be quiet! The tsaddik is about to speak."

The tsaddik opened wide his eyes. He looked around and sighed.

"In the beginning God created heaven and earth," he began, then his voice broke and only his lips were moving, and then once again the voice flowed forth, as in the desert: "And God said: Let there be light!"

Silence fell.

All around the countryside cocks began to crow. The old ones in full rotund voices, the young ones in a high-pitched, staccato screech.

"And there was light!" sang the redhead.

"And God saw the light," sang the cantor.

"And there was evening and morning," sang the youth.

"On the first day!" concluded the handsome one.

"Light! Light!" The redhead grabbed his arms.

"Hallelu-jah, hallelu-jah, hallelu-jah. With sounds and trumpets praise ye God! The night is passing. The day is coming! Let us sing: He led us ..."

"He led us," took up the fat man on short legs. "He led us from sorrow ..."

"He led us from sorrow," sang the Hasidim, "to joy. From darkness into the bright light."

"From sunrise to sunset praised be the name of the Lord," intoned the handsome one, lovingly stroking his locks.

"The mountain leaps like a ram when the night is gone, the hill skips like a lamb when the night is gone," sang the cantor, trying out his voice. "Why does the mountain leap like a ram? Because the night has passed. Why does the hill skip like a lamb? Because the night has passed."

"The day will bring us food and drink, with God's help," said the tallest Hasid, with his face white as a linen sheet with

186

holes cut out for the mouth and the eyes, and bowed low. "The day will bring us double profits, with God's help. The day will bring us health and strength, with God's help. The day will bring bridegrooms to the daughters of the poor, and pregnancy to barren wives. All the best to all the Jews, and let us say amen!"

"Weeping is the guest of the night, and day is like a wedding in a new house," cried the most handsome one.

"Hallelu-jah, hallelu-jah, hallelu-jah!"

"At night the Pharaoh and Aman plotted how to destroy the sons of Israel, but in the daytime the Pharaoh was drowned in the Red Sea, in the daytime Aman was hanged on the gallows. The Almighty raised His hand high, and the white hand towered over all. Such will be the fate of Israel's enemies. Rose of Jacob, thou wilt grow in the garden of Eden, but the strangers will find themselves under the earth."

"The cloud shudders with joy, on the right the Angel Gabriel, on the left the Angel Raphael, close the shutters of the moon and remove its silver crown of stars and put on the golden crown with the diamond which shone in Noah's ark and on Abraham's neck," chanted the beardless youth, flashing his bloodshot eyes.

"Let us sing! Let us sing!" encouraged the Hasid with the lopsided shoulder.

"Hallelu-jah, hallelu-jah, hallelu-jah! Let us praise God with harmony and trumpets!"

"God has saved us."

"When there is as much day in night as night in day, when the hour of the morning Calling of the Name is yet to come, then death is balanced with life," said the tallest one, with his face white as a linen sheet with holes cut out for the mouth and eyes.

"Let us sing! Let us sing!" interrupted the redhead.

Now the full voice of the cantor resounded.

Hallelu-jah, hallelu-jah, hallelu-jah!
Weeping will fill the night, joy will return at dawn.

Sin will rise in the night, absolution will return at dawn.
A cry will rise in the night, it will be heard in the morning.
Fear will fill the night, hope will return in the morning.
Death will appear at night, resurrection will come in
the morning.

The cantor changed the tune.

"Blessed art Thou, O Lord our God, King of the Universe, who with a sneeze extinguisheth fire like a candle. And let us say: Amen!"

"Amen!"

"This is against the rules," said the redhead, stamping his foot. "This is not allowed! It's his invention! We must cleanse ourselves. Come, let's dip ourselves in water."

"Come, let's dip ourselves in water," said the beardless youth, clapping his hands.

"A delight! A delight to be a Jew!" called the handsome one, stroking his golden locks and smiling broadly.

"Let's go to the stream!" called the beardless youth.

"Where is that stream? Who knows?" asked the fat man on short legs.

"Now is the time when the water is best. The moment before sunrise," said the beardless youth, smacking his lips.

"They're having a good time," said Soloveytchik.

"Gershon, show them where the stream is," said Old Tag, and walked over to the wattle fence.

The Hasidim were already crossing the meadow, so Gershon ran after them. They went in single file, with the exception of the redhead, who supported the tsaddik, whose hand was on his shoulder. Old Tag followed them with his eyes.

The wind bounced off the alder wood and pulled at the skirts of their caftans, revealing their white stockings, now damp from the dew. It was already daylight.

Are the Hasidim dancing on the green grass? Each has put his hand on the shoulder of the preceding one, as the tsaddik has done with the redhead's shoulder. The Hallowed Flock! Give them, as you would give children, paper flags with a red apple pushed onto the stick, and a little candle stuck to the apple, and they will play with them, like children. It is good for them; they can dance round a table. And when they decide to drink vodka, the whole house of prayer trembles with delight, rocks like a ship on black waters; for it is permitted to get drunk once a year and to shout: "Long live the people of Israel! Long live the Hallowed Flock!" "The first people among all the peoples is eternal!"

Swallows flew out from under the roof of the cow-shed. Frightened by the red glow in the darkness, they would no longer return, as they had done before.

Yevdocha was driving out the cows. The roan one lifted her tail and splayed her legs, the white one rubbed herself against the fence.

"Have you taken the milk to the kitchen?" asked Tag.

"I have," mumbled Yevdocha.

"The daughter-in-law is still asleep."

"What's that to me?"

"Are you sore about something?"

"Why?"

"Perhaps it would be better not to drive them out today."

"Why not?"

"Don't stay away long today."

"Why?"

"Perhaps I'll go to town today."

"What for?"

"Stay here and keep an eye on my daughter-in-law and granddaughter."

"When will you return? In the evening?"

"I don't know."

"Well . . ."

"I shall try to return as soon as possible."

"All right. . . ."

"I shall wait here. Leave the cows or bring them back at once."

"Why?"

"I want to give you my keys."

"What the devil for? I don't want them!"

The girl wanted to walk away.

"Wait!" Old Tag caught her hand.

Yevdocha pulled it away.

"Leave me alone, you old devil!"

"Yevdocha, listen to what I have to say. . . ."

"Leave me alone, people are watching."

The chaplain came down to them from the main road.

"Good morning!"

"Good morning," answered Old Tag.

"Get back! Get back!" Yevdocha screamed at a cow.

"I've come from town," said the chaplain, wiping his forehead and neck with a handkerchief. "I've come from town," he repeated.

"From town?"

"From hell, if you'd like to know."

"Are the fires still burning?"

"Yes. Here and there."

"But they seem to be dying out."

"Maybe."

Both turned their eyes to the silver streak in the east: the clouds of smoke had thinned out; the red glow had faded and turned a light pink.

"It's daylight already. Maybe things will quiet down now. The fire's dying out," said Old Tag.

"God is merciful."

Yevdocha kept shouting at the cows, which had now strayed across the stream and into the mud.

"Thank goodness it's daylight at last. What day is it? Friday?"

"Friday. . . . They have hanged Boom," said the chaplain.

Tag stood still, his arms heavy.

"We ran into some Cossacks. I was driving the trap, with Asya's body. Boom was walking alongside. They said they were looking for him. They thought it was his sister. They let me go free."

"I knew it, I felt it. . . ."

"I begged them, I pleaded, I threatened."

190

"Boom, of all people . . . He wasn't the one who killed . . . It wasn't him!"

"I went with the Baroness to see the commandant. A lot of good it did."

"But he wasn't the one who killed!"

"I did what I could."

"Blessed be the True Judge."

"My feet are giving way, let's sit down somewhere."

The gate was open. They entered the inn and went to the guest hall, which was still dark. Tag drew the curtains. Somebody must have extinguished the hanging lamp. Probably Yevdocha. She must also have removed the black shawl.

Tag half opened the door to the bedroom.

"Boom is no more. . . ."

The chaplain sat at the long table.

"I wanted to help. He was a good boy. Why did I take that body? The older a man gets the more stupid he becomes." The chaplain sighed.

"Perhaps you'd like some milk, Father?"

"Thank you. It's always the same with you Jews. Whenever you try to do some good, you wind up doing the opposite. A curse, for all I know. I thought to myself, the poor boy, I'll take his dead girl to the burial ground, I'll help him bury her, say a prayer for her soul no matter if it's in a Jewish cemetery." The chaplain rubbed his forehead. "Only now do I begin to understand the words: 'Follow me, and let the dead bury their dead'."

Old Tag went to the kitchen and got a glass of milk. He put it on the table in front of the priest.

"Please, Father, drink it. It's still warm, a fresh batch."

The chaplain shook his head.

"Please, Father, I'm worried about my daughter-in-law and granddaughter."

"That's why I've come. I want to take you all to my place. You can stay with me for a few days."

"I must go to the commandant."

"What for? It won't do any good now."

"I must tell them that they've hanged an innocent man."

The chaplain raised his eyes to him.

"Boom was here in the inn all the time. He sat by the girl's body. That's what I must tell him. I must go to the commandant."

"They won't let you in. The guards won't let you in."

"They must. Boom was innocent; may his innocent blood fall like a stone upon their souls."

"It won't do any good now. Why take any chances when you don't have to? You're not so young any more. Why don't you sit down?" The priest was starting to lose his temper.

Old Tag did not move. He stood, his face turned toward the bedroom.

"This is the end of everything, and not only for me," said Old Tag to himself.

"You're a stubborn old man. If you go alone, they certainly won't let you in."

Old Tag came up to the table.

"How old are you?" asked the chaplain. "There's a year's difference between us, isn't there?"

"Two years. It's nothing."

"At the time it seemed a lot. Once again it's become a lot. Do you remember how afraid you were of me? And I felt sorry for you." The priest took the glass of milk in both his hands, but he did not lift it.

"Sorry? Why?"

"You sat in your school, knee-deep in the Old Testament, and had no idea that you were in danger of going to hell."

"I don't follow you."

The priest smiled slightly. He sighed.

"Don't you know that souls without baptism go to hell after death?"

"What difference does it make where they go after death? Isn't it all the same?"

"It's not all the same. First of all, no two deaths are the same. Much more so than life."

"Does this mean that not only can we look forward to a worse life, but even a worse death? Maybe it's true. It's because God loves us so much."

"Do you remember how I tried to save your soul in those days, do you remember?"

"No, I don't. I don't remember anything."

"'He that believeth and is baptized shall be saved: but he that believeth not shall be damned.'"

"With us, one also says 'shall be damned'. Only with us life is a punishment greater than hell. A rotten life: disease, poverty, which is worse than any disease, and, worst of all, death itself. This is punishment enough."

"Everybody is afraid of death. The Christians are helped by their faith."

"It's becoming harder and harder to have faith."

"Do you know why? Because people don't love God enough. Not for nothing is it written: 'To believe in Jesus Christ is to love Him.' And something else—to love one's neighbour."

"You should take it easy, Father."

"All right, I'll stop now. And you—do you believe in God?"

"I try to."

"So you see, is your God different from ours? Do you remember how we used to meet in the yard? I often thought of you. When I was serving at Mass, I used to think that you would be damned. I wanted to save your soul. Today I know it was childish and ridiculous. And every time I sang 'Hosanna' and saw children with palm leaves, I wondered why you didn't love Jesus. Because 'the fetters of Old Jerusalem where fear reigned are broken, and the time of the New Testament has come where love reigns.' I couldn't make much sense out of these words, yet I kept rushing out to meet you."

"Moses! Jerusalem! Our holy names."

"Don't be afraid. Our common God will give us absolution."

"I'm not afraid. I couldn't any more, even if I wanted to. I'm very sorry, Father."

"For goodness' sake! Believe in what you will, how you will! Let's not talk about it. I didn't come here to have a discussion."

"What are you driving at, Father? You know that I'm a Jew and shall remain a Jew till the day I die. A Jew always remains a Jew. Even if he gets baptized."

"You're different from the others."

"All Jews are alike. Like no other nation. I'm no different from other Jews."

"You want to go to town? What for?"

"Now I'll tell you something, Father. The enemy's here, the enemy's there. We're surrounded by enemies. What am I to do? The Jews are looked upon as enemies too, and it probably will always be that way. My inn is rocking on black waters like a small boat. Will it or won't it be saved? It's as if the Tsar had declared war against me alone. All right. So now I'm going to town to tell the commandant how things were: You have hanged Boom, who was innocent. Maybe something can still be done. Save what can be saved. I'm waiting until it becomes completely light."

"You won't bring Boom back to life."

"That doesn't matter any more."

"Believe me, Boom's death has affected me deeply. But how could I have refused his request?"

"It's a great misfortune when the body of a dead person disappears from a house. And it happened here, under my roof! In my house! And where is the body now?"

"The Cossacks took it away, together with my trap."

"What d'you mean, 'took it away'?"

"They took it by force."

"What did they do with the body?"

The priest spread his arms wide.

"The commandant must give it back. So that she can be buried as she should, according to our customs."

"Not even he can help you any more."

"What did they do with the body?"

"They poured petrol on it and threw it into the fire. So people told me, I didn't see it myself."

"May their name be erased for ever!"

The chaplain crossed himself.

"And did Boom see it?"

"I don't know."

"What a price we have to pay! Anyone who wants can come into our houses, kill and dishonour us. What a price we have

194

to pay for having been chosen by God. What a price we have to pay for our God!"

"I wanted you to be one of us. Do you remember?"

"I don't remember."

"You were studying in your school with the windows just above the ground."

"What are you talking about?"

"I waved to you. I called out to you with my whole childish heart."

"What are you talking about, Father?"

"'Look at me! Look at me!' I called."

Old Tag buried his face in his hands.

"Other people saw me, but you, hardened in sin . . ."

"In sin? In what sin?"

". . . but you, hardened in sin, pretended not to have seen me. . . ."

"And what next?"

"I broke a window. I kicked it with my foot."

"Oh yes, that's possible."

"The teacher and his assistant came out to catch me and punish me. I had heard various stories about Jews which Christian children are told in order to frighten them. I escaped. But you, too, escaped home at the same time. I saw you look around for me."

"I was afraid you'd come to the inn. . . ."

"Another time, I went to the house of prayer."

"Another time . . .?"

Old Tag got up from the table and walked over to the window.

"Yes, it was another time," repeated the chaplain.

Old Tag pushed the shutters open. A stream of air flowed in, saturated with smoke and soot.

The highway was quiet. The powdery dust stirred slightly. The hussar's horse killed the day before had disappeared. The peasants from Duliby had already hauled it away and skinned it by now. They would give the meat to the dogs or eat it themselves. If a goy from Duliby should kiss you, count your teeth afterward: it is a village of thieves.

195

How many stacks of hay had they not stolen from his field!

The countryside was awake. The cows were lowing in the neighbouring farms, the geese and hens were cackling. Human voices could be heard, and the barking of dogs. As yesterday, as the day before. As if nothing had happened in the world. Only Axelrad's mill was silent.

Over the town the smoke still swirled. The sky was red from the rising sun: the smoke was purple.

The chaplain lowered his head and folded his hands as in prayer.

It was the Day of Atonement. And the priest rose in his pulpit saying: "You serpents, generation of vipers, how will you flee from the judgement of hell?" Can it be the fault of the young boy from the inn? "Then shall they deliver you up to be afflicted and shall put you to death: and you shall be hated by all nations for my name's sake." One child's heart, frail like Jesus' boat, was drowning in tears and calling out to another. On the threshold, in the open door, he was struck by the heat and stale air. In the vestibule on a stone floor, long Jewish candles were alight, and inside the room candles were burning in earthenware pots. Wax was dripping from the candlesticks and the chandelier hanging from the ceiling. His shirt stuck to his back. The Jews in silver-braided striped shawls, which covered their heads down to their eyes, could not see anything. The stranger could penetrate into the centre of the room, up to the platform with little columns and a gallery. The paintings on the walls were shiny with damp: Noah's ark, the animals boarding it meekly in pairs up a gangway, two lions, two tigers, two elephants, two giraffes; the ark was green, the animals were yellow. And a mountain spouting fire from its top, and from the fire a hand sticking out, holding two tablets with Hebrew letters. A green sea and a lot of heads, drowning, one next to another, covered by curly waves. The light of the candles played on the waving shawls and swaying heads. A curtain was parted and the little door of the Jewish tabernacle was opened. The Torah appeared, clothed in coloured velvet with golden crowns and hands with outspread
196

fingers embroidered on it in golden thread, similar to the hands one sees on the gravestones of Jewish priests. A great shout and lament arose. The praying men left their places on the benches and, amidst soft groans and supplications, fell prostrate on the floor. The small Jewish boy from the inn stood next to his father, who was also lying on the floor and calling to his God. The boy looked around and closed a large prayerbook with frayed yellowing pages. His heart must have heard the other heart. The boy turned slowly. He looked to see where to place his foot and cautiously stepped among his coreligionists plunged in despair. Under the shawls their backs were trembling. The boy was leaving the synagogue for ever. The eldest of the Jews, who was half kneeling on the steps in front of the tabernacle, would get up, tear his robes, and pronounce an anathema. His father would pull him by the ear, tear his trousers off, and in the presence of all would beat him until he bled. And the red-faced men around them would shout: "More, more!" The elder was already getting up from the steps, the other men were getting up too, rising from the dirty floor. The hand of the Jewish boy which he held in his was wet with perspiration. They ran out of the house of prayer. The autumn sun blinded them; the air smelled of hoar frost steaming from fallen leaves. The little square in front of the house of prayer was bright and empty. The doors of the one-storey houses were shut. A pump was squeaking somewhere. A Jewish maid or the wife of a caretaker was pumping water into a bucket. The streets were deserted, life stood still, commerce had ceased. Not a single peasant had come up from the country. All the world knew that it was the Jewish Day of Atonement. In the Orthodox church the candles were burning, but there was no one inside. From the yellow trees the horse chestnuts fell. He picked them up and filled his pockets and handed some to the Jewish boy, who did not want them. Dogs were running about in orchards barking at them when they walked past the fences. Someone called out to them. The street, lined with houses on one side only, was likewise deserted. Around the barracks tall grass was growing on damp ground. He used to go skating there in the winter. In the barracks yard soldiers in blue uniforms were marching up and down. An officer could be heard shouting.

He was tightly holding the Jewish boy's sweaty hand. It was not far to go. They must pass the General Hospital, where nuns were pushing paralysed patients in wheel chairs. On benches outside, convalescents in white hospital gowns were sitting in the sun. The boy's hand slipped from his own. The inn was closed. Hens were cackling and wallowing in the dust. The mud bank was never dry, the water in the stream was ice cold. They waded in in their boots. Don't be afraid, it won't take long. I'll just take off your hat and the velvet skullcap. The water drawn from the stream is poured over the Jewish boy's head, splashing down his cheeks: "*Ego te baptizo in nomine Patris et Filii et Spiritus Sancti.*" The young boy tears himself away, covers his face and his head. "No, no, no!" He runs away. But it's too late, my friend. It has been done! Your soul has been saved. You have become a new creature. The Holy Spirit, which renews the face of the earth, has renewed you, and cleansed you in baptism. In vain are your cries: No! Now you should cry: "And I live; yet not I, but Christ liveth in me: and the life which I now live in the flesh I live by the faith of the Son of God, who loved me, and gave Himself for me."

Old Tag turned away from the window.

"Have you been to see the commandant, Father?"

The chaplain raised his head from over his hands folded in prayer.

"I'm sorry to have interrupted," said Tag.

"Speak! Speak, my son!"

"Could someone try to see him?"

"He could, my friend. We must try to see him."

"I'll go put on my Sabbath caftan. Today's Friday, anyway. Commandants, like God, like people who are neatly dressed."

"Friday, a sad day, the saddest day of the week."

"I'll go and change, then."

"We'll go there together."

"If you feel up to it, Father . . . if you will be so kind . . ."

"I'm not doing it for you."

"That doesn't matter. They might not let me in if I went alone."

"Perhaps not."

"No harm in trying."

"And if they let us in, what'll we tell them?"

"What d'you say to a commandant anyway? All you can do is plead with him. I might even fall on my face in front of him. I might even cry."

"That won't bring Boom back to life."

"I could fast. I could pretend this is the Day of Atonement. It is one, in a way, more real than the real one."

"What will you tell him?"

"Today a commandant is more powerful than God."

"But what will you tell him?"

"One must save what can be saved."

"But what will you tell him?"

"I shall go and change."

"They won't let us in."

"We shall see about that."

"They didn't let me in."

"They'll let us in. We'll tell them that we're bringing something important for them."

"What can be important for them?"

"I shall go alone."

"Oh, you!" The chaplain slammed his hand down on the table.

"Why are you angry, Father?"

"I'm going with you. We'll go together. But we still have time. The commandant might still be asleep."

"We can wait outside the front door. It makes no difference."

"Go and change. And meanwhile I'll wash my face."

"Why don't you drink your milk, Father?"

"Go now, go! On the way, I'll stop by the church."

Through the bare windows the light of early morning flooded the bedroom. Old Tag turned the key in the wardrobe door and took out his Sabbath suit. Changing before going to the synagogue had been a source of joy from his earliest days. To derive pleasure in one's advanced years from the same things as in one's youth is a sign that eternity exists. It means that the outside world exists and continues eternally, that our life is renewed over and over again like nature's four seasons, sunshine and rain, frost and heat. This means peace. In the house of prayer Father had always been greeted by a nod, a witty remark, a wink of the eye. Today you are a father, tomorrow your son will be a father. Everything is known beforehand. Until yesterday, everything had been known in advance, for generations to come. Life revolved quietly like the sun, from morning to evening. The kind of world a man lived in was taken for granted. But last night! It's tough for a man to pull his boots onto feet swollen from a night like that. Such a night! A night of vigil like that of a woman's first confinement. And what kind of fruit would that night bear? What will the newly born day be like? For whom will it be the first, for whom the last? The first day and the last are like the banks of a river, and in the middle flows sin. And I myself was a child and ran about in the meadows like a colt. Although for the Jews, meadows and flowers were only for the girls; the school and the Pentateuch were for the boys. Even so, my mother used to say to me: Go on outside, run your legs off; there'll be time enough for the columns of small print and for nodding over yellowed pages. She was a wise woman for her time. A man doesn't remember the first day of his life. And just as he doesn't know the day of his birth, he must not know the day of his death. O Lord, thanks be to You for it: leave me in ignorance of whether this day is to be my last. Cause not this day to be the last of my life. Make us lose that habit of counting days. The span of life is seventy years. O Lord, make us lose the habit of counting years so that we may not die a little every day. Break us of the habit of thinking. From every thought, death flies out like a black bird. You have given us a soul. Thanks be to You. You have torn it from under Your heart piece by piece, in order to give it to us. How can I praise You enough for it! Like a mother who shares fruit with her young, You have shared Your immortality with us. Good wine must be poured into good jugs. Why, then, do You consider our bodies to be inferior clay, which has risen from

200

dust and will be returned to dust? Is it right that a body should be "the vessel of shame and disgrace"? For so it is said. How can one expect the best wine to remain pure in a vessel like that? The eyes and the heart are the procurers. They tempt the soul, as a bride is tempted before she decides to stand under the wedding canopy. Isn't a lion, which has no soul, no thought and no shame, better off than we are? Isn't a creature which is blind and deaf, and doesn't realize that it is alive or that one day it will die, better off than we are? I don't want to die. I've still got time. You know Yourself that I have plenty of strength, that I have enough of it to last me for another ten years. And what if it is Fate which sends me to town so that I should perish there? What kind of sacrifice is that? You asked for the sacrifice of Isaac, but you did not accept it although Isaac was holy. But I? What am I? Only a speck of dust, only a vessel of shame and disgrace. So if I am to die ... My father breathed his last in my arms. He was telling me all the time: "Come nearer, come nearer." It was impossible to come any nearer. "I am dying, and you?" A son stays alive so that he may say Kaddish after his father's death. On his grave, then every day for a whole year, then on every anniversary of his death. "All right, all right, but I'm dying!" The Kaddish is a prayer that helps you to get to Paradise. "Oh, well!" Father shook his head for the last time. He did not believe that Paradise is for the Jews. Perhaps every dying man believes only in Hell. But before Father died, he asked to be dressed in his Sabbath caftan and to be taken out into the open. To have a look at that corner of the world where his mother gave birth to him.

Yevdocha was coming from beyond the stream. So she was returning earlier than usual. The cat was walking slowly, paw by paw, greedily eyeing the circling swallows, and purring as he always did. The swallows were flying low, skirting the ground. After so many months of drought, there will be rain. It will settle the dust on the road. The cock was standing on tip-toe as if he wanted to see better. The guests at the inn had made room for one another next to the walls; the wives of the Hasidim were leaning against the wall of the main building,

and opposite them Soloveytchik with his family and Blanca
and her photographer husband were dozing under the roof of
the cow-shed. Morning light poured down from the east.
The fires had been put out, only wisps of smoke trailed across
the sky. From behind the clouds, the sun's rays suddenly
sprang forth, lighting the tops of trees in the orchard, the dark
alders beyond the stream, the meadow where the cows were
grazing alone, the stream full of bathing Hasidim. They were
jumping into the water, naked or in white underpants, and
splashing under the bridge; they were swimming where the
water was deepest and shouting. Their cries travelled all the
way up to the inn: "A delight! A delight! A delight to be a
Jew!" From under the bridge a thin rivulet of water flowed in
the dried-out river bed. The autumn rains would fill it up to
the muddy banks. Then it would be possible to swim in a
large arc from under the black alders up to Axelrad's mill.
Fortunately, there was no prohibition against water. Instead of
making hundreds of prohibitions, Moses might just as well
have written in the Torah: Everything that is attractive to the
eye and tasteful to the palate is permissible to all the peoples
of the world, but prohibited to Jews. If Moses—whose name
means "pulled out" of the river—had not been saved by water,
who knows if the Jews would be allowed to swim? We owe a
lot to that Egyptian river. To it we also owe several thousand
years of wandering and misery which all began with that small
rush basket. It all began with water. Sin, too, came out of
water. On that day the sun was already setting. He was alone
on the bank of the river when a naked girl emerged from it.
Her legs were red from the cold, and so they have remained
ever since. "What is your name?" "Yevdocha." "Where do you
come from?" "From the village." "What do you do?" "Look
after cows." "Would you like to work for me?" "I would."
Before her death, his wife told him: "You might have waited
until I was gone."

He turned away from the window. On the floor lay Asya's
sheet next to the brass candlesticks. Over these candlesticks
his mother had cried every Friday evening. Tiny and frail, she
had survived her husband and ten children. She herself took

each of them to the burial ground, wrapped in linen. "What can I do? Where can I turn?" She had wrung her hands when a child died. Of twelve children only he and his sister were left. It was because of her that the chaplain had come to the inn before he was ordained. She had inherited him from Tag. He had outgrown childhood, but he still escaped to a dark corner whenever his mother lit small candles for her living and dead children in the brass candlesticks. At first she cried softly, then it grew louder. This is how Mother Rachel weeps when she rises at night from her grave on the road to Bethlehem to take leave of her sons going into exile. "Let thy voice cease from weeping and thy eyes from tears and the children shall return to their own borders." "Gird your loins, rise and speak to them everything I order you, do not fear their faces, for I shall make you unafraid of their faces...." The time has come for the morning Litany. "I confess to Thee, O living and everlasting King..."

Old Tag beat his breast:

> For the sin which we have committed before Thee under
> compulsion of our own free will
> And for the sin which we have committed before Thee
> in hardening of the heart;
> For the sin which we have committed before Thee
> openly or secretly;
> For the sin we have committed before Thee by the
> sinful meditating of the heart;
> For the sin we have committed before Thee by
> association with impurity;
> For the sin we have committed before Thee by
> confession with the mouth alone.

Somebody knocked at the door. It was the priest. He stuck his head in.

"Let's go!"

Old Tag blinked.

"Won't you take leave of your family?"

Old Tag nodded.

"I have done so already."

"Let's go."

Tag came out of the bedroom.

"We'll go in a minute."

He closed the bedroom door and locked it.

In the guest hall Tag stopped in front of the cupboard. He opened the top drawer and put in a shabby wallet, tied with a piece of string, a bunch of large keys and various smaller keys. He left the drawer slightly open.

The priest turned toward the window.

"You didn't finish your milk, Father."

"I must stop by the church on the way."

He was now facing Tag. For a moment they looked into one another's eyes. Tag lowered his head. He began to look again for something in one of the cupboard drawers.

"Listen," said the chaplain, "will you come into the church with me?"

"Yes."

"You mean you'll enter my church?"

"Why not? You're coming with me to see the commandant, aren't you?"

"That's not the same thing!"

"There are no rules when it comes to saving a human life."

"And what if the commandant puts us in jail?"

"Nobody will do that to a priest."

The chaplain shrugged his shoulders.

"On whose behalf shall we speak?" he asked.

"I don't know. I don't understand."

"Who is sending us?"

"No one is sending me. I'm going of my own accord."

"Will you join me in church? I'm going to confess. What about you?"

"With us, there is only one confession, a prayer before dying. I have already said it."

Old Tag closed the drawer. The chaplain went out first; Tag followed.

Yevdocha was standing in the hall.

"Where're you going?" she asked.

"To town." Old Tag hung his head.

"What for?"

"I've told you already."

"I won't let you!"

Old Tag said nothing.

"I won't let you," repeated the girl.

"We're going together." Tag pointed with his eyes to the priest.

"Let him go alone!"

"I'll be back. I won't be long."

"You're lying."

"Be good to Minna and Lolka."

"They'll take our cows! They'll take everything!"

"I'll buy some meat and fish in town for Saturday."

"I don't want your fish!"

"Out of the way. I must be off." Old Tag pushed her aside.

Yevdocha caught his arm.

"You old devil! You old devil!"

Tag embraced her and pressed her head against his breast.

"I'll come back. The keys are in the drawer; the money is in the wallet. Give everything to Minna. Be good to her."

Yevdocha pushed him away.

"Go! You old devil. Let 'em kill you there!"

The priest was not in the hall; he was waiting in the road.

Tag secured the gate with the hasp.

"Let's go," he said.

They started off toward the town.

Yevdocha rushed out of the inn, stood in the middle of the road, and shouted after them:

"You devil! You old devil!"